MAY 16 2000

SF
Anderson, Poul
The day the sun stood
still

DEMCO

# THE DAY THE SUN STOOD STILL

# THE DAY THE SUN
# STOOD STILL

*Three Original Novellas of Science Fiction*

by

Poul Anderson

Gordon R. Dickson

Robert Silverberg

*With a Foreword by*
*Lester del Rey*

THOMAS NELSON INC.
Nashville          New York

00-809810

Manufactured in the United States of America

# Introduction

This trio of science-fiction novellas is published here for the first time. Each story considers in detail the reaction of society to a unique and astonishing event—a miracle; and their similarity of theme is no accident, for the three writers were asked to deal with the same situation. A brief essay by the well-known author and editor Lester del Rey provided the basic challenge; each writer, having no knowledge of what his colleagues were doing, then interpreted del Rey's suggested theme in his own way. The outcome is a group of stories by three of science fiction's most expert authors, illuminating many facets of a single concept.

# Table of Contents

# Foreword

## Lester del Rey

Man does not live by bed and bread alone. He is—so far as we know—the only animal motivated by faith. Even those among his race who lack the will or need to believe must recognize this; for six thousand years of history, his ability to have absolute belief in what he cannot know has been one of the dominant factors determining his individual and mass conduct.

Yet for every thing there is a season and a time to every purpose under the heaven: a time to tear down and a time to build up; a time to believe and a time to know. Already, despite Scopes, knowledge has eroded many foothills of ancient belief.

And there came a time when man was sore troubled and beheld among his kind throughout all the lands a weakening of the faiths. Then appeared a great leader, crying: Gird up your loins and be united in a mighty voice at my signal, that there be a sign in the heavens. And the multitudes of divers faiths, even unto twice a billion, hearkened unto him; and at the appointed hour there went up a great shout, asking that a sign be vouchsafed unto them, that the unbelieving should heed.

And for a day and a night (less $1 \times 12^{-4}$ sidereal day) the earth moved not around the Sun, neither did it rotate. And the laws of momentum were confounded. Then Earth again took up its appointed course. And nothing otherwise was changed.

Except, of course, some of the ways of man.

To the men who depended on evidence and rationality, there would now have to be a recognition of a Power beyond the laws established for the universe, a Power that would respond to the cry of mankind—and perhaps one small clue, such as that of using the duodecimal system, to permit some rational theorizing.

To the men who had based their lives on inner faith, there would now be external evidence—evidence that must weaken the need for mere faith as a means of salvation and require new examination of their orthodoxies, whether eschatological or cultistic, traditional or humanistic.

Every society throughout our history has had some faith as one of the great shaping forces of its existence. Even the men who profess no faith today are rooted into and adapted to a social matrix based upon faith. Our languages reflect this, from our curses to our most philosophical writings. And, of course, we have faith in such things as the conservation of angular momentum. To a major extent, we walk by faith, not by sight.

What kind of a world might exist were the basis of faith replaced by certain knowledge?

# A Chapter of Revelation

## POUL ANDERSON

*Poul Anderson's stories began appearing in science-fiction magazines a couple of years after the end of the Second World War, when he was still a physics major at the University of Minnesota. Quickly he built a reputation for vigorous prose and rigorous exploration of ideas, and has enjoyed an enthusiastic following among science-fiction fans for more than twenty years. His best-known novels include* The High Crusade, Three Hearts and Three Lions, Brain Wave, *and* Tau Zero, *and he is one of the very few authors to have received the Hugo award of the World Science Fiction Convention more than twice. He lives near San Francisco with his wife and daughter.*

(Chairman Wu Yuan of China warned today in an internationally telecast address that the presence of American warships in the Yellow Sea is an intolerable threat and provocation. "Unless this trespass upon the territorial waters of the People's Republic cease forthwith," declared the head of the Chinese state, "it will become necessary to take measures fraught with the gravest consequences." At a special press conference called within hours of the speech, U.S. Secretary of Defense Jacob Morris insisted that the American fleet is staying well outside the twelve-mile limit and is in that area only in response to the Korean crisis. Heavier fighting was reported along the 38th parallel, but officials refused to give newsmen any details.)

Simon Donaldson stumbled a bit as he entered the living room. His wife glanced up from her seat before the television. "Why home so early?" she asked—and then, having looked more closely into his face, rose and hurried to him.

"I knocked off," he mumbled. "Wasn't getting anything done. Couldn't think." She reached him. He caught the warm slenderness of her and held it close. "Oh, God, darling!"

She, understanding, did not try to kiss. Because they were both tall, she could not well lay her head on his breast; but her cheek rested on his shoulder and his nostrils filled with the clean scent of her hair. He ruffled it.

"Yeah," she said after a while. "I'm getting scared too."

"We'd better not delay any longer. Tonight we load the camping gear in the car. Tomorrow you buy groceries and start north."

"Not without you, buster."

"You'll have to. I can't get away. Listen, Johnny's only ten, Mike's only eight. We owe our kids their lives."

"*And* their dad. Why can't you phone in sick and come along?"

"Because—" Donaldson sighed. "Our project's at a critical stage. I can't tell you more. Look at it this way. I'm a soldier in the technological war. The war that's being fought in the laboratories, on the proving grounds, to keep the balance of power stable enough that the war of missiles won't get fought. My friends on the Hill aren't running. Neither can I, if I want to keep any self-respect."

Gail stepped back a pace. Her eyes, blue beneath yellow bangs, sought his. "I know about lead times," she said. "Whatever you're developing can't be in production for five or ten years. The Korean business is this minute."

"Things may not explode," he said. "However, I want you three at Fort Ross, outside the fallout ellipse, for a week or so . . . in case."

She forced a smile. "What say we relax over a drink, so we can have dinner instead of a refueling stop, and argue later?"

Exhaustion overwhelmed him. "Okay."

Nevertheless his gaze followed her rangy gait until she had disappeared in the kitchen. After twelve years of marriage he went on considering himself lucky: he, awkward, rawboned, bespectacled, perpetually rumpled, a competent physicist and a bravura chess player but bookish, given to long rambles alone, no good at small talk—he got Gail Franklin!

And Mike and Johnny. A subdued clatter from the rear of the house showed they were at play, probably building further on their imaginary world Rassolageeva, not much chilled by that which lay across the world Earth.

Donaldson lit a cigarette, inhaled raggedly, prowled to the picture window and stared out. His house stood well aloft on the range that forms the eastern side of Berkeley. From there he saw over roofs and trees, gardens and uninhabited slopes gone tawny with summer, immense beneath a still more enormous blue, down to the cities. He could not see Lawrence Radiation Laboratory, where he worked, but he glimpsed the Campanile, poised on the University campus like a spaceship ready for long voyages. The Bay gleamed sapphire and emerald, through a trace of mist snow-like under sunlight, San Francisco dream-vague on the farther shore but the Golden Gate Bridge arching clear to vision in a few fine brushstrokes that could have been done by a Chinese artist. . . . *Chinese, God help us, nonexistent God. The great mother of the East and the son and heir of the West, with guns at each other's temples.*

"—our next guest—"

The too-hearty voice scratched Donaldson's nerves. He moved to switch the television off, then stayed his hand. *Maybe I need a counterirritant, till Gail has the anesthetic mixed,* he thought. *Besides, she likes this show. What's it called? Oh, yes, "Pulse." Local talk program. People write in and whozis picks whoever seems likeliest to help fill the bored housewife's hour. No, I'm being unjust. After all, the show is popular, including among bright folk like Gail. It beats dangling on the lips of some half-hysterical news commentator.*

"Mr. Louis Habib of Oakland," the MC (Dawes, yes, that was his name) announced. Teeth glittered above his modish tie. "How do you do, Mr. Habib. Welcome to 'Pulse.' "

"Th-thank you." The other man could scarcely be heard. Stage fright, doubtless. He must have something a bit unusual to offer, if he hadn't been weeded out in audition. Donaldson peered at the screen. Habib was stiffly and shabbily clad, squat, dark, big-nosed, balding. His eyes were his best feature, the long-lashed gazelle eyes of the Levant.

"Let me see, Mr. Habib, you have a garage, don't you? The Motor Man Garage, 1453 Murphy Street, Oakland, right? Commercial pause, ha-ha. Well, tell us something more about yourself, if you please. You're married?"

"Yes. I'm not important, though," the short man blurted. "M-

m-my message . . . no, too big a word . . . what I'm here about
—that's what matters."

"Our audience does like to get acquainted," Dawes said. "Your
idea, the letter you wrote, is certainly very interesting, but we
want to get to know the man behind it."

"It's not my idea," Habib stated in a kind of desperate valor.
Donaldson made out how sweat channeled the makeup they had
put on him. "It's as old as . . . oh, Moses, or older, I dunno. And
I'm not important. Nor are you."

That rocked Dawes back sufficiently for Habib to confront the
camera. His look seemed to spear the watcher. "Listen, please
listen," he begged. "Sure, I'm married. Three children. Friends. A
whole world. Everything to lose. Same as you, all of us. This thing
in Asia—this way the human race's been living on the edge of the
pit, far back's I can remember, and I'm forty-four. What's wrong?
We're crazy, that's what. Else we'd see how no . . . uh . . . i-de-
ology, no power, no pride, nothing's worth blackening this beautiful world we got and frying little children alive."

Dawes tried to get back control. "As I understood your recom-
mendation, Mr. Habib, you do not propose we surrender."

The round head shook. "No. We can't. Or we won't. I realize
that. Don't say we should, either. There aren't many countries
left with any freedom in them. Though maybe a lot don't agree
with us about what freedom is, any more than we agree with their
notions.

"But arguments don't mean we, the Chinese, the Russians, anybody has to fight. Least of all fight with weapons that won't leave
much to quarrel about, afterward. We could, uh, settle somehow.
Live and let live. Except we don't. Why? Because we're crazy.
And what's made us crazy? I think it's that we don't know God."

Dawes, in a valiant effort to restore smoothness: "You indicated, Mr. Habib, you feel man has a need of faith as great as his
need for food. He craves to believe in something higher than himself, something he can give himself to because it gives meaning to

the universe. At the same time, you are not a conventional evangelist. Am I right?"

"Sort of." Habib continued looking straight into the camera, out of the screen. "I'm not a Bible thumper. Haven't been in church for years. But, well, I always figured there has to be a spirit behind creation. People used to believe. That didn't, uh, necessarily make them good or kind or wise, I know. But then, they had nothing but faith to go on."

He lifted a finger. "That's my point," he said. "In the long run, faith wasn't enough. Maybe it should've been, but it wasn't. When science didn't find any reason to suppose the world was more than atoms and chance, why, faith eroded away. And people felt, well, empty. So they started inventing faiths, like communism or fascism in politics, or these nut cults you see around. But those just made 'em crazier, same's they went crazy when the old Catholic religion was, uh, challenged. Then they burned heretics and witches and they fought like devils. Today we make concentration camps and atomic rockets and we fight like devils.

"And maybe we Americans—and, uh, western Europeans too, I guess—maybe we're the worst off. We haven't got faith in anything, not even progress. Why's this country been so terrified, these past days? Isn't it on account of nearly everybody thinks, in his heart, he thinks nothing exists worth dying for?"

A curious power filled the stumbling words. Donaldson found himself listening and weighing, barely aware that Gail had returned with two martinis and was likewise quiet at his side.

"You suggest—" Dawes began.

"We need a sign," Habib told them. "We need proof, scientific proof, the only kind we can accept any more, proof that God is."

He hunched forward where he stood, fists clenched at his sides. "We won't get it free," he said, hoarsely now. Sweat soaked through his jacket. "Maybe we won't get it at all. Then we'll just have to live, or die, as best's we can. But why not ask for a sign? Ask for some proof that there is a God, Who cares; that there is something bigger and brighter than our squabbles, our greeds, our want to make our fellowmen into copies of us. Then maybe we can begin to see those things for what they are, and—"

He did not quite ignore Dawes, but rather hurried on before the host should get a chance to soften his one occasion: "Let's pray together. That way, if the sign happens, we'll know God listens. A week from today. Tuesday noon. Midsummer. Around the world, whenever noon comes to you. Stop a minute and pray for a sign. If you don't believe, well, then speak your wish to yourself—your wish we will be shown while time remains. Even if you're an atheist, can't you dare to hope?"

*Wednesday 15 June*
(Dr. Nikio Sato, head of the Radiological Institute at the University of Tokyo, has confirmed that monitoring teams under his leadership have detected the explosion of "a sizable nuclear device not far southwest of Cheju," an island below the Korean Peninsula. The news blackout imposed by Washington, Peking, Seoul, and Pyongyang continues.)

Louis Habib entered the shop almost timidly. Joe Goldman, his assistant, was laying out tools. "Hi, boss," the mechanic said.

"How're you?" Habib started to remove his jacket. Morning sunlight streamed in the entrance, hit a fresh oil slick on the concrete floor, and melted in rainbows. Morning traffic rumbled and whirred past in the street. Smog was already acrid. "Gonna be bad today, the air," Habib said. "Wish I was out fishing."

"Yeah, if you know a stream the pollution hasn't killed." Goldman cleared his throat. "I, uh, heard about your show yesterday. My girl friend saw it."

"Oh, that." Habib hung up his jacket and took his coverall off its hook. His ears smoldered. "Damn fool thing to do, I guess."

"Hey, now, you can't mean that, Lou."

Surprised at the young man's vehemence, Habib dropped his glance and said with difficulty, "No, sure, I meant it, all right.

Only I never—well, I sort of wrote in on, uh, impulse, and my jaw really hit the floor when they called and asked. . . . I'd never've had the nerve myself. But Helen insisted. You know how women are. Especially when I was promised twenty-five bucks for appearing and the dentist's gotten a little impatient about his bill."

"Seems like a good idea, though," Goldman said. "What can we lose? I think I'll phone in and ask 'em for a replay one evening when I can watch."

"Aw, Joe, come off it."

"No, seriously, Lou. I don't go to services and I'm a good customer for ham sandwiches. But things look so ugly. My girl says— Anyhow, okay, next Tuesday noon I'll take a minute off to ask for a sign. If we're still here."

"Well, well . . . thanks." Habib buttoned his coverall fast. "Meanwhile, the transmission in that Chevy *is* here."

He took refuge in his hands.

*Thursday 16 June*
(President Reisner admitted today that the American fleet in the Yellow Sea has suffered heavily from a missile described as being "in the hundred-kiloton range." He denounced the Chinese move and vowed "appropriate response." Peking had made public several hours earlier that it launched the weapon at units it declared were "in flagrant violation of territorial waters, preparing for a seaborne invasion of the People's Republic of Korea." Heads of state around the world issued pleas for restraint, and Secretary-General Andrei Dekanović called an emergency session of the United Nations.)

Simon and Gail Donaldson stood, fingers clasped together in hurtful tightness, and stared down at the night cities. Lamps, windows, electric placards were nearly lost among headlights, which did not move and did not move.

"No," he said. "We put it off yesterday and now we're too late. Be as dangerous to join that stampede as to stay here."

"What can we do, then?" she whispered.

"Keep your packsack loaded and the bedrolls handy. Be ready to hike with the boys into Tilden Park, hills between you and the Bay. Hope too many people haven't gotten the same idea."

"At once?"

"No. The enemy might settle for a counterforce strategy, and the fallout from places like Vandenberg and Hamilton might not blow this way. Or, conceivably, a general war will be avoided. We sit tight for a while."

"And pray?"

"If that'll make you feel any better."

"I'm not getting religion, Si. But that funny little man on TV the other day—What harm can a prayer do?"

"What harm can anything do, by comparison? Sure. I'll join you. Probably be home anyway. The Lab's tumbling into chaos much faster than I expected."

*Friday 17 June*

(United States bombers today launched an atomic attack on Chinese rocket bases on the Shantung Peninsula. President Reisner declared that the weapons used were of strictly limited yield, for the strictly limited purpose of taking out installations which, he said on television, had "murdered an estimated ten thousand American sailors and left a greater number in the agonies of burns, mutilations, and radiation sickness." He pledged no further strikes unless further provocation occurred and called for a conference to settle the Korean problem and "other issues which have brought civilization to the rim of catastrophe.")

The network representative scanned the room, as if an assessment of it would explain what he had just heard. It remained a room: yellow-plastered, wood-paneled in the pseudo-Maybeck style of older Eastbay houses; furniture which years of use had contoured to individual bodies; threadbare carpet; obviously homemade drapes; television set; a few harmless paperback novels and how-to books, newspaper, *Life*, *Reader's Digest*; no Bible in view; some family pictures, a mountainscape clipped out of a magazine and framed; everything clean but unfussy.

"Maybe you don't understand, Mr. Habib," he said. "We're not simply offering to fly you to New York and pay you money. We're giving you a chance to present your, ah, appeal before the whole North American continent. Maybe the whole world."

The short man shook his head and drew on his cigar. "No, thanks," he repeated. "I don't want the publicity. If my, uh, suggestion seems to've, uh, caught on . . . if it's spreading around . . . why, that's plenty. I'm no preacher. When Mr. Dawes asked me to come back—"

"But this is *national*, Mr. Habib!"

"Yeah. And a fine idiot I'd look, stuttering in front of a couple hundred million people. Right, Helen?"

His wife squeezed his arm. "You never were much of a public speaker, Lou." To the representative: "Be warned, sir, and don't waste your time. Once his mind's made up, he can give cards and spades to a mule."

The representative considered her. She was of Mexican descent, though California born: cheekbones wide and high, flared nostrils, almond eyes, olive complexion, hair sheening black. Those features had a delicacy; she must have been damn good-looking when she was young, before she put on weight, and she wasn't bad yet. "You're invited too, of course, Mrs. Habib," he said.

She laughed. So little laughter was heard of late that the noise startled him. "What have I to tell them? I'm a Unitarian, mainly because several of my friends are. Lou doesn't belong to any church."

The representative looked past them at their children. He'd been briefed. James, seventeen, skinny, long-haired, a frequently self-proclaimed conservative, that being the latest style in adolescent rebellion; Stephanie, twenty, student at California College of

Arts and Crafts, who had inherited her mother's plumpness and her father's face; Richard, twenty-two, likewise plain and stocky, but the most promising of the lot since he was studying for the Episcopal ministry. . . . Behind his parents' backs, he smiled slightly and shook his head.

"You've got to tell them something!" the representative exclaimed. "What would be an unmistakable sign, a miracle nobody could explain away?"

"How should I know?" Habib answered. He squirmed. "I, uh, no, who'm I to tell God what He ought to do? But . . . well—no, I won't."

"Go ahead," his wife urged gently. "It's not a bad idea."

"J-j-just a thought," Habib said. (How luminous his eyes were.) "You know, we, well, we're back in a very crude stage now, I think. We've got a lot of fine science and, uh, technology, but we've put behind us all that thinking, that experience, over thousands of years—you know, theology, that nobody except a few like my son cares about any longer. We've really no better notion of God than, uh, some Hebrew nomad before Abraham. I know I don't. We've got to start over. Not the still, small voice, but something big, flashy—oh, like, how's the line go? 'Sun, stand thou still.' If God would stop the sun a while, maybe we'd get the idea. Because we sure can't understand a Sermon on the Mount any longer. Don't you agree?"

A reporter from the Oakland *Tribune*, quietly present, made a note.

*Saturday 18 June*
(Soviet Premier Nikolai Isaeff today asserted that his country would stand firmly beside China in any major conflict with the United States. He warned that further attacks upon the Chinese mainland could bring massive retaliation by Russian forces now fully mobilized.)

They weren't demonstrating before the White House. Not ex-

actly. They were praying. Most of them were black. Their chant
was so many-throated that it rolled past the fence, over the lawn
and through the wall, into the bones.

"They could get out of hand, Mr. President," the Secret Service
officer fretted. "We can hold them off, naturally, but the casualties . . . Are you sure we shouldn't disperse them?"

"That would make casualties too," William Reisner replied.
"No, let them stay. They don't menace anything except Pennsylvania Avenue traffic." His lips dragged upward. "I might follow their
example, come the time."

*Sunday 19 June*
(Pope Benedict, in a sermon delivered at St. Peter's, today
added his voice to the growing number of religious leaders who
have urged their followers to pray for a token of God's presence
at noon on Tuesday. At a press conference afterward, he was
asked whether or not he meant noon, daylight saving time. "Follow your clocks," he said wearily. "God made time but man made
the hours. Unless God help us, it may be man will end them.")

"Not the Tibetans, what remains of them," said the head of the
political police. "Nor the Russians. Their reactions might have
been foreseen. But the thing has spread like cholera across our
own country."

"How did it happen?" Chairman Wu responded. He forestalled
a reply. "Do not answer. There is no single, simple answer. Not in
an age of transistor radios and relay satellites. The fact is, the average Chinese is as reluctant as anyone else to see his children
turned to corpses and his land to ash. He grasps at archaic straws."

"What shall we do, honored leader?"

"Do? Why, nothing. Let them beat their gongs, burn their incense, yes, flock to their churches and pagodas if they wish. When
no sign comes—but when their government, a few mortal men
armed only with courage and correct principles—when *man* rides
out the storm—they will have had a most valuable lesson."

*Monday 20 June*

(President Reisner has declared martial law throughout the United States. National Guard units, now federalized, are instructed to restore order among hordes fleeing the cities.)

"No power," Donaldson said. "Well, we've got candles."

"No fresh groceries," Gail told him. "Store's been bought out." She paused. "Remember, when we were first married and poor, what I could do with potatoes? We have quite a few spuds left."

He looked out into darkness. "You sure we shouldn't start walking?"

"Quite sure. To judge from what news I hear. No, darling, we stand fast and wait for tomorrow noon."

He regarded her in astonishment. "You know," he said after a moment, "I believe you're seriously expecting a miracle."

"Aren't you?" she asked.

"No. Certainly not. A miracle's a suspension of natural law. Can't happen."

"But you will join the boys and me. Won't you?"

"Oh, yes. Psychological effect. The idea does seem to've traveled fast and far. And Szilard once defined a miracle as an event with less than ten percent probability. Okay, us, the Europeans, Asians, Africans, Australians, everybody, let's hope together. The little man was right as far as that goes. We do need something bigger than ourselves to live by."

*Tuesday 21 June*

(*Help.*
*Namu amida Butsu.*
*Om mani padme hum.*
*Hare Krishna.*
*Eli, Eli.*
*Ullah akbar.*
*Our Father Who art in Heaven.*

*Minoké ago Legba.*
*Cosmos.*
*Man.*
*Luck.*
*Give us a sign.*
*Help.*)

The strangest thing had been the way things kept going. For the most part, the riots, the panic flights, the destructions and breakdowns happened to you on TV and in the paper. Oh, you saw the smoke pall above West Oakland, and a troop carrier growl by full of Guardsmen who looked pitifully young under their helmets, and the looted remnants of a couple of shops in your own neighborhood; various businesses were closed and traffic had thinned and mail delivery was irregular; electricity was often out for hours in a row; your wife took what foods she could find after tramping from market to market, at police-guarded prices, or gave in to backdoor slinkers who had the goods at a thousand-percent markup; you quit using the phone, since lines were always jammed —but you and most of those like you continued on your rounds. You worked, you coped, you ate and bathed and went bowling on your usual night, you actually joked (thinly) and slept (badly) while the hours wore into days.

Joe Goldman had demanded, "What's holding us here?"

"Our jobs," Louis Habib had replied. He chose his words with care. "I won't get mad if you light out. I do advise you against it. The countryside can't support as many as have run. You'd be just another animal, to herd into a refugee camp and try to feed somehow. You'll help, instead of adding a burden, if you stand pat."

Goldman shifted a wad of chewing gum around in his mouth. "How can I be less of a man than my boss?" He grunted.

Over Habib's objections, he did insist on having a radio tuned to the news Tuesday. While they worked, the descriptions came in, hour by hour: crowds had gathered in Piccadilly Circus, a special service had been held on a battleship in mid-Atlantic, Times

Square was jammed with humanity as on a silent New Year's Eve, rain fell in Chicago but nevertheless a gathering. . . . "Don't you want to go downtown?" Goldman inquired. "Or maybe back to your folks?"

"No," Habib said. His heart stuttered. *God has to be everywhere, and we one in Him. Right? I don't know. That damn fundamentalist preacher who's been pestering us* . . . "At the Mormon Tabernacle in Salt Lake City—"

Bells around the Bay. No sirens; that would have been gruesomely dangerous. Noon bells, though, tinkling, mewing, clanging, striding. Cars, buses, walkers come to a halt. Heads bowed, heads uplifted to a blank sky. A shadow across the shop floor, cast by the pillar of a hydraulic lift. *God, Spirit, Whoever made the world, You can't have made it in vain. Show us. Please. Stop the sun, or do what else is best, but show us that You are, because we've failed ourselves and nobody is left except You.*

"Sun, stand thou still," Joe Goldman muttered.

Afterward he and Habib avoided each other's eyes and spoke no more than they must. Neither ate his lunch. Disappointment was too thick in their gullets.

Earth spun eastward, nightward. About four forty-five in the afternoon, the first wild rumor came out of the radio. Habib stood a moment. Then he laid a wrench on the floor, at the exact point where shadows joined of a rack and the automobile it upbore. He and Goldman watched for several minutes before they were quite sure that the shadow had stopped. Goldman broke into harsh, inexperienced sobs. Habib stowed tools, locked doors, got into his car, and drove home. At least, his body did.

*Wednesday 22 June*

(For one sidereal day, a trifle more than twenty-four hours, the sun remained moveless, at zenith in mid-Pacific, precisely over the International Date Line.

Rather, Earth's rotation period was slowed to a value identical with Earth's year. As nearly as could be told, this happened instantaneously. It is certain that none of the sensitive instruments prepared and manned by what scientists had not gone more or less mad for the duration were able to measure any finite time in which the old spin was resumed at the end of that endless day.

Nothing else changed. The planet moved on in orbit, as did its moon. [This made every calendar in existence obsolete. But if Earth had actually stopped, Luna would have fled, become an independent globe on a wildly eccentric path. As was, its light fell icy on otherwise lightless Washington, New York, Brasília, Buenos Aires, London, Paris, Rome, Capetown, Cairo, Tel Aviv, Leningrad, Moscow, New Delhi.] Weather and tide patterns grew somewhat confused, but the term was insufficient for disaster to be generated. Wildlife was troubled; circadian rhythm disturbed, untold organisms went hungry until the familiar night-and-day returned; but few, if any, died.

Man took the matter worse. A thousand generations of historians would fail to record the whole of those hours and their immediate aftermath. Yet death, devastation, injury, collapse were held within astonishingly close bounds. It helped that worldwide dread had, beforehand, brought about worldwide activation of disciplined forces—police, firemen, militia, political cadres, private organizations. Then, too, the magnitude of what happened, the infinitely greater magnitude of what it meant, stunned violence out of all save the most foolish and brutish. Oftener than not, loss occurred because minds were turned elsewhere than to everyday [everynight] maintenance work.

The pilgrimages by torch to the Ganges, by candlelight to the Western Wall and the Mosque of Omar, by furnacelike sunlight to Our Lady of Guadalupe, were not frantic in any true sense of that word. They were awesome: men, women, children by the millions flowing together and becoming a natural force.

Nor did everyone enter such a tide or such a congregation. Some cleaved to the routines, others to the purposes which had always been their lives.)

Helen Habib thrust a sandwich into her husband's grasp. He took it without noticing, where he sat by the window in his old armchair and stared out at the empty pavement.

She shook him. "Lou, you must eat," she said.

He blinked at her. "Now?" he answered, as if from very far away.

"Yes, now. When we've no faintest idea of what will come next. Eat. I'll make coffee."

"How long?" whimpered Stephanie in her corner while a marble-fronted clock, brought from Lebanon by her great-grandfather, bonged midnight. Around the house lay afternoon, listless leaves upon trees, shadows that did not stir. A dog loped by, outrageously unaffected.

"How should anyone know?" Richard retorted.

"You, dad," she said for the fiftieth or hundredth time. "You prayed for this. So pray for sunset."

"Yah, yah," Jimmy jeered. He was hunkered before the television, trying to get a program. But there had been no broadcasts for hours except replays of a tape whereon President Reisner told America to stay calm. "Just like that."

Dick's knuckles stood white around a Book of Common Prayer. Back and forth he paced. One shoe squeaked. "You seem to think your father's a magician, Steffie," he lectured, likewise repeating himself. "I tell you, divine inspiration is something else."

Habib shook his whole body. "Me? Inspired?" Their attention snapped to him; he had scarcely spoken before. "Can't be."

"The Lord chooses whom He will, father," Dick said; and then: "No! I've got to get off this pomposity. I was a glorified agnostic, a social-gospel churchman who saw God, if ever I saw Him, as a—what'd somebody call it once?—a kind of oblong blur." Breath sucked between his teeth. "'It is a fearful thing to fall into the hands of the living God.'"

"But me!" Louis Habib climbed to his feet. The sandwich dropped on the floor. He groped, as if blind, toward Helen. "Me," he pushed out of his lips. Sweat ran off him; they could smell the sharpness. "Me who figured there must be a God, but till the war scare never thought it made much difference—not since I was a kid, when I used to make fun of the sisters in my mind—hell, when I wrote that letter, I really thought we needed faith. Not that we needed God. The difference—"

He caught both his wife's hands and stood before her weeping. "I cheated on you once, Helen. I'd've done it more if the chance had come. Sometimes when a pretty girl went past, I'd imagine—I, I, I play poker, I go off bowling or fishing when maybe you'd rather have me home, I vote the straight party ticket b'cause that's easier'n thinking, I've chiseled on the income tax as much's I had the guts to, though th-th-that's not much—"

She kissed him. Nobody quite noticed the pain which had crossed her. "If you've nothing worse to confess, Lou, stop moping and . . . and eat, blast it!"

A drumbeat on the door called their minds away. Dick looked relieved. He went and opened it. A neighbor stood on the porch. "Why, hello, Mr. Olstad. Come in."

The man entered behind a shotgun.

"What?" Dick sprang back. Stephanie shrilled. Jimmy started to lunge, checked, and retreated, hands high. Their parents stood in the middle of the floor, moving no more than the shadows.

"Okay." Olstad's cheeks were unshaven, his hair uncombed. He croaked rather than spoke. The twin barrels of his gun jittered about. "Bring back the night."

Habib could merely gape through his tears.

"You did this, damn you." Olstad stabbed the gun in his direction. "I remember. Well, undo it. Or I'll kill you."

"Stop." Habib let go of Helen, thrust her behind him and took a step toward the intruder. "I did . . . maybe I did suggest praying for this sign . . . first, I mean. Or maybe not." As the words came forth, strength seemed to rise in him. He squared his shoulders. "Ideas like that get in the air. We never really know who begins them. Sam, do you believe one monkey like me can control this planet? That any one man can? I heard a commentator guess a billion people were praying. *They* were heard. Not me."

"Then start them praying again," Olstad said.

"Sure," Habib answered. "Glad to. Tell me how."

For a minute they faced each other. Suddenly Olstad pitched the shotgun through a window. Glass rang and tinkled; one chamber crashed off on the lawn. "Martha's half out of her head!" he screamed. "Billy's not come back from his Scout trip! What'm I s'posed to do?"

Habib went to him, gave him a brief hug, and said, "You start by having a drink, Sam. I've got a little Jack Daniels somewhere."

There was not much talk until after Olstad had left. Then Jimmy ventured, "Uh, dad, that went cool. You know, though, we could get a whole lynch mob. Couldn't we?"

"What do you propose?" Habib asked.

"Well, we hide out, like with friends or—"

This time the rapping was more controlled. Jimmy darted into his room for a sheath knife. When he came back, he saw his father confronted by two men. They were dressed like solid citizens, young and hard.

"Mr. Habib?" one said. "How do you do. We're from the Federal Bureau of Investigation." He flipped a wallet open to show his credentials. "You will all come along with us."

*Thursday 23 June*

(Heads of state around the world called for public thanksgiving at the return of day and night. Most agreed that mankind has indeed been granted an unmistakable sign that a personal God exists. Exceptions included the government of China, which had no immediate comment other than broadcasts and wall posters directing citizens to resume their duties, and the Kremlin, which issued a terse statement that "this extraordinary phenomenon must be soberly and scientifically evaluated.")

Gail Donaldson had spent most of those twenty-four hours

holding fear at bay in Mike and Johnny. When they, exhausted, fell asleep, she rejoined her husband in the living room but soon dozed off herself. Waking from fitful dreams, she found him still at the picture window, his eyes locked west across the afternoon light on the waters. Her attempts to talk foundered on his frozenness.

When finally the sun moved again, she had once more been preoccupied with the children. "Look, we're getting our night back! Soon you'll see the stars." On the whole, she thought, she had succeeded in making this experience a marvel to them rather than a root of future terrors. Simon's shock remained to be dealt with.

While the eastern range turned purple and the Bay argent, the ruddy globe sank beyond the Golden Gate and Venus gleamed above, she made drinks for them both and brought them to him. He accepted his, not altogether as mechanically as he had taken the food she prepared. Twilight smoked around them.

She raised her glass and grinned lopsidedly. "Here's to God."

"Uh." Donaldson stared at her for a moment, and at his martini, before he made jerky response. "Yeah."

"No disrespect intended, of course," she said. "I simply . . . am ignorant yet . . . about sacraments."

"You believe?"

"What, don't you?"

"I don't know." His hand trembled, so that the drink slopped over.

"The evidence, darling. You prayed too."

"I, well, I took part in a rite. Yes. My thought was, if people around the world could unite in an appeal . . . at this time in history . . . I mustn't hang back. Yes, I hoped for a miracle, but in Szilard's meaning. A mass conversion of some kind, conversion to sanity. Instead, we got—" His gesture chopped at the dusk. City lights were twinkling forth; large patches of darkness lay between, but no doubt full service would presently be restored and meanwhile the sky stood clear.

"Why're you so bothered?" she asked. "You never were a dogmatic atheist."

"No," he said slowly, scowling, though at least becoming restored somewhat to his old self, even to a touch of humor. "An agnostic, i.e., a polite atheist. I did believe in a natural order. That the universe, however mysterious, made sense."

"What's that line from Eddington? The universe is not only queerer than we know, it's queerer than we can imagine. Something like that. Isn't a God one more element of an always strange cosmos?"

"Not the same kind of element." His tone roughened. "I've heard and read too much drivel through the years, about how quantum uncertainties or evolution or whatnot prove there has to be a Creator or an afterlife or whatnot—when in fact they prove nothing of the sort. And what's happened now doesn't prove a God either. It only mocks all reason. A discontinuity. An impossibility. Either the laws of nature are subject to meaningless suspensions—are, maybe, mere statistical fluctuations in howling chaos—or else a Being is able to abrogate them at whim—and in either case, *we'll never understand.*"

"Do we have to?"

"I have to," he told her. "That was the horror of the war building up. You know how I rejected peace petitions and the like for the garbage they were, and held that old-fashioned realism, plus basic goodwill, gave us a fighting chance of winning through to a better order of things. Then Korea erupted, and suddenly events were beyond human comprehension or control. Disaster seemed inevitable regardless of anyone's wish, knowledge, power. Our helplessness was nearly as hard for me to take as the blowup itself would be."

He had been sipping while he talked. In his worn state, the alcohol took quick hold and hastened his tongue: "We may have been rescued, temporarily anyhow. But the helplessness is now like burial under a mountain. Think! If Earth can slow down its spin and then regain it—more than six times ten to the twenty-first tons of mass, accelerated instantaneously, which is even a logical contradiction; and no released energies to melt the ground and boil the oceans, not so much as a hurricane or a quake—which means that cornerstones of physics like conservation of energy and momentum were removed, and later replaced, with no noise, no fuss, no trace—How can we ever dare look to the future?

"A child might, on impulse, rescue a beetle about to drown. Later, on impulse, he might step on it. Or if there is a plan behind all this, what?" Donaldson shuddered. "Arthur Machen once defined absolute evil as when a rose begins to sing."

"You're no more certain of evil or chaos than you are of good and . . . and an order that includes purpose," Gail said. "Less, in fact." She set down her glass and offered him the reality of her hands.

He tossed off his own drink, straightened, and said, "Maybe. Maybe the impossibility . . . can be fitted in . . . somehow."

"That has to be your working hypothesis, doesn't it? And you're just the man to do the work." She kissed him.

He said at last, "Thanks more than I'll ever be able to speak, for giving me back some guts." After a hesitation, he added, "Do you mind if . . . if I go back to the lab already tomorrow?"

"Of course not, silly. You need to." After dinner she fed him a sleeping pill and held him in her arms till he drowsed.

—That had been the Wednesday sunset which ought to have come on Tuesday. Driving the winding hill streets on the belated early morning of Thursday, Donaldson dialed a local educational radio station, hoping for more than the inanities which blatted on every other waveband, save for those which played half a dozen religious compositions to death. A professional voice:

"—indubitably a conscious decision, therefore a conscious intelligence, stood behind the event. Would some blind, random process have halted the globe so that midnight fell exactly over our arbitrary prime meridian? And I suspect more was intended than that token. Consider. Almost the maximum land surface was held in darkness: the eastern United States, South America, Africa,

Europe, most of Asia. True, the western United States enjoyed day, if 'enjoy' is the proper word; but most of China did also, as if to balance the two great antagonists. Does not a strong hint lie in the fact that mainly the part of Earth which stayed beneath the sun was innocent Oceania?

"Perhaps we have been given a symbol in the very dating. Besides the solstice, with all its associations, we have the occurrence lasting from Tuesday to Wednesday. Or, in Romance languages, from the day of Mars to the day of Mercury. In either case, from the god of war to the god who conducts away the souls of the newly dead. A warning? I don't know. I can merely suggest we close our ears to the rising chorus of partisan claims and, in this respite which has been given us, humbly set about our affairs in a more decent fashion than hitherto."

At the head of Cyclotron Road, Donaldson was inspected closer than usual by the guard at the gate. "Shucks, Bob, you know me," he protested.

"I don't know what I know," the guard answered. "Lemme have your badge a second, please."

The physicist found his office empty; the secretary he shared with a couple of other men hadn't reported in, nor had they. The laboratory he chose was likewise hushed. Instruments stared, apparatus loomed like idols of an abandoned faith. He wasn't sorry. It was good to use his own fingers on an elementary job. For a start, he wanted to measure terrestrial magnetism. The suspension of rotation must have affected it . . . maybe. . . . He sought his office again, phoned the main switchboard, found a girl on duty and asked her to put him in touch here and there across the country, as soon as possible. Beneath every shakenness he thought: *If ordinary laws did otherwise prevail, a fresh value of H, at a lot of different points around the planet, should give us insights about the core that we might never have had.*

A man in Army uniform, colonel's insignia, entered. "Dr. Donaldson?" He held out his hand. "My name's Heinrichs, Ed Heinrichs. Excuse the intrusion, but this is important. They told me in Administration that of the workers here who're present today, you're our best bet."

Donaldson gave him an uneasy clasp. "What's the problem?"

"Well—" The colonel was no model of assurance either. He shifted his feet and stared at the floor. "The fact of the matter is . . . you know this Habib fellow? The guy who seems to have started it all?"

"I know who he is," Donaldson said warily.

"Well, we've got him here. And his family." The colonel raised a palm. "No, please hear me out. What else can the government do? We have to try to get some idea of what's happened, what's likely to happen, and he's our only handle on it. Isn't he? Besides, he needs protection. If you'll tune in the news on TV, you'll probably see a helicopter shot of the mob around his house. Not a hostile mob, so far, anyway. More like a . . . an old-time revival meeting, I guess, except the quietness is eerie." He gulped. "The police have the house cordoned off. They didn't get to Habib's garage in time. That's been stripped. Right down to the ground. Souvenir hunters, relic hunters, I don't know what."

Donaldson recalled the brisk medieval trade in pieces of the True Cross.

"Anyhow," Heinrichs said, "the word from Washington was to take the whole family into protective custody for a while. Could be Russian or Chinese agents after them. Or ordinary psychos. We can house them here, temporarily, secretly. A scientist—"

His eyes did not command, they pleaded.

*Friday 24 June*

(I. M. Leskov, noted astronomer and member of the Soviet Academy of Sciences, today proposed that the pause in Earth's spin was due to beings from outer space. "We cannot equate superstition and explanation," he declared in a statement which had the cautious endorsement of the Kremlin. "The requirement of minimum hypothesis practically forces us to assume that what happened resulted from the application of a technology centuries beyond ours. I find it easy to believe that an advanced civilization, capable of interstellar travel, sent a team to save mankind from the carnage threatened by an imperialism which that society outgrew long ago.")

William Reisner sat still behind his desk for some time before he said, most quietly, "I don't want to suppose you're insane, Stan. I'd rather suppose I misheard you. Would you repeat?"

Gray-faced, the spokesman for the Joint Chiefs of Staff answered, "You didn't hear me out, Mr. President. True, the Korean fighting is still in abeyance. But the Chinese are using the chance to pour in reinforcements. Besides troops, mobile ICBM's. I have the reports here, air reconnaissance, space surveillance, ground-based intelligence. They understand as well as we do, no ICBM is worth a spent bullet, except for wanton butchery, till we reprogram every computer and adjust every navigational system. I don't give that tacit cease-fire another week. They have an overwhelming superiority in manpower and armor."

"But we have the same in bombers."

"Even so—"

"We retaliated for what they did in the Yellow Sea," Reisner said. "A so-called preventive strike is something else again. Its proper name is murder."

"There is also such a thing as responsibility toward our own men and allies. I don't argue for hitting their cities. I advocate it, but know better than to argue for it. A sharp, local warning *now*—"

"Will either make Peking respect our will enough to negotiate . . . or confirm Peking's belief that we are monsters who cannot be negotiated with. How about morale, discipline, organization among the Chinese? They must be pretty badly shaken themselves."

The military man shrugged and said bitterly, "Did you catch the news from the Middle East, Mr. President? Seems that Palestinian mullah who's preaching a jihad against Israel . . . seems he's got men swarming to him, yelling that Allah has shown He wills it. And that militant rabbi in Haifa—"

"I know," Reisner interrupted. "Still another consideration. We dare not spread ourselves too thin. But I asked you about the state of the Chinese."

"I can't tell you, sir. In spite of a hundred contradictory predictions from as many psywar experts, I've no idea what shape the American reaction will take, let alone the Oriental. I was just pointing out that the . . . miracle . . . didn't include putting brotherly love into all human hearts."

"Yours, Stan?"

"Sir, I'd go to chapel occasionally, but God always seemed comfortably distant from it. Today . . . He's here. Only what is He? I keep thinking of Jehovah the Thunderer—the Crusades—Don John at Lepanto, saving Christendom with sword and cannon—Suppose we sent a couple hundred squadrons over North Korea to buzz them? Simply buzz them; no shooting, no bombing, unless they shoot first."

*Saturday 25 June*
(A startling new theory about the stoppage of Earth's rotation was published today in China over the signature of Chairman Wu Yuan. According to it, the occurrence may have been a matter of ESP. "Such phenomena as telepathy [mind-reading], telekinesis [moving objects by mental power], and precognition [foreknowledge of the future] are claimed by many reputable scientists to have been observed in the laboratory," said the widely distributed pamphlet. "The mind of man may have tremendous abilities, once liberated from the blinkers of the past. More than a third of the contemporary human race is guided by Marxism; more than half this number has for more than a generation been under the tutelage of wholly correct principles. Thus the massed concentration of the peace-loving peoples may well have triggered cosmic energies to produce those events which

have halted the imperialists in their bloody track and thrown them wallowing back into the basest superstitions.")

Richard Habib sat down uneasily at first, in Donaldson's office, till the physicist opened a drawer and took out a bottle. "Care for some?" Donaldson invited. "Frankly, I need a drink."

"Wouldn't mind, thanks," the young man replied, almost too low to hear.

Whisky gurgled into Dixie cups. "Water down the hall if you want," Donaldson said. "No ice or soda handy, I'm afraid."

"This is fine, thanks."

Silence hemmed them in. Few were at the Radlab today and none, seemingly, in this building. The room lay bleak, hardly relieved by a picture of Gail and the children on a desk, a Peanuts cartoon Scotch-taped to a wall, a window open to mild air, sunlight, and concrete.

Donaldson sat down, lit a cigarette, filled his lungs with what he knew was carcinogenic pungency, and said, "I hope you're not too uncomfortable. They had to improvise quarters."

"Not bad, sir."

"Call me Si, will you? I'm, uh . . . you realize I was co-opted? I don't think they're right to hold you incommunicado like this, and I'm leaning on them to change that. Until they do, however—"

Richard Habib nodded. He was dressed in incongruously colorful sports shirt and slacks. Well, he hadn't been ordained as yet, had he?

Donaldson glowered at his ashtray. "The thing is," he said, word by word, "I'm a lousy choice. Too stiff. I've spent the last couple of days trying to get acquainted with your father, your mother. You saw the result."

"You're too shy, really, sir," Dick said.

Startled, Donaldson glanced up. After a moment, wryly, he replied, "Uh-huh. I've requested they bring my wife in on this. She understands people. Meanwhile, okay, I want to get on with my job . . . more because that's essential to my own sanity than for any other reason . . . but what is my job?"

"An impossible one, I'm afraid," the young man told him in a sober voice.

"Could well be. We can take EEG's and tissue samples and I don't know what from your father, we can give him psychological tests till hell wouldn't have it—" Donaldson stopped. Dick uttered a chuckle. Donaldson swallowed and plowed on: "For the time being, while they scramble around in Washington drawing organizational charts, Project Habib, *c'est moi*. My word's bound to carry weight in proportion to what results I can show before the bureaucrats descend on us. Well, I'm as anxious as you to keep the proceedings humane, to respect the rights of your father and his family. I'm also anxious to get some answers, or at least a notion of what the unanswerable questions are."

"I'm no authority."

"You are your father's son. And an almost-graduate of a seminary. And, they tell me, broad-minded. That makes you the natural lead piece in this game. Won't you tell me what you think happened?"

"A miracle." Dick's gaze was direct and calm. "I mean in the sense that Thomas Aquinas used, *praeter naturam* or *supra et contra naturam* or, in plain English, a supernatural thing. Therefore unexplainable by science. But verifiable by it."

"Hm?" Donaldson drew hard on his cigarette, grimaced, and took a sip of whisky. It glowed on the way down. *If you want quotations,* he thought, *I'll give you "Malt does more than Milton can."* Aloud: "I guess I see what you mean. Spell it out, though, will you?"

"What happened was a genuine, physical, observable event." Dick leaned into his chair, which creaked, looked out the window, and spoke with care. "I've had to come to terms myself, these past few days. Suddenly what had looked like a nice cozy symbol became reality. Well, it's happened before. Hume was more willing to assume that testimony had erred or lied than that the laws of nature had been set aside. On the other hand, the Roman Church in modern times has taken pains to investigate alleged miracles, establish their empirical authenticity. As Saint Paul did in the beginning."

Donaldson waited.

"First Corinthians," Dick said. "By now I have the passage memorized. He realized that the Resurrection is the central fact of Christianity. If you can believe that a corpse rose from its tomb, walked and talked, ate and drank and lived for forty days, why, then you can swallow anything, ancient prophecies, virgin birth, wedding at Cana, instant cures of leprosy—those are mere detail. The Resurrection is what matters. 'And if Christ be not raised, your faith is vain; ye are yet in your sins.' Paul went to considerable trouble to find eyewitnesses; he names them and lists the reasons for trusting them."

After a second he continued, "And that was a subtle miracle. I think my father caught onto one truth when he remarked that today we're so far gone into spiritual savagery that nothing except the most primitive, public sort of demonstration could touch us."

Donaldson took off his glasses, which made the world blurry, and polished them. He needed something to do. "As if we'd flunked quantum mechanics and been sent back to roll balls down inclined planes?"

Dick smiled. "I suppose. You must know better than I how much science is taken on faith. How many crucial experiments have you carried out yourself?"

"Uh-huh. Or how many theoretical developments have I traced the math of, step by step? Precious few. Still, in principle I can. Or could, till this week." Donaldson hunched forward. "Science always had its differences of interpretation. Einstein never did feel the Bohr-Heisenberg discontinuities could be right, though he had no fast proof. Remember? 'Raffiniert ist der Herr Gott, aber boshaft ist Er nicht.' "

"I'm afraid I don't know German."

"Oh, take the usual version. 'God does not play dice with the world.' Well, has He here? If He's been around at all? Or suppose He exists, suppose He did what He did for a purpose, like to save us from ourselves. Why this way? He could better have put some sanity into us."

"And taken away our free will," Dick responded. "Turned us into puppets. No, I think He would rather give us a fresh chance to make our own salvation."

"Free will!" Donaldson's fist thumped hurtfully hard on his desk. "We could spend a whole day rehearsing the tired old arguments about that pseudo-problem." He stubbed out his cigarette as if it were a personal enemy. "Salvation? What is salvation? Playing harps through eternity? Or simply being righteous? I've read a little biblical commentary too. In most of the Old Testament, they don't seem to have imagined we live past the grave." He gulped more liquor. "*What* God wrought the miracle, if any did? The Christian God? If so, what version? A medieval one surrounded by saints and angels, a Calvinist one Who plans to cast most of us into perdition, a simpering Positive Thinker, or what? How do we know it wasn't the Jewish God . . . one of the Jewish gods? Or Moslem, or any of a thousand Hindu deities, or what?"

"We don't know," Dick said. "Except by faith. Saint Paul grasped that as well as the need for facts—the absolute necessity of faith if we're to have any intellectual coherence. Read his Epistle to the Hebrews, for instance."

"And so we're back where we began!" Donaldson shouted. "Faith! Believe and be saved! What to believe? Take your choice of dogmas, each full of logical holes big enough to drive a camel through; or meaningless 'nonsectarian' mush; or science, a painfully built and always changing house, made by human hands alone—which has just had the foundations knocked from under it!"

*Sunday 26 June*

(As this day moved around the globe, churches were filled to overflowing. Where no more room was available, outdoor services were attended by thousands each. This was as true of most Communist countries, including the Soviet Union, as of the West. Non-Christian faiths draw similar hordes on their own special days. Rumors of a vast religious revival in China seep past a censorship which has put foreign journalists under virtual house arrest. On the whole, sermons have urged rededication to peace; but some have emphasized other matters.)

*Los Angeles.* The Reverend Matthew Thomas Elliott paused for a sip of water, which presented his aquiline profile to the television camera, before he tossed back a lock of hair with the well-known gesture of his head, leaned across the pulpit, and said into the faces and faces that crammed the auditorium:

"All right, my people, now I'm going to speak plain, the way God wants me to speak. I know it's going to shock the liberals. Oh, you'll hear them squeal like stuck pigs, exactly the way the Commies want them to squeal. And the children of Shem won't like it any more than the children of Ham; you know what I mean? But God has made me His vessel. If He spoke His own will—and how could He speak plainer than by stopping the sun as He did for Joshua, Joshua who fought the good fight—if He spoke loud and clear on behalf of His chosen people, honest working Americans, the people of His promised land that the Comsymps want to give over to the hosts of Moloch—if God spoke, can Matthew Thomas Elliott remain silent? Can you? Let's hear you, folks. Let's hear you speak out for the Lord!"

The "Amen!" shivered the walls.

*Oakland.* Brother Hughie Aldrich looked up, as if to see Heaven beyond the banners which hung from the ceiling. He let silence grow until the breathing of his crowd was like surf, their sweat like incense. Then, slowly, he looked downward and caught their eyes.

"What did God stop?" his famous organ tones demanded of them. "The world? Oh, yes. But that was a tiny thing. What He really stopped was this rich man's war that was getting started when the bombs of white Amerika"—he formed the K with his fingers, a gesture that had become his trademark—"struck our Chinese brothers. The rich man's war on the poor, the white man's war on the black, the brown, the yellow, the red. Well, brothers and sisters, we've been given the sign we prayed for in our agony. If the Man can go so far that God Himself has to cry 'Halt!' . . . why, then the Man can start undoing part of the misery, slavery, poverty, torture, and death he's visited on us these past four hundred years—he can do that or perish, perish beneath the wrath of God and the people!"

"Right on!" chanted back at him. "Right on! Right on! Right on!"

*Sacramento.* "And who was the prophet chosen by God?" asked the lay speaker. "Was he some wild radical? Was he some dirty dropout? No, friends, he was a law-abiding, free-enterprise American businessman, struggling to pay the taxes to support his bloated government the same as you and I must struggle. Could God have given us a clearer sign of His will?"

*San Francisco.* "What has become of Louis Habib?" cried he who delivered the keynote address. "Where is he? What have the capitalists done with him, his wife, his children? Why have they hidden him away from the people? Because they're afraid of the message an honest workingman has to bring us, the same as fascist Rome was afraid of the message a carpenter named Jesus had to bring. If we don't want another crucifixion, we'd better act fast."

*Portland.* "In the presence, brethren, in the very presence of this awesome manifestation of God's power, Satan's agents continue to gnaw like rats at the heart of faith, morality, and society. These atheists, evolutionists, free-love swine, boozers, tobacco smokers, dope fiends still try to hide from us the plain truth of God's word as revealed in the Holy Bible. Why else have they cast His chosen prophet into a nameless dungeon?"

*Seattle.* "Like, God's told the establishments what He thinks of 'em. Every establishment, dig? Every last unhuman suppressive polluting corporate monster, in America, in Russia, in China, in Europe. When He stopped the Earth spinning, He told them, 'Rotate.' Now they're scrambling to save their corruption. That's why Louis Habib, our guru, ain't here today. You dig?"

*Tijuana, San Diego, Bakersfield, Eugene, Walla Walla, Vancouver, Honolulu, and points north, south, east, and west.* "When God's word came to me and I called upon the people of the world—"

*Peking.* "After Chairman Wu's thought had massed the minds of the peace-loving peoples of the world—"

*Monday 27 June*

(The Soviet government today announced its willingness to take part in a great power conference for the purposes of defusing the Korean powder keg and working out arrangements for arms control and broadly based international cooperation. Public unrest and spontaneous meetings throughout the country, in defiance of prohibitions and calls to official rallies, are believed to have influenced the Kremlin's decision. There has been no direct Soviet response to riots in the European satellites, from which most Russian forces have withdrawn in the course of the last few days. Since these have not been deployed in the western USSR, observers think they are hurrying to the Manchurian border in alarm at the massive Chinese buildup.)

Alice Haynes Prescott, wife of the Senator, frequent contributor to magazines, television panelist, former United States ambassador to Belgium, president of the Women's League for Social Justice, vice-president of Americans United for Law and Order, inevitable on every best-dressed list, beamed with long but dazzling teeth and said, "You can't imagine how hard it was to learn where you were and be admitted. My husband the Senator and I had to—if I may use the expression reverently—move heaven and earth."

"Nice of you," Louis Habib mumbled.

She patted his hand. "The arrogance! The sheer stupidity! Though" (a delicate moue) "I must say I would expect no better of the present Administration."

"Oh, they did what they figured was right. We've not, uh, been mistreated. In fact, the Donaldsons are damn nice—begging your pardon."

She measured out a laugh. "Well, quite as I thought. The holy man is human."

He swallowed and looked from her. It was bright, gusty weather. Clouds scudded small on a wind which roared in the eucalyptus trees. Sun-flecks and leaf shadows danced on crackly-carpeted ground; pungency whirled through the air, which was cool. Below spread the Radlab complex, and hills toppled down into Berkeley, the Bay danced aglitter, San Francisco rose white, Marin County lifted heights that were blue-hazed with distance.

He had grabbed the chance to go for a walk when this woman desired it. The two guards who came behind didn't spoil the day much. Now he wished he'd crawled into the darkest corner of the quarters hastily rigged for his family and shoveled old newspapers over himself.

"I'm not a holy man," he said, half strangled. "I've told 'em and told 'em till the words turn me sick. I got no visions, not then, not since, never. I don't feel any different. Sure, I'm glad to learn there is a God and we matter to Him . . . I guess we do. But I don't know anything about Him, I tried to say daily prayers but felt too silly, I'm no kind of priest and don't want to be."

"I understand, Lou. You're the man of genius, exactly as I described him in my article for *Civilization* magazine. The real geniuses have all been unpretentious men and women, you know. When somebody is bombastic, like the composer Richard Wagner, it proves he isn't a genius."

"Who says I thought of the idea first?" He waved his arms. "I been watching TV, what times they aren't quizzing me or putting me through their stupid tests. Quite a lot of guys claim they had the original notion. Could be. Why not? An idea sort of floats around when the time is ripe, don't you think?" He pounced at what seemed an opportunity. "In fact, Mrs. Prescott, the more I think about it, the more sure I am that I was a Johnny-come-lately. This guy back east, says he was pushing for everybody to pray together these past three years—sure, I'll bet I heard about him somewhere and, uh, subconsciously . . . No?"

She shook her head firmly. The wind had displaced no hair upon it. "No, dear," she smiled. "Cranks and false prophets we have always among us. They don't count. The overwhelming majority of the Free World knows that the inspiration came to you. Vox populi, vox Dei. That's Latin and means, 'The voice of the people is the voice of God.' "

"Uh, I don't know much, uh, theology, but I doubt—"

"Besides," Alice Haynes Prescott told him, "you have a patriotic duty. Don't you realize what would happen if you, the American seer, disowned yourself? Haven't you heard of Wu Yuan's preposterous assertion that he is responsible for the event? You can't let such a madman go unchallenged, especially when the international situation is so critical. My husband the Senator is preparing a major speech on the subject; that's why he isn't here today. For my part, I intend to make good use of my appearance on the "Forefront" show Wednesday night. And you must back us up in the clinches, Lou."

"Well . . . well, I never went in for politics, Mrs. Prescott."

"Alice." Again she patted his hand. "Never fear. Some of the most talented speechwriters in the country will be at your disposal. And—don't breathe a word of this, Lou—Rance Rockstone called me personally from Hollywood and offered his services in any coaching you might need. No, not a peep out of you. I know this sounds terribly, terribly insincere, but the fact is you can't put your sincerity across without professional help. Besides, Rance is one of the most sincere persons alive. You'll find out."

"We better go back," he said. "I better ask my wife."

"Oh, come along a while. A lovely day. Naturally, you should consult Helen. I want to myself. I'm sure she'll have thousands of good ideas for the gala we'll give in Washington to celebrate your arrival, as soon as my husband the Senator has won your release from here. And your children . . . what fine young persons. Did you know that I'm on the board of the Minerva Foundation? Among other things, it gives college scholarships to deserving students, very generous ones, if I do say so."

*Tuesday 28 June*

(The call for a People's Crusade, a mass descent on Washington to insist on "peace and equal rights under God," is gathering adherents from all walks of life with terrifying speed. By now an estimated million individuals are on the move, and more are added every hour. Authorities express concern at the health hazard and at the violent tone of many spokesmen, like one who declared, "This is Armageddon." Already they have trouble maintaining order, especially when groups of would-be demonstrators encounter such militant newly formed rivals as White Americans for Christ, Angels of the Judgment, United Anarchists, and the Religious Freedom League [atheist].

In a press conference, President Reisner deplored what he termed mass hysteria. He also warned against a quieter but, he said, still stronger tendency for workers to quit their jobs and seek a religious life of some kind. "When vital and complex negotiations on the highest levels are to be undertaken," he stated, "the American government must not be weakened at home." He refused comment on the rumor that desertions from the armed services are taking place at such a rate that many units have become completely ineffective.)

"Similar phenomena are not unknown in history." The psychiatrist had to raise his voice above the cocktail-party hubbub. The smoke made him cough a bit. "Consider the medieval dancing manias or the Reformation witch hunts. Today, thanks to global electronic communications, a piece of news, an attitude—a conversion—can spread at the speed of light."

"Everybody saw the sun halted in its course," the chemistry professor pointed out.

"Yes, yes. The difference from the past, had it occurred in the past, is this. Virtually no individual, certainly no community, could decide in privacy and at leisure what it meant or how to react. Everybody saw, or at least heard on a radio, the most spectacular things that everybody else was doing. Of course you get a lemming effect! The trend's been visible for decades. It changed the character of politics before you or I were born. Today, however, it's gained a new order of magnitude. Some fascinating depth-psych studies wait to be done." The psychiatrist grimaced. "If we survive."

"Oh, I'm sure we will," the professor said comfortably. "I can't imagine the miracle was passed for any reasons except two, and one of them was to prevent us from destroying ourselves."

"What was the other?"

"To give us further information about reality." The professor held his glass out to a passing waiter. While a filled one was handed him, he chose a canapé. "You know I was not a devout man before the event," he said. "And I don't suppose I am yet, in any conventional sense. I've positively no intention of becoming a Mormon. Nevertheless, the Mormons do have something in their doctrine of continual revelation: the idea that the Cosmic Force (which term I prefer, tentatively) has not given us any last word but speaks further to us when it deems us ready for the next stage of comprehension."

"Hm. Pretty noncommittal this time around, I'd say."

"No, no. Far from it. You see, we were given a scientifically measurable phenomenon, precisely in an era of sophisticated instrumentation and analytical techniques. I expect a flood of papers on every aspect. For example, I happen to know that personnel aboard our manned space laboratory took close observations on changes in its orbit due to the pause in terrestrial rotation. Not to speak of meteorology, continental drift, solar wind, et cetera. Now let's organize these data in various ways, crank them through suitable computers in search of patterns—d'you see?"

The psychiatrist blinked. "You hope to . . . find clues to the nature of God?"

"Precisely," said the professor. "I don't claim a coded message is buried in fluctuations of the Van Allen belts. Such things are conceivable and we must check them out. But the fact that the Cosmic Force has operated in *this* manner rather than *that*— d'you see? Just as man went from astrology to astronomy, he's about to move from theology to theonomy." He nudged his companion. "Ah, please keep this confidential, but I've put my grad students to work and I expect soon to have a proposal which'll make NSF spring for as hefty a grant as ever was dreamed of. Really, you ought to get something in yourself before the rush begins."

*Wednesday 29 June*
(In a lightning predawn move, Israeli troops struck deeply into Jordan and Syria. Premier Levi ben-Zvi asserted that the massacre at Jericho was only the last straw and his government intends to reach a final solution of the fedayeen problem. He warned that if Egypt or any other nation makes a move in the holy war which muezzins have been preaching throughout the Arab world this week, "Israel will take what measures are indicated." He did not rule out the use of tactical nuclear weapons, which he revealed his country possesses. Defense Minister Rachmael Hertz stated bluntly, "Last week, after three thousand years, again the Lord God of Hosts made Himself known to us.")

"What can we do?" Helen Habib implored. "Tell me what we can do."

Gail Donaldson was quiet a while. They were, for once, alone in the apartment. Their husbands were in conference and the

Habib children had been allowed a picnic, under supervision. *Mine are in care of my parents*, passed through her awareness. *Why have they been spared when these were not?*

On one side of the room, a window gave on a view of the bevatron building. Occasionally someone passed by. Work was resuming, an incredible business as usual. The sun was harshly bright, the air still and hot, but Helen refused to turn the conditioner on, though sweat ran over both their skins. "I've got to have that much natural," she had said.

At length Gail, who was seated, gave a direct look to the other woman, who paced back and forth before her. "I really have no right to counsel you," she murmured. "You're older. No, I don't mean calendar ages. They aren't important. But I suspect you've seen more of life than I have."

"Well, I can tell you about making a way from field work in the Central Valley to lower middle class in Oakland," Helen replied. "No information about how to be famous in that, is there? You're the only person I trust who might know." Her lips drew back, her voice rose. "Oh, help me!" Echoes bounced flatly off bare walls.

"Well." Gail decided she could be more soothing if she leaned back and pretended to be at ease. Damn, how the chair stuck to blouse and shorts and thighs! "Simon has a method of standing off from a problem to study it."

"He hasn't seemed any too calm either," Helen flung at her.

Gail winced. "No. Your man has no monopoly on troubles." She gathered will and words. "I'll try the system anyhow. First you spell the whole business out, item by item. Most seem too obvious to be worth bothering with, but that's misleading. What we need is the relationship between them."

Helen stopped, raised crook-fingered hands, and nearly screamed, "Santa María, hasn't this analyzing any end?"

"You asked for my help." Gail hoped she sounded as humble as she felt. "I'm doing my poor best."

"I'm sorry." Helen sat down on the edge of another chair. "Please go on."

"M-m-m. Because Lou is . . . associated . . . with what happened, everybody assumes he must have special talents or a direct line to God or something. Everybody except him."

"And me. I've told you that. I haven't seen a halo over him or . . . or any change, except that he's tired and worried and sorry. Why, I was the one who pushed him to write that letter and afterward go on that show. And I'm in no state of grace."

"What do the children think?"

"I can't tell. Who can tell about children? Maybe they don't know themselves. Dick prays a lot, Jimmy sulks a lot, and I think poor Steffie daydreams about how she'll be sought after when she returns to college."

"Okay," Gail said. "An officialdom that couldn't imagine what else to do hustled you here. Maybe that was unwise. Yet what can police, civil service, elected politicians do about a miracle? Play cautious; and, as long as Lou was sequestrated, make the effort to find out if there was in fact anything unique about him. A foolish, futile effort, seen by hindsight. Like quarantining the original lunar astronauts. But the stakes being what they were in either case, how could you not take every possible niggling precaution?"

"I know," Helen said. "He's made me understand and forgive, a little. We're lucky Simon was put in charge. We'd hoped, though—"

"Hoped you'd soon be released?" Gail shook her head. "Dear, Lou can no more escape being the first man who told us to ask for a sign than Neil Armstrong can escape, ever, being the first man on the moon. So don't fight it. Use it."

"That's what we can't," Helen whispered. "I'm afraid, I'm afraid."

"Let's keep on laying out the facts," Gail said. "Obviously your detention here is temporary. Half of humanity is aclamor to know what's become of you. President Reisner *must* be seen on television with Lou."

"That horrible woman—"

"Never mind her. I find her rather pathetic. Lou has incomparably more power, if only he can use it right. Which is what I'm getting at. Not simply that the Habibs can better themselves in a material way. Though what harm if you do? Mainly, however, think what an influence for good he can be. Suppose—oh, suppose he called for real, enforceable universal disarmament and real, meaningful justice for the poor and oppressed. He doesn't have to parrot what some scriptwriter hands him, you know."

"I'm afraid he will." Helen's fingers writhed in her lap. "Gail, he's—he's innocent. He never went to college. He did most of his Army hitch in Iceland, of all forsaken places. Afterward he met me and we got married, and ever since, it's been work, first in a filling station—night school to become a mechanic—then in a garage, then to make his own business go. He's never had any enemies. When somebody pushed him, he'd just go quiet and immovable, and the person couldn't get angry. He doesn't read much; a bit of popular history has been the most intellectual stuff he's ever gotten through. What he likes best on television is pro football. He goes bowling and fishing with his friends. Vacations, we usually go . . . went . . . go auto camping." She bit her lip. "Never mind the rest. Ordinary too." Louder: "Put him in Washington among important fast-talking people and what can he do?"

"To a large extent," Gail said softly, "that will depend on you, Helen."

"Who am I?" Both rose to their feet. Helen was crying. "I told you I'm no saint. I'm not even bright."

"Between us, dear, I think you're considerably more bright than your husband."

"M-m-maybe. But—Gail, there's been nothing between us since . . . since before. . . . It's been like living with a shadow. And everybody back east, waiting for him, wanting him to use. . . . Yes, women, why not admit I . . . I . . . I'm scared of them? I shouldn't be, but I am." Helen sought her companion's arms. "I miss him, I miss him."

Gail stroked the dark hair while tears mingled with the sweat on her shoulder. "You'll have to fight, Helen," she said. "I'll try to help you plan. In the end, though, nobody but you can fight on your side. Not even God."

*Thursday 30 June*

(The vote of no confidence which toppled the government of India has ominous implications, according to knowledgeable observers. The new parliament is sure to contain a number of the Kali worshipers, who are making converts at a wildfire rate. Their truculence may well cause a reaction in Pakistan, already alight with Moslem fervor kindled by the "night of Allah" and fanned to a blaze by the Middle Eastern war. Other experts, while hoping conflict can be averted, foresee a turning away from what one called "rational-technological civilization" toward more traditional modes throughout southern Asia.)

"Well," Donaldson said, and knew how inanely he spoke, "soon you're off."

"Yeah." Louis Habib reached in his shirt pocket for a fresh cigar. The office smelled stale from those whose stubs overflowed the ashtray. But dusk blew in a window, cool and quiet. Early stars twinkled forth. They could be seen above darkened buildings, because Donaldson had only one small lamp lit on his desk.

Its glow was lost in the lines and hollows lately carved over his countenance. "Don't worry about Dick, Jim, Steffie," he said, still repeating himself. "We're glad to have them stay with us till you and Helen get back. And I don't think they'll meet any trouble. A lot of nuisance, yes, but nothing serious."

Habib's own gaze was dull. "You're too kind."

"Not in the least." Donaldson became busy polishing his glasses. "We like them. And . . . to tell the truth, Dick's in a position to help me."

"A boy?"

"Wiser than me, in the area where I most need wisdom. You, uh, you can't have failed to notice, I'm a shaken man these days."

Habib squinted at Donaldson, lit his cigar, and blew a couple of smoke rings before he said slowly, "I have noticed. Your religion fell apart last week, didn't it?"

"I've about decided that it did."

"Think Dick's church has the answer?"

"No. Or, at any rate, I can't bring myself to make the . . . the commitment. Too much seems to fly straight upwind of reason. And, without the creed, what use the rites?" Donaldson hesitated. "Your son told me the same. He believes, now. But he said to me, God wouldn't be honored by an act of autohypnosis on my part."

"What's he doing for you, then?"

"O-oh, listening, mainly. Like my wife. Dick, though, Dick knows the books. He can point out where these questions have been raised before, century after century. I . . . My problem is, Lou, and I'm surely far from unique—I have to make sense out of a universe which somehow contains both the data of science and the fact of what took place. I can't accept the Russian spacemen or the Chinese psionics. They're too *ad hoc*. Dick's helping me reconcile myself to the idea of a sentient, supernatural order of creation."

"Good." Habib's voice turned harsh. "But he'd better do some explaining away of his own."

"Hm?"

"Let him figure out how the same world can hold a God who's a loving Father, and what we see on every newscast or in every cancer ward."

"That problem is as old as Akhnaton."

"Who? Never mind. We have to live it today." Habib slammed fist into palm. In anguish: "What'm I supposed to do?"

*Friday 1 July*

(British and Irish troops are waging a vain struggle against fanatical Christian Liberation Front gangs rising throughout Northern Ireland and invading from the south. "Untrained and poorly armed though they are, barriers and tear gas are not stopping them, admitted Eire Premier John Ward. "Yet if we open fire, it will be a political as well as a moral catastrophe." In a statement issued from secret headquarters, CLF leaders scorned Pope Benedict's demand that they order an end to terrorism on pain of excommunication. "Irish Christianity was Celtic before it was Catholic," they maintained. "It will be Celtic anew. God's purpose is clear.")

Nobody knew whence the preacher had come, nor even his full name. He called himself simply Ivan, a simple worker on a nearby kolkhoz until an insight, which he dared not believe was divine, came to send him forth. He had been addressing the regiment at sunset for the past three days. The first time, a political officer had tried to arrest him, and was hauled away by a score of hands. Ivan told the men to show mercy. He reproached them next evening when he learned the political officer had been found dead of a dozen bayonet stabs. Then Colonel Kuprin decreed that every law-abiding Soviet citizen had a right to be heard and every soldier not on duty a right to listen; and he came too, with his staff.

Mikhail Grigorovitch Saltykov had to strain to hear. Ivan spoke softly, though his voice carried, and a wind had sprung up, chill and murmurous across the mournful plain. Mikhail, who was only a private and a small man, stood well back in the mass of his comrades. He was glad of that. It was a warmth amidst the blowing bleakness, and a comfort to feel human bodies around one at this hour when the sun slipped from sight.

Bearded, unkempt, raggedly clad, Ivan stood on a tank. The waning light cast him dark across a greenish western sky. Eastward a few stars appeared in gray-purple heaven. Mikhail shivered. He had been in his home village on furlough when It happened. Throughout that night without end the stars had stood unmoving, numberless, keen and terrible over the fields, and poor old Nikolai Ilyitch had gone mad.

Ivan pointed beyond camp, to the river, which shone like polished metal, broken by sandbars, and to the murky mass of the Chinese camp on the far side, where lanterns began to glow.

"—our brothers," he said. "All men are our brothers. Have you not heard the word of Jesus Christ? He damns himself like Cain who hates and slays his brother. Could our Lord not have called down the hosts of the angels to avenge His wounds? Instead, he reproved Peter for drawing a sword upon one man. For that man was a common soldier, and so was very precious to God.

"Our leaders have explained to us that the Earth was stopped in its course upon the great day by wise and kindly beings from yonder." He pointed aloft, and Mikhail discovered those lights were not really inhuman, they were almost like the lanterns over the river. "These beings would rescue us from our sinful folly. The Party has made it quite plain. I, a common man, a simpleton, have nothing to add except this: That those good guardians must have been here before. Our Lord Jesus Christ must have been chief among them. The Resurrection was no less real because it was done by scientific means, nor was our Lord less holy because he descended from a planet and returned thence."

Ivan laid a hand on the cannon that jutted forth beside him. "Well, comrades," he said, "I explained this much yesterday, and you, who are more learned than me, seemed to feel it is reasonable. Now I wish to ask a further question. If the masters from the stars are here again, *is this not the Second Coming of Jesus Christ which was foretold?*"

A gasp went into the wind.

"And if that be true," Ivan's patient sentences continued, "what is required of us? What except repentance for evil deeds, resolution to do better, and that love for our fellows which God and the Party alike tell us is our duty as well as our joy?

"Comrades, do not fear wrath and burning. It is unthinkable that the star masters would ravage a helpless Earth. We ourselves were about to do that, before we were stopped. Therefore, what need to fear other men? They too are stopped from drawing the sword. The motherland now needs something else than defense.

"What Jesus Christ Returned wants is simple. Lay down your arms. Go home to your dear ones. Work until our Russia has been made a temple fit for the Lord."

*If we did!* flashed through Mikhail. *If we did! A long march back, but singing all the way; and at the end, Marina, you!*

*Saturday 2 July*
(The junta which has seized power in Argentina is extending its control from Buenos Aires to the hinterland with little difficulty. Its pledge to "restore order and the holy Catholic faith" is popular. The situations in Brazil and Chile remain confused.)

Outside, the White House lawn was ringed by soldiers. Beyond its high iron fence, the crowd had become inhuman through sheer mass. William Reisner wondered how many would die today, packed like that in the suffocating Washington summer. Every once in a while a trooper fainted, was borne off and replaced. The mass was orderly—thus far—unlike too many elsewhere. It made noise, a scraping mumble which penetrated the whir of the air conditioner.

He released the hand of Helen Habib. "Do be seated," he told her and her husband.

"Thanks . . . uh . . . thank you, Mr. President," the man said. They obeyed stiffly.

Reisner settled down too, more at ease. It occurred to him that to them the aides and Secret Service men were not part of the Georgian decor. Their eyes, flickering about, reminded him of a wounded deer he'd once found and dispatched. (A quarter century ago? Impossible.) "I hope you had a pleasant trip," he said.

"Yes, thank you, Mr. President." Louis Habib was barely audible.

His wife showed more animation: "I'd never been on a plane before. To start out on Air Force One! And afterward a helicopter!"

*No way to get you from National to here except by chopper,* the President thought. He donned a smile. "We aim to please. I hope you'll be satisfied with your guest apartment. Whatever you need, tell the gentleman who'll conduct you there shortly." He paused. "I know you're tired. I've been through time-zone changes myself. But I did want a quiet, private chat, as private as one can be in this job, before the VIP storm breaks."

"The what?" Habib coughed. "Oh, yes. VIP." His tone lifted in pitch. "We're not, sir. Isn't there any way to convince people of what's true? I'm not holy, not smart, nothing."

"As a matter of fact," Reisner said, "I am convinced." That caught them. He laughed; a politician learns how to do so at need. "If you tell me you had no miraculous visions, no flash of inspiration, merely an idea that others may well also have had, I believe you."

"Well, tell them!" exploded from the wife.

Reisner sighed. "I'm afraid you're wrong on one detail, Mr. Habib. You're not 'nothing.' For better or worse, you're identified with the miracle. Let's try to make it for better."

"How?"

"It won't be too rough. After we finish here, I'd like you to appear briefly on a balcony, just wave and accept the cheers. As for your scheduled press conference, we've screened the reporters very carefully. You'll be asked nothing embarrassing, nothing that will commit you to any particular position."

"But Tuesday night—" Habib gulped.

Reisner nodded. "Yes. Your televised speech. That's the payoff. You're bound to have the largest audience in history, and the most desperately anxious to follow any lead you give."

"I haven't got anything."

"Haven't you? It can be supplied. I hear that Senator Prescott has, ah, kindly volunteered assistance."

Blood beat in Helen's Indian visage. "I read that 'draft speech' his wife gave Lou," she snapped.

"And?" Reisner hinted.

"It's not a bad speech," Louis Habib said lamely.

Helen fleered. "It's a damn clever speech, if you think you ought to give God's personal endorsement to Senator Prescott's being elected the next President."

"Uh, honey, I didn't see—" The words trailed off. "Well, I'm only a knucklehead."

"I wouldn't agree," Reisner lied. "You get the point, I'm sure. Inevitably, everyone wants your prestige to serve his personal or partisan ends."

Habib ceased squirming. His eyes said, *You too.*

"Yes," Reisner confessed. "Of course I'd like to be reelected. I hope to do it on my merits, not on the cheap. The future of the United States is rather more important than the future of my career."

They waited.

"I needn't remind you how difficult and dangerous this period is for the country," he said. "At the same time, we've never had more dazzling opportunities. Suddenly the morale, the entire organization of our rivals is disintegrating. Abroad. At home— that's another story." Reisner bridged his fingers and proceeded in his most judicious manner: "You can stand before the cameras Tuesday, Mr. Habib, and utter platitudes like 'Love thy neighbor.' Nice, safe, noncontroversial, and empty. Or you can come out for or against specific things that specific persons are trying to do. That will make you enemies as well as friends. But it might bring about the survival of your country.

"We'll discuss this in more detail tomorrow, after you've caught your breath. Meanwhile, you'll find a typescript in your suite. It's rather thick, I'm afraid, and heavy going—because it has the facts, the statistics, hard information rather than pious generalities—but I'll be grateful, America will be grateful, if you'll study it and let me know your reaction."

*Sunday 3 July*

(South African authorities admitted they were helpless in the face of the general strike by nonwhite workers which has paralyzed the nation. Native leader Bastiaan Ingwamza told correspondents: "That night under the unmoving stars, we heard God say, 'Enough.' Now, His will be done. Whether they shoot us down or let us starve or give us our ordinary rights as we ask, an end will come to the evil." Prime Minister Marcus de Smet declared in an official statement: "The government is willing to negotiate and to right wrongs as fast as possible. However, this cannot happen quickly. An industrial economy cannot function when the uneducated are set equal to the educated or when a separation which many hold to be divinely ordained is struck down. Collapse would be inevitable. Certain orators who have helped bring on the strike have openly said collapse is desirable.")

The head of the political police cried, "But we have some loyal troops left! And the missiles! Now, to lose this very moment when the American fleet is departing and the Russian armies are melting away—"

Chairman Wu Yuan answered lifelessly, "We cannot afford a victory."

"What? Honored leader, I fail to grasp your thought."

"When every day more units mutiny, when at home more millions every day reject—or, worse, ignore or laugh at—official orders . . . do you seriously propose we spend what strength we have in Korea? No. I am recalling those brigades. The Koreans will have to liberate themselves." Wu sagged back. "I doubt they will. If reports of what is going on among them are to be trusted."

"Is anything to be trusted any longer?" the other man asked out of his despair.

"I do not know," Wu sighed. "I do not know. I was quite sincere in my idea, my dream, that man had moved the planet, man stood on the threshold of transcendence. Who would have guessed that . . . the thing . . . would turn the people to the past? Would make them serve their ancestors and read the *Tao-te-ching* and the *Analects* aloud to eager thousands, and divide the col-

lectives up among families where once more Grandfather is lord
—and this within less than a month—?"

"Mere panic. They will come to their senses."

"I doubt it."

"They can be led."

"Can they? How shall we even reach them?"

The police head gave the chairman a narrow look. His own
courage was returning. "You seem to feel this government will
not endure," he said.

"Oh, it will, I suppose. We can limp along in a fashion, as one
more set of warlords among the many who will soon rip our land
apart. . . . China, China! What has Heaven done to you?"

The chairman covered his face and wept. The police head
fingered his sidearm. It might prove necessary to replace the chairman. That was a gamble, however; it risked a struggle for succes-
sion which could, indeed, bring the state down in ruin.

Night thickened beyond the windows.

*Monday 4 July*
(In a grisly parody of Independence Day celebrations, fires in
Baltimore, Newark, and Cincinnati raged out of control as firemen were checked by rioters. Street battles in Chicago, between
extremists of the right and left convinced God is on their sides,
mounted in frequency and ferocity. To date, the armored division
which rings Washington against the People's Crusade converg-
ing on it has not suffered serious attack. But tension increases.)

They lay in each other's arms, in darkness, and whispered.

"Helen, what'm I going to say?"

Her breath touched his ear, her warmth enfolded him. "What's
right Lou. You're that kind of guy."

"What is right? How can I know? God, God, whatever I say,
human beings'll die because of it."

Her voice turned dry. "Well, read your speech."

"Which speech?—I guess I forgot to tell you. After the reception today, I found two more slipped into my coat."

"No surprise." She stroked his hair a while, until she had the strength to give him strength. "I think you should scrap them all."

"What can *I* say?" He shuddered.

"You'll know."

"Huh? God's not with me!"

"You're with yourself, Lou. Let them hear a good man. You are one." Helen chuckled most softly. "I'm sure of that. I have experience."

"You. You." He clung to her as the children had done when they were small and hurt. "I love you."

"Regardless of what happens tomorrow," she said, "they've been wonderful years. Thanks for them, darling."

*Tuesday 5 July*

(Distinguished Harvard economist Martin Bielawski warns of possible national collapse. "Spreading lawlessness is only a symptom," he stated in a public lecture. "True, it may destroy us, as fever may destroy a sick person. Yet fever is not the sole symptom of a disease, nor are any symptoms its cause. What appears to be happening is this. Across the whole world, a God-starved generation has encountered the supernatural and become, overnight, God-intoxicated. Fanaticism is an ugly manifestation. It can be countered. What cannot be controlled is the seemingly benign, peaceful absorption of millions in their newfound faith. The job, the state, the obligations and satisfactions of temporal existence no longer impress them as of any great importance. The exodus from the cities, in search of utopian rural simplicity, is high in the news. But more significant is the exodus within the cities. Thousands each day quit their work in favor of something less demanding, something that leaves them time and energy to explore their own souls. Intelligent, educated persons, in positions of responsibility, are especially prone to this change of heart, as might be expected. No doubt, in its fashion, it is commendable. But industrial society cannot survive much of it. Consider the power blackouts, the stock-market nosedive, and the virtual breakdown of banking and credit systems this past week. Such disintegration feeds upon itself; those who had not intended to resign from their jobs will soon lose them. We rejoice to see hostile governments turning impotent. We forget that our own is equally mortal.")

Louis Habib's talk was set for nine P.M., which was six on the West Coast. His children and the Donaldsons ate an early dinner. It was interrupted by a reporter who wanted to watch them watching the screen. Gail had to be downright nasty before they were rid of him.

She drew the curtains so that the image would be brighter. Because of sparse auto traffic and the shutdown of most factories, the air above the streets was clear. Fog rolled in through the Gate and across the Bay, which at sunset would become a bowl of molten gold.

The young Habibs poised mute, altogether vulnerable. Her own boys sprawled bottoms up on the floor, eagerly awaiting whatever they were to see. *Your future lives, perhaps,* she thought. The uselessness of her wish to guard them made a pain in her throat. Simon sat chain-smoking but otherwise calm. She switched on the set, adjusted the color, and lowered herself to a chair beside his.

"—the new, new, new product—"

Her older son made an obscene comment.

"John!" she exclaimed. "Where'd you learn such language?"

He grinned. "From my father." In chilling scorn, he jerked a thumb at the commercial and said, "Big, grown men still think that garbage matters."

She wanted to send him out, but the station break ended. "—Ladies and gentlemen, the President of the United States."

Through all the makeup and mannerism, Reisner looked weary

unto death, Gail thought. His introduction was good: brief, reasonably free of clichés, frank about the fact that the speaker disavowed prophethood. "Nevertheless, his modesty cannot conceal his wisdom. Though he may disagree, it is my honest belief, shared by millions, that he is at least partly responsible for the tremendous event of two weeks ago. Mankind waits to hear him. To his country, to humanity, I have the honor of presenting Louis Habib."

A camera swung about. For a moment the man stood small and alone at a lectern. Then the zoom lens brought him in, as if he were shoved through a tunnel, until his face filled the screen. It was also a tired face; but the nervousness, the near-terror that Gail remembered were gone.

"Good evening," he said.

He lifted a sheaf of papers. The optics hastily backed up to give a wider view. "Here's the speech I was supposed to read," he went on. He strewed it across the floor. "Sorry."

"Good for you, dad!" yelped his younger son.

"Oh, no." His daughter shrank into herself.

His older son drew the sign of the cross. Gail's hand sought her husband's, found it and clung.

"Never mind who wrote those pages," Habib was saying. "I had quite a few scripts given me. Pretty well done, too. Any of 'em would've sounded better than I will. I decided, though, if you figured you'd be hearing me, the only fair thing to do was speak my own piece."

The picture blanked. PLEASE STAND BY flashed on the screen. "They can't!" Gail protested.

"They'll realize that in a minute," Simon Donaldson said grimly.

Sight and sound returned: "—trouble is, I haven't got any real piece to speak. No message from on high. No solutions to your problems. No comfort for your griefs.

"Look," said the plodding voice, "the men who wanted to use me for a mouthpiece are a lot smarter than me. And I suppose they mostly are decent. They want me to, uh, endorse platforms or candidates or ideas . . . whatever . . . whatever they think is best for the country, for the world. Maybe they're right, some of them. But they can't all be right.

"For instance, well, President Reisner, who's been very kind, President Reisner has a program which amounts to, uh, restoring the same old rickety balance of power." The camera panned to the introducer, seated behind the speaker, and caught him appalled. Habib smiled. "Understand, he means well. And maybe we should stick with the devil we maybe know. But a big publisher, a gentleman named Link, wants the United States to make itself world boss. Senator Leverett feels that God wants us to put ourselves under the command of the United Nations. Senator Prescott says we have to, uh, institute a consortium. I'm not sure what that means. Congressman Lippert says we've got to drop everything else and go to the aid of Israel. Congressman Flaherty says we have a sacred mission to liberate Northern Ireland. Congressman Bradford says we have to guarantee every citizen five thousand dollars a year. And so on and so on, including those who didn't get a chance to approach me.

"Well, like I said, none of these gentlemen are crooks, and could be one of them is right. Only how can I tell which? How can you?"

Habib stuck hands in pockets of the suit that, tailored for him, had instantly lost its superb fit. Between thin strands of hair his scalp caught a highlight. "Now I'll tell you what I think," he said, "if you'll please bear in mind it's just me thinking, an ordinary dumb guy who's probably dead wrong. I think we must've been mighty close to wrecking the world. Else why did God pass a miracle? He sure didn't for the Ukrainians under Stalin or the Jews under Hitler or the Tibetans under Mao. Maybe He gives us a leg up now and then, like the Bible says, and this was the latest. Or maybe He had to save this beautiful planet from us. And you know, it could be He's not saving it for us. Get the difference? We could be a kind of dinosaur, or become one if we don't take care."

He drew breath. "I wonder if maybe it isn't the world that God loves," he said. "The whole of it. Everything that is. Mountains, bugs, and trees the same as people. I wonder if maybe we shouldn't stop supposing we're the center and, uh, the purpose of everything. If maybe we shouldn't stop hiding God behind a mask shaped like a human face."

He stood silent for a space, took his hands out, shrugged, and smiled. "I don't know," he said. "I can't tell you what to do. Can anybody? Thanks and good night."

The cameras followed him as he stumped offstage.

*Wednesday 6 July*

(The Salvation Army today announced plans for monastery-like communities. A statement issued at national headquarters said: "Our recruits are so fantastically numerous since God last manifested Himself that we have no place for most of them in our usual work among the urban needy. At the same time, the number of those needy is growing as the current financial panic deepens into a depression. Federal and state governments are in such difficulties that we dare not assume they can cope much longer with the problem. Therefore men must turn from impersonal 'welfare' and 'charity' to that *caritas*, love of man within the love of God, enjoined by Scripture. We plan to use the added personnel whom divine grace has brought us on large farms—since land is being deeded and willed us all over North America—to produce necessities for distribution among the poor. It is hoped that many of the poor, in turn, will wish to join this effort.")

"Okay," the Secret Service agent said. "End of the line."

Habib rose. The airplane enclosed him and Helen; beyond, the airport was bare concrete. "Uh, I thought—" he began.

The agent grinned. "Thought a limousine 'ud chauffeur you to your house? Sorry. The President said return you to Oakland."

The President had said little more than that.

Sweat studded the agent's forehead. "I oughtn't to blab this," rasped from him. "But I will. I'm probably going to quit my job anyway. Habib, you had your chance to save the country, and you flushed it down the drain. Do you really expect any more red carpets? I have three small kids of my own, Habib."

"But . . . what could I do . . . how could I know . . . ? And we *weren't* looking for a limousine!"

"Come." Helen took her man's arm. "Thanks for the ride, sir."

When they were outside, she remarked, "People don't like being told they have to make their own lives and success isn't guaranteed. But you were right to tell them."

They trudged across hardness, beneath an empty sky. Two stood at the fence behind the terminal. Recognition startled Habib. "Hey, Si and Gail! Let's go!" He jogged. Passing the gate, he hugged them both.

It had taken repeated attempts to telephone them from Washington. Connections were scatty.

It was worth the trouble. A clean wind blew and the hills lifted lion-colored.

Gail Donaldson said unevenly, "I'm afraid we have bad news. The police guard on your home was withdrawn last night. Nothing's left. Looted and burned."

Habib and his wife regarded each other. She managed a smile. "Well, we have insurance."

"I hope your insurance company isn't one of those that've filed bankruptcy." Simon Donaldson blinked hard behind his glasses. "Whatever happens, we'll always have an extra potato in the pot."

Habib wrung his hand for a moment before, again, clasping Helen's. Gail explained, "There're quite a few onlookers around our own place. They don't know when or how you were due back, but figure it must be soon. That's why Simon and I left everybody else behind and went off by ourselves as if to go shopping. At that, we were followed, but shook those cars by ducking around an Army convoy."

"Are they mad at us?" Helen asked quickly.

"No," Donaldson said. "Contrariwise. Expectant. Hopeful. Big 'Welcome Back' signs. Doubtless you will have to beware of the embittered disillusioned. But some faiths are unshaken."

"I tried to tell them—" Habib slumped. They walked to the car in silence. It stood almost alone in the parking lot. On the freeway he stirred and said, "Maybe God was also trying to get a simple message across. Maybe He's always been trying."

Helen stroked his cheek.

Donaldson took the Gilman Street exit into Berkeley. Though other automobiles were few, he found the way crowded. From the campus area had overflowed processions of candle-bearing Christian penitents and yellow-robed, shaven-headed, joyfully chanting and dancing Krishna worshipers. Householders stood at their doors and watched. Some joined in.

When the ground began to climb, the pavement grew clear and they drove among rose gardens. Habib gusted a sigh. "Good to be home," he said.

"What are your plans?" Gail inquired.

"Oh . . . to rebuild. House and business both."

"Frankly," Donaldson said, "I'm not sure a garage is a sound investment any longer. I wouldn't be surprised but what I finish my life as a teacher in a one-room country school."

"No odds to me," Habib said. "Any area needs men who can make machinery behave. A pity for you."

"Not necessarily," Donaldson replied. "It could beat designing weapons—a job I'll gladly drop when everybody else does. I don't want to sound Pollyanna. Still, I could perhaps even do some research. The end of huge apparatus and huge organization, if it comes, doesn't have to spell the end of discovery."

Louis Habib laid an arm around Helen. "Nor the end of being happy," she said.

They rounded a curve. Donaldson cursed and stamped on the

brakes. Gail choked off a yell. "That many—that fast? Who told them? Get away from here!"

He threw the gears into reverse and backed. He was too late. The fringes of those ten thousand human beings who surrounded his place had seen him, and called to the rest.

They engulfed the car. The doors came off beneath their reaching. The faces were only eyeballs and mouths, the voices mostly a shriek through stench. Here and there a word slashed past.

"Help."

"Tell us what God wants."

"Why won't you?"

"Get the Jews out of Palestine."

"What should we pray for next?"

"Listen, I got this great idea."

"Help."

"I have the secret of the ages."

"I am chosen to bear your son."

"Get the Jews out of Russia."

"I understood what your sermon really meant."

"Lead us against the missile bases."

"Help."

"I'm starving."

"I'm blind."

"I'm afraid."

"I'm alone."

"My little girl has leukemia."

"Help."

The hands laid hold on Louis Habib, dragged him forth and plucked, while the bodies closed in. Donaldson broke a jaw with his fist, a rib with his shoe, and somehow got Gail and Helen down under the car. It rocked beneath surging impacts. The one man's screams were soon over. Then the mob stampeded, as a herd of bison stampedes. Belated police vehicles arrived to halt the damage, succor the wounded, and bear away the trampled, unrecognizable dead.

*Thursday 7 July*

(David Greenfeather, president of the newly formed American Council, today explained its purposes in a broadcast from Santa Fe, N. M. "We are by no means an exclusively Indian group, nor are we romantics trying to raise from the dust a past that never was," he said. "No, we welcome everyone of every race, color, or creed. We hope to make use of advanced scientific knowledge, for example in plant genetics, if not of an elaborate technology that is doomed to crumble. We do seek to regain the values of our forebears, values we believe are necessities of survival in the coming era. They include a renunciation of lust for the merely material—there will not be many material goods for a long time to come; a readiness to suffer and die when needful—it often will be; a sense of intimate community with a few dear neighbors—megalopolis is a dry husk; at the same time, a oneness with the entire living world and the living God." His speech, which had been widely looked forward to, went unheard in numerous areas because of power failures and civil disturbances. But it is expected that mimeographed or hand-copied pamphlets will be made available.)

Near sunset, Donaldson parked his new station wagon. "This looks ideal," he said.

They were well into the Sierra, well off the highway on a deserted dirt road. The site was a meadow among pine trees, dropping sharply down to a valley. Someone must formerly, lovingly have dwelt here, for water trickled from an iron pipe out of the hillside into a moss-grown trough. It tasted of earth and purity.

"How long do we stay?" Helen Habib asked.

"As long as seems prudent," Donaldson told her. "Couple weeks, maybe. We've supplies for that. Afterward, if the radio says things haven't calmed down, we search for a pleasant village."

"You shouldn't do this much for us."

"It's also for ourselves, Helen. I don't think the future lies in the cities."

She went off for a while, alone, walking like an old woman. But later she insisted on helping pitch camp, cook dinner, and clean up. Her oldest son was much beside her; Jimmy and Steffie hung back, awkward. John and Mike rollicked, of course, under the eyes of Gail's parents.

Only once did Helen speak of the day before. She was scrubbing a pot when, apropos of nothing but silence, she said, "Dick, you're educated about these things. Did he have to die?"

"Everyone must," the young man answered. He paused. "If you mean, did he have to be martyred, I think not. Most prophets, in most faiths, lived to a ripe age. Today's people . . . couldn't understand. Let's hope later generations will be able to." He squeezed her shoulder. "He is, mother."

"He was, anyway." She raised her head. "I can live on that."

Tired from their journey, all but Donaldson and Gail were soon in the tents and asleep. Those two walked about.

"Do you really believe, Si," she wondered, "we're in for a new Dark Age?"

"No," he said. "It's not predestined, at least. Nothing is. For all I know, we're coming out of one. I do expect the great empires to fall, ours among them. Whatever civilization rises on the ruins won't be like any the world has seen before. And that, however painful, may show us a new side of our souls."

They reached the cliff edge and stopped. The moon had risen, bright enough that only a few stars appeared. The pines were tall shadows with sweet breath; the spring murmured and chimed; underfoot, the valley fell away in tremendous distances which upheaved themselves on the farther side to a snowpeak that seemed afloat in the violet night. The air was cold. Gail leaned against her man, seeking warmth.

"After all," he said, "changes are bound to follow a miracle."

She replied slowly, "When will we see that we've always lived in a miracle?"

# Thomas the Proclaimer

## ROBERT SILVERBERG

*Robert Silverberg is one of the most productive of science-fiction writers. Since 1953 he has published some two dozen novels and innumerable short stories; in addition he has edited anthologies and written many works of nonfiction on scientific and historical themes. His best-known novels include* Tower of Glass, Thorns, Downward to the Earth, *and* Son of Man. *In 1956 and 1969 he received the Hugo award, and in 1970 he was voted the Nebula trophy of the Science Fiction Writers of America for the year's best short story. That year, also, he was American Guest of Honor at the World Science Fiction Convention held in Heidelberg, Germany. He was President of the Science Fiction Writers of America in 1967–1968. He and his wife are both native New Yorkers and make their home there today.*

## 1. Moonlight, Starlight, Torchlight

How long will this night last? The blackness, though moon-pierced, star-pierced, torch-pierced, is dense and tangible. They are singing and chanting in the valley. Bitter smoke from their firebrands rises to the hilltop where Thomas stands, flanked by his closest followers. Fragments of old hymns dance through the trees. "Rock of Ages, Cleft for Me." "O God, Our Help in Ages Past." "Jesus, Lover of My Soul, Let Me to Thy Bosom Fly." Thomas is the center of all attention. A kind of invisible aura surrounds his blocky, powerful figure, an unseen crackling electrical radiance. Saul Kraft, at his side, seems eclipsed and obscured, a small, fragile-looking man, overshadowed now but far from unimportant in the events of this night. "Nearer, My God, to Thee." Thomas begins to hum the tune, then to sing. His voice, though deep and magical, the true charismatic voice, tumbles randomly from key to key: the prophet has no ear for music. Kraft smiles sourly at Thomas' dismal sounds.

> Watchman, tell us of the night,
> What its signs of promise are.
> Traveler, o'er yon mountain's height,
> See that glory-beaming star!

Ragged shouts from below. Occasional sobs and loud coughs. What is the hour? The hour is late. Thomas runs his hands through his long, tangled hair, tugging, smoothing, pulling the strands down toward his thick shoulders. The familiar gesture, beloved by the multitudes. He wonders if he should make an appearance. They are calling his name; he hears the rhythmic cries punching through the snarl of clashing hymns. *Tho-mas! Tho-mas! Tho-mas!* Hysteria in their voices. They want him to come forth and stretch out his arms and make the heavens move again, just as he caused them to stop. But Thomas resists that grand but hollow gesture. How easy it is to play the prophet's part! He did not cause the heavens to stop, though, and he knows that he cannot make them move again. Not of his own will alone, at any rate.

"What time is it?" he asks.

"Quarter to ten," Kraft tells him. Adding, after an instant's thought: "P.M."

So the twenty-four hours are nearly up. And still the sky hangs frozen. Well, Thomas? Is this not what you asked for? Go down on your knees, you cried, and beg Him for a Sign, so that we may know He is still with us, in this our time of need. And render up to Him a great shout. And the people knelt throughout all the lands. And begged. And shouted. And the Sign was given. Why, then, this sense of foreboding? Why these fears? Surely this night will pass. Look at Kraft. Smiling serenely. Kraft has never known any doubts. Those cold eyes, those thin wide lips, the fixed expression of tranquillity.

"You ought to speak to them," Kraft says.

"I have nothing to say."

"A few words of comfort for them."

"Let's see what happens, first. What can I tell them now?"

"Empty of words, Thomas? You, who have had so much to proclaim?"

Thomas shrugs. There are times when Kraft infuriates him: the little man needling him, goading, scheming, never letting up, always pushing this Crusade toward some appointed goal grasped by Kraft alone. The intensity of Kraft's faith exhausts Thomas. Annoyed, the prophet turns away from him. Thomas sees scattered fires leaping on the horizon. Prayer meetings? Or are they riots? Peering at those distant blazes, Thomas jabs idly at the tuner of the radio before him.

". . . rounding out the unprecedented span of twenty-four hours of continuous daylight in much of the Eastern Hemisphere, an endless daybreak over the Near East and an endless noon over Siberia, eastern China, the Philippines, and Indonesia. Meanwhile western Europe and the Americas remain locked in endless night. . . ."

". . . then spake Joshua to the Lord in the day when the Lord delivered up the Amorites before the children of Israel, and he said in the sight of Israel, Sun, stand thou still upon Gibeon; and thou, Moon, in the valley of Ajalon. And the sun stood still, and the moon stayed, until the people had avenged themselves upon their enemies. Is this not written in the book of Jasher? So the sun stood still in the midst of heaven, and hasted not to go down about a whole day. . . ."

". . . an astonishing culmination, apparently, to the campaign led by Thomas Davidson of Reno, Nevada, known popularly as Thomas the Proclaimer. The shaggy-bearded, long-haired, self-designated Apostle of Peace brought his Crusade of Faith to a climax yesterday with the worldwide program of simultaneous prayer that appears to have been the cause of . . ."

> *Watchman, does its beauteous ray*
> *Aught of joy or hope foretell?*
> *Traveler, yes; it brings the day,*
> *Promised day of Israel.*

Kraft says sharply, "Do you hear what they're singing, Thomas? You've got to speak to them. You got them into this; now they want you to tell them you'll get them out of it."

"Not yet, Saul."

"You mustn't let your moment slip by. Show them that God still speaks through you!"

"When God is ready to speak again," Thomas says frostily, "I'll let His words come forth. Not before." He glares at Kraft and punches for another change of station.

". . . continued meetings in Washington, but no communiqué as yet. Meanwhile, at the United Nations . . ."

". . . Behold, He cometh with clouds; and every eye shall see Him, and they also which pierced Him: and all kindreds of the Earth shall wail because of Him. Even so, Amen . . ."

". . . outbreaks of looting in Caracas, Mexico City, Oakland, and Vancouver. But in the daylight half of the world, violence and other disruption has been slight, though an unconfirmed report from Moscow . . ."

". . . and when, brethren, when did the sun cease in its course? At six in the morning, brethren, six in the morning, Jerusalem time! And on what day, brethren? Why, the sixth of June, the sixth day of the sixth month! *Six—six—six!* And what does Holy Writ tell us, my dearly beloved ones, in the thirteenth chapter of Revelations? That a beast shall rise up out of the sea, having seven heads and ten horns, and upon his horns ten crowns, and upon his heads the name of blasphemy. And the Holy Book tells us the number of the beast, beloved, and the number is six hundred three score and six, wherein we see again the significant digits, *six—six—six!* Who then can deny that these are the last days, and that the Apocalypse must be upon us? Thus in this time of woe and fire as we sit upon this stilled planet awaiting His judgment, we must . . ."

". . . latest observatory report confirms that no appreciable momentum effects could be detected as the Earth shifted to its present period of rotation. Scientists agree that the world's abrupt slowing on its axis should have produced a global catastrophe leading, perhaps, to the destruction of all life. However, nothing but minor tidal disturbances have been recorded so far. Two hours ago, we interviewed Presidential Science Adviser Raymond Bartell, who made this statement:

" 'Calculations now show that the Earth's period of rotation and its period of revolution have suddenly become equal; that is, the day and the year now have the same length. This locks the Earth into its present position relative to the sun, so that the side of the Earth now enjoying daylight will continue indefinitely to do so, while the other side will remain permanently in night. Other effects of the slowdown that might have been expected include the flooding of coastal areas, the collapse of most buildings, and a series of earthquakes and volcanic eruptions, but none of these things seem to have happened. For the moment we have no rational explanation of all this, and I must admit it's a great temptation to say that Thomas the Proclaimer must have managed to get his miracle, because there isn't any other apparent way of . . .'"

". . . I am Alpha and Omega, the beginning and the ending, saith the Lord, which is, and which was, and which is to come, the Almighty. . . ."

With a fierce fingerthrust Thomas silences all the radio's clamoring voices. Alpha and Omega! Apocalyptist garbage! The drivel of hysterical preachers pouring from a thousand transmitters, poisoning the air! Thomas despises all these criers of doom. None of them knows anything. No one understands. His throat fills with a turbulence of angry incoherent words, almost choking him. A coppery taste of denunciations. Kraft again urges him to speak. Thomas glowers. Why doesn't Kraft do the speaking himself, for once? He's a truer believer than I am. He's the real prophet. But of course the idea is ridiculous. Kraft has no eloquence, no fire. Only ideas and visions. He'd bore everybody to splinters. Thomas succumbs. He beckons with his fingertips. "The microphone," he mutters. "Let me have the microphone."

Among his entourage there is fluttery excitement. "He wants the mike!" they murmur. "Give him the mike!" Much activity on the part of the technicians. Kraft presses a plaque of cold metal into the Proclaimer's hand. Grins, winks. "Make their hearts soar," Kraft whispers. "Send them on a trip!" Everyone waits. In the valley the torches bob and weave; have they begun dancing down there? Overhead the pocked moon holds its corner of the sky in frosty grasp. The stars are chained to their places. Thomas draws a deep breath and lets the air travel inward, upward, surging to the recesses of his skull. He waits for the good lightheadedness to come upon him, the buoyancy that liberates his tongue. He thinks he is ready to speak. He hears the desperate chanting: *"Tho-mas! Tho-mas! Tho-mas!"* It is more than half a day since his last public statement. He is tense and hollow; he has fasted throughout this Day of the Sign, and of course he has not slept. No one has slept.

"Friends," he begins. "Friends, this is Thomas."

The amplifiers hurl his voice outward. A thousand loudspeakers drifting in the air pick up his words and they bounce across the valley, returning as jagged echoes. He hears cries, eerie shrieks; his own name ascends to him in blurry distortions. *Too-mis! Too-mis! Too-mis!*

"Nearly a full day has passed," he says, "since the Lord gave us the Sign for which we asked. For us it has been a long day of darkness, and for others it has been a day of strange light, and for all of us there has been fear. But this I say to you now: BE . . . NOT . . . AFRAID. For the Lord is good and we are the Lord's."

Now he pauses. Not only for effect; his throat is raging. He signals furiously and Kraft, scowling, hands him a flask. Thomas takes a deep gulp of the good red wine, cool, strong. Ah. He glances at the screen beside him: the video pickup relayed from the valley. What lunacy down there! Wild-eyed, sweaty madmen, half naked and worse, jumping up and down! Crying out his name, invoking him as though he were divine. *Too-mis! Too-mis!*

"There are those who tell you now," Thomas goes on, "that the end of days is at hand, that judgment is come. They talk of apocalypses and the wrath of God. And what do I say to that? I say: BE . . . NOT . . . AFRAID. The Lord God is a God of mercy. We asked Him for a Sign, and a Sign was given. Should we not therefore rejoice? Now we may be certain of His presence and

His guidance. Ignore the doom-sayers. Put away your fears. We live now in God's love!"

Thomas halts again. For the first time in his memory he has no sense of being in command of his audience. Is he reaching them at all? Is he touching the right chords? Or has he begun already to lose them? Maybe it was a mistake to let Kraft nag him into speaking so soon. He thought he was ready; maybe not. Now he sees Kraft staring at him, aghast, pantomiming the gestures of speech, silently telling him, *Get with it, you've got to keep talking now!* Thomas' self-assurance momentarily wavers, and terror floods his soul, for he knows that if he falters at this point he may well be destroyed by the forces he has set loose. Teetering at the brink of an abyss, he searches frantically for his customary confidence. Where is that steely column of words that ordinarily rises unbidden from the depths of him? Another gulp of wine, fast. Good. Kraft, nervously rubbing hands together, essays a smile of encouragement. Thomas tugs at his hair. He pushes back his shoulders, thrusts out his chest. Be not afraid! He feels control returning after the frightening lapse. They are his, all those who listen. They have always been his. What are they shouting in the valley now? No longer his name, but some new cry. He strains to hear. Two words. What are they? *De-dum! De-dum! De-dum!* What? *De-dum! De-dum! De-dum, Too-mis, de-dum!* What? What? "The sun," Kraft says. The sun? Yes. They want the sun. "The sun! The sun! The sun!"

"The sun," Thomas says. "Yes. This day the sun stands still, as our Sign from Him. BE NOT AFRAID! A long dawn over Jerusalem has He decreed, and a long night for us, but not so very long, and soon sped." Thomas feels the power surging at last. Kraft nods to him, and Thomas nods back and spits a stream of wine at Kraft's feet. He is aware of that consciousness of risk in which the joy of prophecy lies: I will bring forth what I see, and trust to God to make it real. That feeling of risk accepted, of triumph over doubt. Calmly he says, "The Day of the Sign will end in a few minutes. Once more the world will turn, and moon and stars will move across the sky. So put down your torches, and go to your homes, and offer up joyful prayers of thanksgiving to Him, for this night will pass, and dawn will come at the appointed hour."

How do you know, Thomas? Why are you so sure?

He hands the microphone to Saul Kraft and calls for more wine. Around him are tense faces, rigid eyes, clamped jaws. Thomas smiles. He goes among them, slapping backs, punching shoulders, laughing, embracing, winking ribaldly, poking his fingers playfully into their ribs. Be of good cheer, ye who follow my way! Share ye not my faith in Him? He asks Kraft how he came across. Fine, Kraft says, except for that uneasy moment in the middle. Thomas slaps Kraft's back hard enough to loosen teeth. Good old Saul. My inspiration, my counselor, my beacon. Thomas pushes his flask toward Kraft's face. Kraft shakes his head. He is fastidious about drinking, about decorum in general, as fastidious as Thomas is disreputable. You disapprove of me, don't you, Saul? But you need my charisma. You need my energy and my big loud voice. Too bad, Saul, that prophets aren't as neat and housebroken as you'd like them to be. "Ten o'clock," someone says. "It's now been going on for twenty-four hours."

A woman says, "The moon! Look! Didn't the moon just start to move again?"

From Kraft: "You wouldn't be able to see it with the naked eye. Not possibly. No way."

"Ask Thomas! Ask him!"

One of the technicians cries, "I can feel it! The Earth is turning!"

"Look, the stars!"

"Thomas! Thomas!"

They rush to him. Thomas, benign, serene, stretching forth his huge hands to reassure them, tells them that he has felt it too. Yes. There is motion in the universe again. Perhaps the turnings of the heavenly bodies are too subtle to be detected in a single glance, perhaps an hour or more will be needed for verification, and yet he knows, he is sure, he is absolutely sure. The Lord has with-drawn His Sign. The Earth turns. "Let us sleep now," Thomas says joyfully "and greet the dawn in happiness."

## 2. The Dance of the Apocalyptists

In late afternoon every day a band of Apocalyptists gathers by the stinking shore of Lake Erie to dance the sunset in. Their faces are painted with grotesque nightmare stripes; their expres-sions are wild; they fling themselves about in jerky, lurching steps, awkward and convulsive, the classic death-dance. Two immense golden loudspeakers, mounted like idols atop metal spikes rammed into the soggy soil, bellow abstract rhythms at them from either side. The leader of the group stands thigh-deep in the fouled waters, chanting, beckoning, directing them with short blurted cries: "People . . . holy people . . . chosen people . . . blessed people . . . persecuted people. . . . Dance! . . . Dance! . . . The end . . . is near. . . ." And they dance. Fingers shooting electrically into the air, elbows ramming empty space, knees rising high, they scramble toward the lake, withdraw, advance, withdraw, advance, three steps forward and two steps back, a will-you-won't-you-will-you-won't-you approach to salvation.

They have been doing this seven times a week since the begin-ning of the year, this fateful, terminal year, but only in the week since the Day of the Sign have they drawn much of an audience. At the outset, in frozen January, no one would bother to come to watch a dozen madmen capering on the windswept ice. Then the cult began getting sporadic television coverage, and that brought a few curiosity seekers. On the milder nights of April perhaps thirty dancers and twenty onlookers could be found at the lake. But now it is June, apocalyptic June, when the Lord in all His Majesty has revealed Himself, and the nightly dances are an event that brings thousands out of Cleveland's suburbs. Police lines hold the mob at a safe distance from the performers. A closed-circuit video loop relays the action to those on the outskirts of the crowd, too far away for a direct view. Network copters hover, cameras ready in case something unusual happens—the death of a dancer, the bursting loose of the mob, mass conversions, another miracle, anything. The air is cool tonight. The sun, delicately blurred and purpled by the smoky haze that perpetually thickens this region's sky, drops toward the breast of the lake. The dancers move in frenzied patterns, those in the front rank approaching the water, dipping their toes, retreating. Their leader, slapping the lake, throwing up fountaining spumes, continues to exhort them in a high, strained voice.

"People . . . holy people . . . chosen people . . ."

"Hallelujah! Hallelujah!"

"Come and be sealed! Blessed people . . . persecuted people . . . Come! Be! Sealed! Unto! The! Lord!"

"Hallelujah!"

The spectators shift uneasily. Some nudge and snigger. Some, staring fixedly, lock their arms and glower. Some move their lips in silent prayer or silent curses. Some look tempted to lurch forward and join the dance. Some will. Each night, there are a few who go forward. Each night, also, there are some who attempt to burst the police lines and attack the dancers. In June alone seven spectators have suffered heart seizures at the nightly festival: five fatalities.

"Servants of God!" cries the man in the water.

"Hallelujah!" reply the dancers.

"The year is speeding! The time is coming!"

"Hallelujah!"

"The trumpet shall sound! And we shall be saved!"

"Yes! Yes! Yes! Yes!"

Oh, the fervor of the dance! The wildness of the faces! The painted stripes swirl and run as sweat invades the thick greasy pigments. One could strew hot coals on the shore, now, and the dancers would advance all the same, oblivious, blissful. The choreography of their faith absorbs them wholly at this moment and they admit of no distractions. There is so little time left, after all, and such a great output of holy exertion is required of them before the end! June is almost half spent. The year itself is almost half spent. January approaches: the dawning of the new millennium, the day of the final trump, the moment of apocalypse. January 1, 2000: six and a half months away. And already He has given the Sign that the end of days is at hand. They dance. Through ecstatic movement comes salvation.

"Fear God, and give glory to Him; for the hour of His Judgment is come!"

"Hallelujah! Amen!"

"And worship Him that made heaven, and earth, and the sea, and the fountains of waters!"

"Hallelujah! Amen!"

They dance. The music grows more intense: prickly blurts of harsh tone flickering through the air. Spectators begin to clap hands and sway. Here comes the first convert of the night, now, a woman, middle-aged, plump, beseeching her way through the police cordon. An electronic device checks her for concealed weapons and explosive devices; she is found to be harmless; she passes the line and runs, stumbling, to join the dance.

"For the great day of His wrath is come; and who shall be able to stand?"

"Amen!"

"Servants of God! Be sealed unto Him, and be saved!"

"Sealed . . . sealed . . . We shall be sealed. . . . We shall be saved. . . ."

"And I saw four angels standing on the four corners of the Earth, holding the four winds of the Earth, that the wind should not blow on the Earth, nor on the sea, nor on any tree," roars the man in the water. "And I saw another angel ascending from the east, having the seal of the living God: and he cried with a loud voice to the four angels, to whom it was given to hurt the Earth and the sea, saying, Hurt not the Earth, neither the sea, nor the trees, till we have sealed the servants of our God in their foreheads."

"Sealed! Hallelujah! Amen!"

"And I heard the number of them which were sealed: and there were sealed an hundred and forty and four thousand of all the tribes of the children of Israel."

"Sealed! Sealed!"

"Come to me and be sealed! Dance and be sealed!"

The sun drops into the lake. The purple stain of sunset spreads across the horizon. The dancers shriek ecstatically and rush toward the water. They splash one another; they offer frantic baptisms in the murky lake; they drink, they spew forth what they have drunk, they drink again. Surrounding their leader. Seeking his blessing. An angry thick mutter from the onlookers. They are disgusted by this hectic show of faith. A menagerie, they say. A circus sideshow. These freaks. These godly freaks. Whom we have come to watch, so that we may despise them.

And if they are right? And if the world *does* end next January 1, and we go to hellfire, while *they* are saved? Impossible. Preposterous. Absurd. But yet, who's to say? Only last week the Earth stood still a whole day. We live under His hand now. We always have, but now we have no liberty to doubt it. We can no longer deny that He's up there, watching us, listening to us, thinking about us. And if the end is really coming, as the crazy dancers think, what should I do to prepare for it? Should I join the dance? God help me. God help us all. Now the darkness falls. Look at the lunatics wallowing in the lake.

"Hallelujah! Amen!"


### 3. *The Sleep of Reason Produces Monsters*

When I was about seven years old, which is to say somewhere in the late 1960's, I was playing out in front of the house on a Sunday morning, perhaps stalking some ladybirds for my insect collection, when three freckle-faced Irish kids who lived on the next block came wandering by. They were on their way home from church. The youngest one was my age, and the other two must have been eight or nine. To me they were Big Boys: ragged, strong, swaggering, alien. My father was a college professor and theirs was probably a bus conductor or a coal miner, and so they were as strange to me as a trio of tourists from Patagonia would have been. They stopped and watched me for a minute, and then the biggest one called me out into the street, and he asked me how it was that they never saw me in church on Sundays.

The simplest and most tactful thing for me to tell them would have been that I didn't happen to be Roman Catholic. That was true. I think that all they wanted to find out was what church I *did* go to, since I obviously didn't go to theirs. Was I Jewish, Moslem, Presbyterian, Baptist, what? But I was a smug little snot then, and instead of handling the situation diplomatically I cheerfully told them that I didn't go to church because I didn't believe in God.

They looked at me as though I had just blown my nose on the American flag.

"Say that again?" the biggest one demanded.

"I don't believe in God," I said. "Religion's just a big fake. My father says so, and I think he's right."

They frowned and backed off a few paces and conferred in low, earnest voices, with many glances in my direction. Evidently I was their first atheist. I assumed we would now have a debate on the existence of the Deity: they would explain to me the motives that led them to use up so many valuable hours on their knees inside the Church of Our Lady of the Sorrows, and then I would try to show them how silly it was to worry so much about an invisible old man in the sky. But a theological disputation wasn't their style. They came out of their huddle and strolled toward me, and I suddenly detected menace in their eyes, and just as the two smaller ones lunged at me I slipped past them and started to run. They had longer legs, but I was more agile; besides, I was on my home block and knew the turf better. I sprinted halfway down the street, darted into an alley, slipped through the open place in the back of the Allertons' garage, doubled back up the street via the rear lane, and made it safely into our house by way of the kitchen door. For the next couple of days I stayed close to home after school and kept a wary watch, but the pious Irish lads never came around again to punish the blasphemer. After that I learned to be more careful about expressing my opinions on religious matters.

But I never became a believer. I had a natural predisposition toward skepticism. *If you can't measure it, it isn't there.* That included not only Old Whiskers and His Only Begotten Son, but all the other mystic baggage that people liked to carry around in those tense credulous years: the flying saucers, Zen Buddhism, the Atlantis cult, Hare Krishna, macrobiotics, telepathy and other species of extrasensory perception, theosophy, entropy-worship, astrology, and such. I was willing to accept neutrinos, quasars, the theory of continental drift, and the various species of quarks, because I respected the evidence for their existence; I couldn't buy the other stuff, the irrational stuff, the assorted opiates of the masses. When the Moon is in the seventh house, etc., etc.—sorry, no. I clung to the path of reason as I made my uneasy journey toward maturity, and hardheaded little Billy Gifford, smartypants bug collector, remained unchurched as he ripened into Professor William F. Gifford, Ph.D., of the Department of Physics, Harvard. I wasn't *hostile* to organized religion, I just ignored it, as I might ignore a newspaper account of a jai-alai tournament in Afghanistan.

I envied the faithful their faith, oh, yes. When the dark times got darker, how sweet it must have been to be able to rush to Our Lady of the Sorrows for comfort! *They* could pray, *they* had the illusion that a divine plan governed this best of all possible worlds, while I was left in bleak, stormy limbo, dismally aware that the universe makes no sense and that the only universal truth there is is that Entropy Eventually Wins.

There were times when I wanted genuinely to be able to pray, when I was weary of operating solely on my own existential capital, when I wanted to grovel and cry out, *Okay, Lord, I give up, You take it from here.* I had favors to ask of Him. God, let my little girl's fever go down. Let my plane not crash. Let them not shoot *this* President too. Let the races learn how to live in peace before the blacks get around to burning down my street. Let the peace-loving enlightened students not bomb the computer center this semester. Let the next kindergarten drug scandal not erupt in my boy's school. Let the lion lie down with the lamb. As we zoomed along on the Chaos Express, I was sometimes tempted toward godliness the way the godly are tempted toward sin. But my love of divine reason left me no way to opt for the irrational. Call it stiffneckedness, call it rampant egomania: no matter how bad things got, Bill Gifford wasn't going to submit to the tyranny of a hobgoblin. Even a benevolent one. Even if I had favors to ask of Him. So much to ask; so little faith. Intellectual honesty *über alles*, Gifford! While every year things were a little worse than the last.

When I was growing up, in the 1970's, it was fashionable for educated and serious-minded people to get together and tell each other that Western civilization was collapsing. The Germans had a word for it, *Schadenfreude*, the pleasure one gets from talking about catastrophes. And the 1970's were shadowed by catastrophes, real or expected: the pollution escalation, the population explosion, Vietnam and all the little Vietnams, the supersonic transport, black separatism, white backlash, student unrest, extremist women's lib, the neofascism of the New Left, the neonihilism of the New Right, a hundred other varieties of dynamic irrationality going full blast, yes, ample fuel for the *Schadenfreude* syndrome. Yes, my parents and their civilized friends said solemnly, sadly, gleefully, it's all blowing up, it's all going smash, it's all whooshing down the drain. Through the fumes of the Saturday-night pot came the inevitable portentous quotes from Yeats: *Things fall apart; the center cannot hold; mere anarchy is loosed upon the world.* Well, what shall we do about it? Perhaps it's really beyond our control now. Brethren, shall we pray? Lift up your voices unto Him! But I can't. I'd feel like a damned fool.

Forgive me, God, but I must deny You! *The best lack all convic-*
*tion, while the worst are full of passionate intensity.*

And of course everything got much more awful than the doom-
sayers of the 1970's really expected. Even those who most dearly
relished enumerating the calamities to come still thought,
beneath their grim joy, that somehow reason ultimately would
triumph. The most gloomy Jeremiah entertained secret hopes that
the noble ecological resolutions would eventually be translated
into meaningful environmental action, that the crazy birth spiral
would be checked in time, that the strident rhetoric of the innumerable protest groups would be tempered and modulated as
time brought them the beginning of a fulfillment of their revolu-
tionary goals—but no. Came the 1980's, the decade of my young
manhood, and all the hysteria jumped to the next-highest energy
level. That was when we began having the Gas Mask Days. The
programmed electrical shutdowns. The elegantly orchestrated international chaos of the Third World People's Prosperity Group.
The airport riots. The black rains. The Computer Purge. The
Brazilian Pacification Program. The Claude Harkins Book List
with its accompanying library-burnings. The Ecological Police Action. The Genetic Purity League and its even more frightening
black counterpart. The Children's Crusade for Sanity. The Nine
Weeks' War. The Night of the Lasers. The center had long ago
ceased to hold; now we were strapped to a runaway wheel.
Amidst the furies I studied, married, brought forth young,
built a career, fought off daily terror, and, like everyone else,
waited for the inevitable final calamity.

Who could doubt that it would come? Not you, not I. And not
the strange wild-eyed folk who emerged among us like dark
growths pushing out of rotting logs, the Apocalyptists, who
raised *Schadenfreude* to the sacramental level and organized an
ecstatic religion of doom. The end of the world, they told us, was
scheduled for January 1, A.D. 2000, and upon that date, 144,000
elite souls, who had "sealed" themselves unto God by devotion
and good works, would be saved; the rest of us poor sinners would

be hauled before the Judge. I could see their point. Although I rejected their talk of the Second Coming, having long ago rejected the First, and although I shared neither their confidence in the exact date of the apocalypse nor their notions of how the survivors would be chosen, I agreed with them that the end was close at hand. The fact that for a quarter of a century we had been milking giddy cocktail-party chatter out of the impending collapse of Western civilization didn't of itself guarantee that Western civilization wasn't going to collapse; *some* of the things people like to say at cocktail parties can hit the target. As a physicist with a decent understanding of the entropic process I found all the signs of advanced societal decay easy to identify: for a century we had been increasing the complexity of society's functions so that an ever-higher level of organization was required in order to make things run, and for much of that time we had simultaneously been trending toward total universal democracy, toward a world consisting of several billion self-governing republics with a maximum of three citizens each. Any closed system which experiences simultaneous sharp increases in mechanical complexity and in entropic diffusion is going to go to pieces long before the maximum distribution of energy is reached. The pattern of consents and contracts on which civilization is based is destroyed; every social interaction, from parking your car to settling an international boundary dispute, becomes a problem that can be handled only by means of force, since all "civilized" techniques of reconciling disagreement have been suspended as irrelevant; when the delivery of mail is a matter of private negotiation between the citizen and his postman, what hope is there for the rule of reason? Somewhere, somehow, we had passed a point of no return—in 1984, 1972, maybe even that ghastly day in November of 1963 —and nothing now could save us from plunging over the brink.

Nothing?

Out of Nevada came Thomas, shaggy Thomas, Thomas the Proclaimer, rising above the slot machines and the roulette wheels to cry, If ye have faith, ye shall be saved! An anti-

Apocalyptist prophet, no less, whose message was that civilization still might be preserved, that it was not yet too late. The voice of hope, the enemy of entropy, the new Apostle of Peace. Though to people like me he looked just as wild-eyed and hairy and dangerous and terrifyingly psychotic as the worshipers of the holocaust, for he, like the Apocalyptists, dealt in forces operating outside the realm of sanity. By rights he should have come out of the backwoods of Arkansas or the crazier corners of California, but he didn't, he was a desert rat, a Nevadan, a sand-eating latter-day John the Baptist. A true prophet for our times, too, seedy, disreputable, a wine-swiller, a cynic. Capable of beginning a global telecast sermon with a belch. An ex-soldier who had happily napalmed whole provinces during the Brazilian Pacification Program. A part-time dealer in boot-legged hallucinogens. An expert at pocket-picking and computer-jamming. He had gone into the evangelism business because he thought he could make an easy buck that way, peddling the Gospels and appropriating the collection box, but a funny thing had happened to him, he claimed: he had seen the Lord, he had discovered the error of his ways, he had become inflamed with righteousness. Hiding not his grimy past, he now offered himself as a walking personification of redemption: *Look ye, if I can be saved from sin, there's hope for everyone!* The media picked him up. That magnificent voice of his, that great mop of hair, those eyes, that hypnotic self-confidence—perfect. He walked from California to Florida to proclaim the coming millennium. And gathered followers, thousands, millions, all those who weren't yet ready to let Armageddon begin, and he made them pray and pray and pray, he held revival meetings that were beamed to Karachi and Katmandu and Addis Ababa and Shanghai, he preached no particular theology and no particular scripture, but only a smooth ecumenical theism that practically anybody could swallow, whether he be Confucianist or Moslem or Hindu. Listen, Thomas said, there *is* a God, some kind of all-powerful being out there whose divine plan guides the universe, and He watches over us, and don't you believe otherwise! And He is good and will not let us come to harm if we hew to His path. And He has tested us with all these troubles, in order to measure the depth of our faith in Him. So let's show Him, brethren! Let's all pray together and send up a great shout unto Him! For He would certainly give a Sign, and the unbelievers would at last be converted, and the epoch of purity would commence. People said, Why not give it a try? We've got a lot to gain and nothing to lose. A vulgar version of the old Pascal wager: if He's really there, He may help us, and if He's not, we've only wasted a little time. So the hour of beseeching was set.

In faculty circles we had a good deal of fun with the whole idea, we brittle worldly rational types, but sometimes there was a nervous edge to our jokes and a forced heartiness to our laughter, as if some of us suspected that Pascal might have been offering pretty good odds, or that Thomas might just have hit on something. Naturally I was among the skeptics, though as usual I kept my doubts to myself. (The lesson learned so long ago, the narrow escape from the Irish lads.) I hadn't really paid much attention to Thomas and his message, any more than I did to football scores or children's video programs: not my sphere, not my concern. But as the day of prayer drew near, the old temptation beset me. *Give in at last, Gifford. Bow your head and offer homage. Even if He's the myth you've always known He is, do it. Do it!* I argued with myself. I told myself not to be an idiot, not to yield to the age-old claims of superstition. I reminded myself of the holy wars, the Inquisition, the lascivious Renaissance popes, all the crimes of the pious. *So what, Gifford? Can't you be an ordinary humble God-fearing human being for once in your life? Down on your knees beside your brethren? Read your Pascal. Suppose He exists and is listening, and suppose your refusal is the one that tips the scales against mankind? We're not asking so very much.* Still I fought the sly inner voice. To believe is absurd, I cried. I must not let despair stampede me into the renunciation of reason, even in this apocalyptic moment. Thomas is a cunning ruffian and his followers are hysterical grubby fools. *And you're an arrogant*

*elitist, Gifford. Who may live long enough to repent his arro-
gance.* It was psychological warfare, Gifford vs. Gifford, reason
vs. faith.

In the end reason lost. I was jittery, off balance, demoralized.
The most astonishing people were coming out in support of
Thomas the Proclaimer, and I felt increasingly isolated, a man of
ice, heart of stone, the village atheist scowling at Christmas
wreaths. Up until the final moment I wasn't sure what I was going to do, but then the hour struck and I found myself in
my study, alone, door locked, safely apart from wife and children
—who had already, all of them, somewhat defiantly announced
their intentions of participating—and there I was on my knees,
feeling foolish, feeling preposterous, my cheeks blazing, my lips
moving, saying the words. *Saying the words.* Around the world
the billions of believers prayed, and I also. I too prayed, embarrassed by my weakness, and the pain of my shame was a stone in
my throat.

And the Lord heard us, and He gave a Sign. And for a day
and a night (less $1 \times 12^{-4}$ sidereal day) the Earth moved not
around the sun, neither did it rotate. And the laws of momentum
were confounded, as was I. Then Earth again took up its appointed
course, as though nothing out of the ordinary had occurred.
Imagine my chagrin. I wish I knew where to find those Irish boys.
I have some apologies to make.


## 4. Thomas Preaches in the Marketplace

I hear what you're saying. You tell me I'm a prophet. You tell
me I'm a saint. Some of you even tell me I'm the Son of God come
again. You tell me I made the sun stand still over Jerusalem.
Well, no, I didn't do that, the Lord Almighty did that, the Lord
of Hosts. Through His divine Will, in response to your prayers.
And I'm only the vehicle through which your prayers were
channeled. I'm not any kind of saint, folks. I'm not the Son of

God reborn, or any of the other crazy things you've been saying I am. I'm only Thomas.

Who am I?

I'm just a voice. A spokesman. A tool through which His will was made manifest. I'm not giving you the old humility act, friends, I'm trying to make you see the truth about me.

Who am I?

I'll tell you who I was, though you know it already. I was a bandit, I was a man of evil, I was a defiler of the law. A killer, a liar, a drunkard, a cheat! I did what I damned pleased. I was a law unto myself. If I ever got caught, you bet I wouldn't have whined for mercy. I'd have spit in the judge's face and taken my punishment with my eyes open. Only I never got caught, because my luck was running good and because this is a time when a really bad man can flourish, when the wicked are raised high and the virtuous are ground into the mud. Outside the law, that was me! Thomas the criminal! Thomas the brigand, thumbing his nose! Doing bad was my religion, all the time—when I was down there in Brazil with those flamethrowers, or when I was free-lancing your pockets in our cities, or when I was ringing up funny numbers on the big computers. I belonged to Satan if ever a man did, that's the truth, and then what happened? The Lord came along to Satan and said to him, Satan, give me Thomas, I have need of him. And Satan handed me over to Him, because Satan is God's servant too.

And the Lord took me and shook me and knocked me around and said, Thomas, you're nothing but trash!

And I said, I know that, Lord, but who was it who made me that way?

And the Lord laughed and said, You've got guts, Thomas, talking back to me like that. I like a man with guts. But you're wrong, fellow. I made you with the potential to be a saint or a sinner, and you chose to be a sinner, yes, your own free will! You think I'd bother to create people to be wicked? I'm not interested in creating puppets, Thomas, I set out to make me a race of *human beings*. I gave you your options and you opted for evil, eh, Thomas? Isn't that the truth?

And I said, Well, Lord, maybe it is; I don't know.

And the Lord God grew annoyed with me and took me again and shook me again and knocked me around some more, and when I picked myself up I had a puffed lip and a bloody nose, and He asked me how I would do things if I could live my life over again from the start. And I looked Him right in the eye and said, Well, Lord, I'd say that being evil paid off pretty well for me. I lived a right nice life and I had all my happies and I never spent a day behind bars, oh, no. So tell me, Lord, since I got away with everything the first time, why shouldn't I opt to be a sinner again?

And he said, Because you've done that already, and now it's time for you to do something else.

I said, What's that, Lord?

He said, I want you to do something important for me, Thomas. There's a world out there full of people who've lost all faith, people without hope, people who've made up their minds it's no use trying any more, the world's going to end. I want to reach those people somehow, Thomas, and tell them that they're wrong. And show them that they can shape their own destiny, that if they have faith in themselves and in me they can build a good world.

I said, That's easy, Lord. Why don't You just appear in the sky and say that to them, like You just did to me?

He laughed again and said, Oh, no, Thomas, that's much too easy. I told you, I don't run a puppet show. They've got to *want* to lift themselves up out of despair. They've got to take the first step by themselves. You follow me, Thomas?

Yes, Lord, but where do I come in?

And He said, You go to them, Thomas, and you tell them all about your wasted, useless, defiant life, and then tell them how the Lord gave you a chance to do something worthwhile for a change, and how you rose up above your evil self and accepted the opportunity. And then tell them to gather and pray and restore their faith, and ask for a Sign from on high. Thomas, if they listen to you, if they pray and it's sincere prayer, I promise you I *will* give them a Sign, I *will* reveal myself to them, and all doubt will drop like scales from their eyes. Will you do that thing for me, Thomas?

Friends, I listened to the Lord, and I discovered myself shaking and quivering and bursting into sweat, and in a moment, in the twinkling of an eye, I wasn't the old filthy Thomas any more, I was somebody new and clean, I was a man with a high purpose, a man with a belief in something bigger and better than his own greedy desires. And I went down among you, changed as I was, and I told my tale, and all of you know the rest of the story, how we came freely together and offered up our hearts to Him, and how He vouchsafed us a miracle these two and a half weeks past, and gave us a Sign that He still watches over us.

But what do I see now, in these latter days after the giving of the Sign? What do I see?

Where is that new world of faith? Where is that new dream of hope? Where is mankind shoulder to shoulder, praising Him and working together to reach the light?

What do I see? I see this rotting planet turning black inside and splitting open at the core. I see the cancer of doubt. I see the virus of confusion. I see His Sign misinterpreted on every hand, and its beauty trampled on and destroyed.

I still see painted fools dancing and beating on drums and screaming that the world is going to be destroyed at the end of this year of nineteen hundred and ninety-nine. What madness is this? Has God not spoken? Has He not told us joyful news? God is with us! God is good! Why do these Apocalyptists not yet accept the truth of His Sign?

Even worse! Each day new madnesses take form! What are these cults sprouting up among us? Who are these people who demand of God that He return and spell out His intentions, as though the Sign wasn't enough for them? And who are these cowardly blasphemers who say we must lie down in fear and weep piteous tears, because we have invoked not God but Satan, and destruction is our lot? Who are these men of empty souls who bleat and mumble and snivel in our midst? And look at your lofty churchmen, in their priestly robes and glittering tiaras, trying to explain away the Sign as some accident of nature! What talk is this from God's own ministers? And behold the formerly godless ones, screeching like frightened monkeys now that their godlessness has been ripped from them! What do I see? I see madness and terror on all sides, where I should see only joy abounding!

I beg you, friends, have care, take counsel with your souls. I beg you, think clearly now if you ever have thought at all. Choose a wise path, friends, or you will throw away all the glory of the Day of the Sign and lay waste to our great achievement. Give no comfort to the forces of darkness. Keep away from these peddlers of lunatic creeds. Strive to recapture the wonder of that moment when all mankind spoke with a single voice. I beg you—how can you have doubt of Him now?—I beg you—faith—the triumph of faith—let us not allow—let us—not allow—not—allow—

(Jesus, my throat! All this shouting, it's like swallowing fire. Give me that bottle, will you? Come on, give it here! The wine. The wine. Now. Ah. Oh, that's better! Much better, oh, yes. No, wait, give it back—good, good—stop looking at me like that, Saul. Ah. *Ah*.)

And so I beseech you today, brothers and sisters in the Lord— brothers and sisters (what was I saying, Saul? what did I start to say?)—I call upon you to rededicate yourselves—to pledge yourselves to—to (is that it? I can't remember)—to a new Crusade of Faith, that's what we need, a purging of all our doubts and all our hesitations and all our (oh, Jesus, Saul, I'm lost, I don't remember where the hell I'm supposed to be. Let the music start playing.

Quick. That's it. Good and loud. Louder.) Folks, let's all sing!
Raise your voices joyously unto Him!

> *I shall praise the Lord my God,*
> *Fountain of all power . . .*

That's the way! Sing! Everybody sing!

## 5. Ceremonies of Innocence

Throughout the world the quest for an appropriate response
to the event of June 6 continues. No satisfactory interpretation
of that day's happenings has yet been established, though many
have been proposed. Meanwhile passions run high; tempers easily
give way; a surprising degree of violence has entered the situation.
Clearly the temporary slowing of the earth's axial rotation must
have imposed exceptional emotional stress on the entire global
population, creating severe strains that have persisted and even
intensified in the succeeding weeks. Instances of seemingly
motiveless crimes, particularly arson and vandalism, have greatly
increased. Government authorities in Brazil, India, the United
Arab Republic, and Italy have suggested that clandestine revolu-
tionary or counterrevolutionary groups are behind much of this
activity, taking advantage of the widespread mood of uncertainty
to stir discontent. No evidence of this has thus far been made
public. Much hostility has been directed toward the organized
religions, a phenomenon for which there is as yet no generally
accepted explanation, although several sociologists have asserted
that this pattern of violent anticlerical behavior is a reaction to
the failure of most established religious bodies as of this time to
provide official interpretations of the so-called "miracle" of June
6. Reports of the destruction by mob action of houses of worship
of various faiths, with accompanying injuries or fatalities suffered
by ecclesiastical personnel, have come from Mexico, Denmark,
Burma, Puerto Rico, Portugal, Hungary, Ethiopia, the Philip-

pines, and, in the United States, Alabama, Colorado, and New York. Statements are promised shortly by leaders of most major faiths. Meanwhile a tendency has developed in certain ecclesiastical quarters toward supporting a mechanistic or rationalistic causation for the June 6 event; thus on Tuesday the Archbishop of York, stressing that he was speaking as a private citizen and not as a prelate of the Church of England, declared that we should not rule out entirely the possibility of a manipulation of the Earth's movements by superior beings native to another planet, intent on spreading confusion preparatory to conquest. Modern theologians, the Archbishop said, see no inherent impossibility in the doctrine of a separate act of creation that brought forth an intelligent species on some extraterrestrial or extragalactic planet, nor is it inconceivable, he went on, that it might be the Lord's ultimate purpose to cause a purging of sinful mankind at the hands of that other species. Thus the slowing of the Earth's rotation may have been an attempt by these enemies from space to capitalize on the emotions generated by the recent campaign of the so-called prophet Thomas the Proclaimer. A spokesman for the Coptic Patriarch of Alexandria, commenting favorably two days later on the Archbishop's theory, added that in the private view of the Patriarch it seems less implausible that such an alien species should exist than that a divine miracle of the June 6 sort could be invoked by popular demand. A number of other religious leaders, similarly speaking unofficially, have cautioned against too rapid acceptance of the divine origin of the June 6 event, without as yet going so far as to embrace the Archbishop of York's suggestion. On Friday Dr. Nathan F. Scharf, President of the Central Conference of American Rabbis, urgently appealed to American and Israeli scientists to produce a computer-generated mathematical schema capable of demonstrating how a unique but natural conjunction of astronomical forces might have resulted in the June 6 event. The only reply to this appeal thus far has come from Ssu-ma Hsiang-ju, Minister of Science of the People's Republic of China, who has revealed that a task force of several hundred Chinese astronomers is already at work on such a project. But his Soviet counterpart, Academician N. V. Posilippov, has on the contrary called for a revision of Marxist-Leninist astronomical theory to take into account what he terms "the possibility of intervention by as yet undefined forces, perhaps of supernatural aspect, in the motions of the heavenly bodies." We may conclude, therefore, that the situation remains in flux. Observers agree that the chief beneficiaries of the June 6 event at this point have been the various recently founded apocalyptic sects, who now regard the so-called Day of the Sign as an indication of the imminent destruction of life on Earth. Undoubtedly much of the current violence and other irrational behavior can be traced to the increased activity of such groups. A related manifestation is the dramatic expansion in recent weeks of older millenarian sects, notably the Pentecostal churches. The Protestant world in general has experienced a rebirth of the Pentecostal-inspired phenomenon known as glossolalia, or "speaking in tongues," a technique for penetrating to revelatory or prophetic levels by means of unreined ecstatic outbursts *illalum gha ghollim ve illalum ghollim ghaznim kroo! Aiha! Kroo illalum nildaz sitamon ghaznim* of seemingly random syllables in no language known to the speaker; the value of this practice has *mehigioo camaleelee honistar zam* been a matter of controversy in religious circles for many centuries.

## 6. *The Woman Who Is Sore at Heart Reproaches Thomas*

I knew he was in our county and I had to get to see him because he was the one who made all this trouble for me. So I went to his headquarters, the place where the broadcasts were being made that week, and I saw him standing in the middle of a group of his followers. A very handsome man, really, somewhat too dirty and wild-looking for my tastes, but you give him a shave and a haircut and he'd be quite attractive in my estimation. Big and strong he is, and when you see him you want to throw yourself into his arms, though of course I was in no frame of mind to do any such thing just then and in any case I'm not that sort of woman. I went right toward him. There was a tremendous crowd in the street, but I'm not discouraged easily, my husband likes to call me his "little bulldog" sometimes, and I just bulled my way through that mob, a little kicking and some elbowing and I think I bit someone's arm once and I got through. There was Thomas and next to him that skinny little man who's always with him, that Saul Kraft, who I guess is his press agent or something. As I got close, three of his bodyguards looked at me and then at each other, probably saying oh-oh, here comes another crank dame, and they started to surround me and move me away, and Thomas wasn't even looking at me, and I began to yell, saying I had to talk to Thomas, I had something important to say. And then this Saul Kraft told them to let go of me and bring me forward. They checked me out for concealed weapons and then Thomas asked me what I wanted.

I felt nervous before him. Such a famous man. But I planted my feet flat on the ground and stuck my jaw up the way Dad taught me, and I said, "You did all this. You've wrecked me, Thomas. You've got me so I don't know if I'm standing on my head or right side up."

He gave me a funny sideways smile. "I did?"

"Look," I said, "I'll tell you how it was. I went to Mass every week, my whole family, Church of the Redeemer on Wilson Avenue. We put money in the plate, we did everything the fathers told us to do, we tried to live good Christian lives, right? Not that we really thought much about God. Whether He was actually up there listening to me saying my paternoster. I figured He was too busy to worry much about me, and I couldn't be too concerned about Him, because He surpasses my understanding, you follow? Instead I prayed to the fathers. To me Father McDermott was like God Himself, in a way, not meaning any disrespect. What I'm trying to say is that the average ordinary person, they don't have a very close relationship with God, you follow? With the church, yes, with the fathers, but not with God. Okay. Now you come along and say the world is in a mess, so let's pray to God to show Himself like in the olden times. I ask Father McDermott about it and he says it's all right, it's permitted even though it isn't an idea that came from Rome, on such-and-such day we'll have this world moment of prayer. So I pray, and the sun stands still. June 6, you made the sun stand still."

"Not me. *Him.*" Thomas was smiling again. And looking at me like he could read everything in my soul.

I said, "You know what I mean. It's a miracle, anyway. The biggest miracle since, I don't know, since the Resurrection. The next day we need help, guidance, right? My husband and I, we go to church. *The church is closed.* Locked tight. We go around back and try to find the fathers. Nobody there but a housekeeper and she's scared. Won't open up. Why is the church shut? They're afraid of rioters, she says. Where's Father McDermott? He's gone to the Archdiocese for a conference. So have all the other fathers. Go away, she says. Nobody's here. You follow me, Thomas? Biggest miracle since the Resurrection, *and they close the church the next day.*"

Thomas said, "They got nervous, I guess."

"Nervous? Sure they were nervous. That's my whole point. Where were the fathers when we needed them? Conferring at the Archdiocese. The Cardinal was holding a special meeting about the crisis. *The crisis,* Thomas! God Himself works a miracle, and to the church it's a crisis! What am I supposed to do? Where does it leave me? I need the church, the church has always been telling me that, and all of a sudden the church locks its doors and says to me, Go figure it out by yourself, lady, we won't have a bulletin for a couple of days. The church was scared! I think they were afraid the Lord was going to come in and say we don't need priests any more, we don't need churches, all this organized-religion stuff hasn't worked out so well anyway, so let's forget it and move right into the Millennium."

"Anything big and strange always upsets the people in power,"

Thomas said, shrugging. "But the church opened again, didn't it?"

"Sure, four days later. Business as usual, except we aren't supposed to ask any questions about June 6 yet. Because they don't have The Word from Rome yet, the interpretation, the official policy." I had to laugh. "Three weeks, almost, since it happened, and the College of Cardinals is still in special consistory, trying to decide what position the church ought to take. Isn't that crazy, Thomas? If the Pope can't recognize a miracle when he sees one, what good is the whole church?"

"All right," Thomas said, "but why blame me?"

"Because you took my church away from me. I can't trust those people any more. I don't know what to believe. We've got God right here beside us, and the church isn't giving any leadership. What do we do now? How do we handle this thing?"

"Have faith, my child," he said, "and pray for salvation, and remain steadfast in your righteousness." He said a lot of other stuff like that too, rattling it off like he was a computer programmed to deliver blessings. I could tell he wasn't sincere. He wasn't trying to answer me, just to calm me down and get rid of me.

"No," I said, breaking in on him. "That stuff isn't good enough. *Have faith. Pray a lot.* I've been doing that all my life. Okay, we prayed and we got God to show Himself. What now? What's your program, Thomas? Tell me that. What do you want us to do? You took our church away—what will you give us to replace it?"

I could tell he didn't have any answers.

His face turned red and he tugged on the ends of his hair and looked at Saul Kraft in a sour way, almost like he was saying I-told-you-so with his eyes. Then he looked back at me and I saw either sorrow or fear in his face, I don't know which, and I realized right then that this Thomas is just a human being like you and me, a scared human being, who doesn't really understand what's happening and doesn't know how to go on from this point. He tried to fake it. He told me again to pray, never underestimate the power of prayer, et cetera, et cetera, but his heart wasn't in his words. He was stuck. *What's your program, Thomas?* He doesn't have any. He hasn't thought things through past the point of getting the Sign from God. He can't help us now. There's your Thomas for you, the Proclaimer, the prophet. He's scared. We're all scared, and he's just one of us, no different, no wiser. And last night the Apocalyptists burned the shopping center. You know, if you had asked me six months ago how I'd feel if God gave us a Sign that He was really watching over us, I'd have told you that I thought it would be the most wonderful thing that had ever happened since Jesus in the manger. But now it's happened. And I'm not so sure how wonderful it is. I walk around feeling that the ground might open up under my feet any time. I don't know what's going to happen to us all. God has come, and it ought to be beautiful, and instead it's just scary. I never imagined it would be this way. Oh, God. God I feel so lost. God I feel so empty.

### 7. *An Insight of Discerners*

Speaking before an audience was nothing new for me, of course. Not after all the years I've spent in classrooms, patiently instructing each season's hairy new crop of young in the mysteries of tachyon theory, anterior-charge particles, and time-reversal equations. Nor was this audience a particularly alien or frightening one: it was made up mainly of faculty people from Harvard and M.I.T., some graduate students, and a sprinkling of lawyers, psychologists, and other professional folk from Cambridge and the outskirts. All of us part of the community of scholarship, so to speak. The sort of audience that might come together to protest the latest incident of ecological rape or of preventive national liberation. But one aspect of my role this evening was unsettling to me. This was in the truest sense a religious gathering; that is, we were meeting to discuss the nature of God and to arrive at some comprehension of our proper relationship to Him. And I was the main speaker, me, old Bill Gifford, who for nearly four decades had regarded the Deity as an antiquated irrelevance. I was this flock's pastor. How strange that felt.

"But I believe that many of you are in the same predicament," I told them. "Men and women to whom the religious impulse has been something essentially foreign. Whose lives were complete and fulfilled although prayer and ritual were wholly absent from them. Who regarded the concept of a supreme being as meaningless and who looked upon the churchgoing habits of those around them as nothing more than lower-class superstitiousness on the one hand and middle-class pietism on the other. And then came the great surprise of June 6—forcing us to reconsider doctrines we had scorned, forcing us to reexamine our basic philosophical constructs, forcing us to seek an acceptable explanation of a phenomenon that we had always deemed impossible and implausible. All of you, like myself, suddenly found yourselves treading very deep metaphysical waters."

The nucleus of this group had come together on an *ad hoc* basis the week after It happened, and since then had been meeting two or three times a week. At first there was no formal organizational structure, no organizational name, no policy; it was merely a gathering of intelligent and sophisticated New Englanders who felt unable to cope individually with the altered nature of reality and who needed mutual reassurance and reinforcement. That was why I started going, anyway. But within ten days we were groping toward a more positive purpose: no longer simply to learn how to *accept* what had befallen humanity, but to find some way of turning it to a useful purpose. I had begun articulating some ideas along those lines in private conversation, and abruptly I was asked by several of the leaders of the group to make my thoughts public at the next meeting.

"An astonishing event has occurred," I went on. "A good many ingenious theories have been proposed to account for it—as, for example, that the Earth was brought to a halt through the workings of an extrasensory telekinetic force generated by the simultaneous concentration of the entire world population. We have also heard the astrological explanations—that the planets or the stars were lined up in a certain once-in-a-universe's-lifetime way to bring about such a result. And there have been the arguments, some of them coming from quite surprising places, in favor of the notion that the June 6 event was the doing of malevolent creatures from outer space. The telekinesis hypothesis has a certain superficial plausibility, marred only by the fact that experimenters in the past have never been able to detect even an iota of telekinetic ability in any human being or combination of human beings. Perhaps a simultaneous worldwide effort might generate forces not to be found in any unit smaller than the total human population, but such reasoning requires an undesirable multiplication of hypotheses. I believe that most of you here agree with me that the other explanations of the June 6 event beg one critical question: Why did the slowing of the Earth occur so promptly, in seemingly direct response to Thomas the Proclaimer's campaign of global prayer? Can we believe that a unique alignment of astrological forces just happened to occur the day after that hour of prayer? Can we believe that the extragalactic fiends just happened to meddle with the Earth's rotation on that particular day? The element of coincidence necessary to sustain these and other arguments is fatal to them, I think.

"What are we left with, then? Only with the explanation that the Lord Almighty, heeding mankind's entreaties, performed a miracle so that we should be confirmed in our faith in Him.

"So I conclude. So do many of you. But does it necessarily follow that mankind's sorry religious history, with all of its holy wars, its absurd dogmas, its childish rituals, its fastings and flagellations, is thereby justified? Because you and you and you and I were bowled over on June 6, blasted out of our skepticism by an event that has no rational explanation, should we therefore rush to the churches and synagogues and mosques and enroll immediately in the orthodoxy of our choice? I think not. I submit that our attitudes of skepticism and rationalism were properly held, although our aim was misplaced. In scorning the showy, trivial trappings of organized faith, in walking past the churches where our neighbors devoutly knelt, we erred by turning away also from the matter that underlay their faith: the existence of a supreme being whose divine plan guides the universe. The spinning of prayer wheels and the mumbling of credos seemed so inane to us that, in our revulsion for such things, we were led to deny all notions of a higher order, of a teleological universe, and we embraced the concept of a wholly random cosmos. And then the Earth stood still for a day and a night.

"How did it happen? We admit it was God's doing, you and I, amazed though we are to find ourselves saying so. We have been hammered into a posture of belief by that inexplicable event. But what do we mean by 'God'? Who is He? An old man with long white whiskers? Where is He to be found? Somewhere between the orbits of Mars and Jupiter? Is He a supernatural being, or merely an extraterrestrial one? Does He too acknowledge a superior authority? And so on, an infinity of new questions. We have no valid knowledge of His nature, though now we have certain knowledge of His existence.

"Very well. A tremendous opportunity now exists for us the discerning few, for us who are in the habit of intellectual activity. All about us we see a world in frenzy. The Apocalyptists swoon with joy over the approaching catastrophe, the glossolaliacs chatter in maniac glee, the heads of entrenched churchly hierarchies are aghast at the possibility that the Millennium may really be at hand; everything is in flux, everything is new and strange. New cults spring up. Old creeds dissolve. And this is our moment. Let us step in and replace credulity and superstition with reason. An end to cults; an end to theology; an end to blind faith. Let it be our goal to relate the events of that awesome day to some principle of reason, and develop a useful, dynamic, *rational* movement of rebirth and revival—not a religion per se but rather a cluster of belief, based on the concept that a divine plan exists, that we live under the authority of a supreme or at least superior being, and that we must strive to come to some kind of rational relationship with this being.

"We've already had the moral strength to admit that our old intuitive skepticism was an error. Now let us provide an attractive alternate for those of us who still find ritualistic orthodoxy unpalatable, but who fear a total collapse into apocalyptic disarray if no steps are taken to strengthen mankind's spiritual insight. Let us create, if we can, a purely secular movement, a nonreligious religion, which offers the hope of establishing a meaningful dialogue between Us and Him. Let us make plans. Let us find powerful symbols with which we may sway the undecided and the confused. Let us march forth as crusaders in a dramatic effort to rescue humanity from unreason and desperation."

And so forth. I think it was a pretty eloquent speech, especially coming from someone who isn't in the habit of delivering orations. A transcript of it got into the local paper the next day and was reprinted all over. My "us the discerning few" line drew a lot of attention, and spawned an instant label for our previously unnamed movement. We became known as the Discerners. Once we had a name, our status was different. We weren't simply a group of concerned citizens any longer. Now we constituted a cult —a skeptical, rational, antisuperstitious cult, true, but nevertheless a cult, a sect, the newest facet of the world's furiously proliferating latter-day craziness.

## 8. *An Expectation of Awaiters*

I know it hasn't been fashionable to believe in God these last twenty thirty forty years people haven't been keeping His path much but I always did even when I was a little boy I believed truly and I loved Him and I wanted to go to church all the time even in the middle of the week I'd say to Mother let's go to church I genuinely enjoyed kneeling and praying and feeling Him near me but she'd say no Davey you've got to wait till Sunday for that it's only Wednesday now. So as they say I'm no stranger to His

ways and of course when they called for that day of prayer I
prayed with all my heart that he might give us a Sign but even so
I'm no fool I mean I don't accept everything on a silver platter
I ask questions I have doubts I test things and probe a little I'm
not one of your ordinary country bumpkins that takes everything
on faith. In a way I suppose I could be said to belong to the discerning few although I don't want any of you to get the idea I'm
a Discerner oh no I have no sympathy whatever with that atheistic
bunch. Anyway we all prayed and the Sign came and my first reaction was joy I don't mind telling you I wept for joy when the sun
stood still feeling that all the faith of a lifetime had been confirmed and the godless had better shiver in their boots but then a
day or so later I began to think about it and I asked myself how
do we know that the Sign really came from God? How can we
be sure that the being we have invoked is really on our side I asked
myself and of course I had no good answer to that. For all I knew
we had conjured up Satan the Accursed and what we imagined
was a miracle was really a trick out of the depths of hell designed
to lead us all to perdition. Here are these Discerners telling us
that they repent their atheism because they know now that God
is real and God is with us but how naive they are they aren't even
allowing for the possibility that the Sign is a snare and a delusion
I tell you we can't be sure the thing is we absolutely *can't be sure*.
The Sign might have been from God or from the Devil and we
don't know we won't know until we receive a second Sign which
I await which I believe will be coming quite soon. And what will
that second Sign tell us? I maintain that that has not yet been decided on high it may be a Sign announcing our utter damnation
or it may be a Sign welcoming us to the Earthly Paradise and we
must await it humbly and prayerfully my friends we must pray
and purify ourselves and prepare for the worst as well as for the
best. I like to think that in a short while God Himself will present Himself to us not in any indirect way like stopping the sun
but rather in a direct manifestation either as God the Father or
as God the Son and we will all be saved but this will come about

*only if we remain righteous.* If we succumb to error and evil we will bring it to pass that the Devil's advent will descend on us for as Thomas has said himself our destiny is in our hands as well as in His and I believe the first Sign was only the start of a process that will be decided for good or for evil in the days just ahead. Therefore I Davey Strafford call upon you my friends to keep the way of the faith for we must not waver in our hope that He Who Comes will be lovingly inclined toward us and I say that this is our time of supreme test and if we fail it we may discover that it is Satan who shows up to claim our souls. I say once more we cannot interpret the first Sign we can only have faith that it is truly from God and we must pray that this is so while we await the ultimate verdict of heaven therefore we have obtained the rental of a vacant grocery store on Coshocton Avenue which we have renamed the First Church of the Awaiters of Redemption and we will pray round the clock there are seventeen of us now and we will pray in three-hour shifts five of us at a time in rotation the numbers increasing as our expected rapid growth takes place I trust you will come to us and swell our voices for we must pray we've got to there's no other hope now just pray a lot in order that He Who Comes may be benevolent and I ask you to keep praying and have a trusting heart in this our time of waiting.

## 9. A Crying of Proclaimers

Kraft enters the room as Thomas puts down the telephone. "Who were you talking to?" Kraft asks.

"Gifford the Discerner, calling from Boston."

"Why are you answering the phone yourself?"

"There was no one else here."

"There were three apostles in the outer office who could have handled the call, Thomas."

Thomas shrugs. "They would have had to refer it to me eventually. So I answered. What's wrong with that?"

"You've got to maintain distance between yourself and ordinary daily routines. You've got to stay up there on your pedestal and not go around answering telephones."

"I'll try, Saul," says Thomas heavily.

"What did Gifford want?"

"He'd like to merge his group and ours."

Kraft's eyes flash. "To merge? *To merge?* What are we, some sort of manufacturing company? We're a movement. A spiritual force. To talk mergers is nonsense."

"He means that we should start working together, Saul. He says we should join forces because we're both on the side of sanity."

"Exactly what is that supposed to mean?"

"That we're both anti-Apocalyptist. That we're both working to preserve society instead of to bury it."

"An oversimplification," Kraft says. "We deal in faith and he deals in equations. We believe in a Divine Being and he believes in the sanctity of reason. Where's the meeting point?"

"The Cincinnati and Chicago fires are our meeting point, Saul. The Apocalyptists are going crazy. And now these Awaiters too, these spokesmen for Satan—no. We have to act. If I put myself at Gifford's disposal—"

"At his *disposal?*"

"He wants a statement from me backing the spirit if not the substance of the Discerner philosophy. He thinks it'll serve to calm things a little."

"He wants to co-opt you for his own purposes."

"For the purposes of mankind, Saul."

Kraft laughs harshly. "How naive you can be, Thomas! Where's your sense? You can't make an alliance with atheists. You can't let them turn you into a ventriloquist's dummy who—"

"They believe in God just as much as—"

"You have power, Thomas. It's in your voice, it's in your eyes. They have none. They're just a bunch of professors. They want to borrow your power and make use of it to serve their own ends.

They don't want you, Thomas, they want your charisma. I forbid this alliance."

Thomas is trembling. He towers over Kraft, but his entire body quivers and Kraft remains steady. Thomas says, "I'm so tired, Saul."

"Tired?"

"The uproar. The rioting. The fires. I'm carrying too big a burden. Gifford can help me. With planning, with ideas. That's a clever bunch, those people."

"I can give you all the help you need."

"No, Saul! What have you been telling me all along? That prayer is sufficient unto every occasion! Faith! Faith! Faith! Faith moves mountains! Well? You were right, yes, you channeled your faith through me and I spoke to the people and we got ourselves a miracle, but what now? What have we really accomplished? Everything's falling apart, and we need strong souls to build and rebuild, and you aren't offering anything new. You—"

"The Lord will provide for—"

"Will He? Will He, Saul? How many thousands dead already, since June 6? How much property damage? Government paralyzed. Transportation breaking down. New cults. New prophets. Here's Gifford saying, Let's join hands, Thomas, let's try to work together, and you tell me—"

"I forbid this," Kraft says.

"It's all agreed. Gifford's going to take the first plane west, and—"

"I'll call him. He mustn't come. If he does I won't let him see you. I'll notify the apostles to bar him."

"No, Saul."

"We don't need him. We'll be ruined if we let him near you."

"Why?"

"Because he's godless and our movement's strength proceeds from the Lord!" Kraft shouts. "Thomas, what's happened to you? Where's your fire? Where's your zeal? Where's my old swaggering Thomas who talked back to God? Belch, Thomas. Spit on the floor, scratch your belly, curse a little. I'll get you some wine. It shocks me to see you sniveling like this. Telling me how tired you are, how scared."

"I don't feel like swaggering much these days, Saul."

"Damn you, swagger anyway! The whole world is watching you! Here, listen—I'll rough out a new speech for you that you'll deliver on full hookup tomorrow night. We'll outflank Gifford and his bunch. We'll co-opt *him*. What you'll do, Thomas, is call for a new act of faith, some kind of mass demonstration, something symbolic and powerful, something to turn people away from despair and destruction. We'll follow the Discerner line *plus* our own element of faith. You'll denounce all the false new cults and urge everyone to—to—let me think—to make a pilgrimage of some kind?—a coming together—a mass baptism, that's it, a march to the sea, everybody bathing in God's own sea, washing away doubt and sin. Right? A rededication to faith." Kraft's face is red. His forehead gleams. Thomas scowls at him. Kraft goes on, "Stop pulling those long faces. You'll do it and it'll work. It'll pull people back from the abyss of Apocalypticism. Positive goals, that's our approach. Thomas the Proclaimer cries out that we must work together under God. Yes? Yes. We'll get this thing under control in ten days, I promise you. Now go have yourself a drink. Relax. I've got to call Gifford, and then I'll start blocking in your new appeal. Go on. And stop looking so glum, Thomas! We hold a mighty power in our hands. We're wielding the sword of the Lord. You want to turn all that over to Gifford's crowd? Go. Go. Get some rest, Thomas."


## 10. A Prostration of Propitiators

ALL PARISH CHAIRMEN PLEASE COPY AND DIS-TRIBUTE. The Reverend August Hammacher to his dearly beloved brothers and sisters in Christ, members of the Authentic Church of the Doctrine of Propitiation, this message from Central

Shrine: greetings and blessings. Be you hereby advised that we have notified Elder Davey Strafford of the First Church of the Awaiters of Redemption that as of this date we no longer consider ourselves in communion with his church, on grounds of irremediable doctrinal differences. It is now forbidden for members of the Authentic Church to participate in the Awaiter rite or to have any sacramental contact with the instrumentalities of the Awaiter creed, although we shall continue to remember the Awaiters in our prayers and to strive for their salvation as if they were our own people.

The schism between ourselves and the Awaiters, which has been in the making for more than a week, arises from a fundamental disagreement over the nature of the Sign. It is of course our belief, greatly strengthened by the violent events of recent days, that the Author of the Sign was Satan and that the Sign foretells a coming realignment in heaven, the probable beneficiaries of which are to be the Diabolical Forces. In expectation of the imminent establishment of the Dark Powers on Earth, we therefore direct our most humble homage to Satan the Second Incarnation of Christ, hoping that when He comes among us He will take cognizance of our obeisance and spare us from the ultimate holocaust.

Now the Awaiters hold what is essentially an agnostic position, saying that we cannot know whether the Sign proceeds from God or from Satan, and that pending further revelation we must continue to pray as before to the Father and the Son, so that perhaps through our devotions we may stave off the advent of Satan entirely. There is one point of superficial kinship between their ideas and ours, which is an unwillingness to share the confidence of Thomas the Proclaimer on the one hand, and the Discerners on the other, that the Sign is God's work. But it may be seen that a basic conflict of doctrine exists between ourselves and the Awaiters, for they refuse to comprehend our teachings concerning the potential benevolence of Satan, and cling to an attitude that may be deemed dangerously offensive by Him. Unwilling to commit themselves finally to one side or the other, they hope to steer a cautious middle course, not realizing that when the Dark One comes He will chastise all those who failed to accept the proper meaning of the revelation of June 6. We have hoped to sway the Awaiters to our position, but their attitude has grown increasingly abusive as we have exposed their doctrinal inconsistencies, and now we have no option but to pronounce excommunication upon them. For what does Revelation say? "I know thy works, that thou art neither cold nor hot: I would thou wert cold or hot. So then because thou art lukewarm, and neither cold nor hot, I will spue thee out of my mouth." We cannot risk being tainted by these lukewarm Awaiters who will not bow the knee to the Dark One, though they admit the possibility (but not the inevitability) of His Advent.

However, dearly loved friends in Christ, I am happy to reveal that we have this day established preliminary communion with the United Diabolist Apocalyptic Pentecostal Church of the United States, the headquarters of which is in Los Angeles, California. I need not here recapitulate the deep doctrinal chasms separating us from the Apocalyptist sects in general; but although we abhor certain teachings even of this Diabolist faction, we recognize large areas of common belief linking us, and hope to wean the United Diabolist Apocalyptics entirely from their errors in the course of time. This is by no means to be interpreted as presently authorizing communicants of the Authentic Church of the Doctrine of Propitiation to take part in Apocalyptist activities, even those which are nondestructive, but I do wish to advise you of the possibility of a deeper relationship with at least one Apocalyptist group even as we sever our union with the Awaiters. Our love goes out to all of you, from all of us at Central Shrine. We prostrate ourselves humbly before the Dark One whose triumph is ordained. In the name of the Father, the Son, the Holy Ghost, and He Who Comes. Amen.

## 11. The March to the Sea

It was the most frightening thing ever. Like an army invading us. Like a plague of locusts. They came like the locusts came up upon the land of Egypt when Moses stretched out his hand. Exodus 10:15 tells it: *For they covered the face of the whole earth, so that the land was darkened; and they did eat every herb of the land, and all the fruit of the trees which the hail had left: and there remained not any green thing in the trees, or in the herbs of the field, through all the land of Egypt.* Like a nightmare. Lucy and me were the Egyptians and all of Thomas' people, they were the locusts.

Lucy wanted to be in the middle of it all along. To her Thomas was like a holy prophet of God from the moment he first started to preach, although I tried to tell her back then that he was a charlatan and a dangerous lunatic with a criminal record. Look at his face, I said, look at those eyes! A lot of good it did me. She kept a scrapbook of him like he was a movie star and she was a fifteen-year-old girl instead of a woman of seventy-four. Pictures of him, texts of all his speeches. She got angry at me when I called him crazy or unscrupulous: we had our worst quarrel in maybe thirty years when she wanted to send him $500 to help pay for his television expenses and I absolutely refused. Naturally after the Day of the Sign she came to look upon him as being right up there in the same exalted category as Moses and Elijah and John the Baptist, one of the true anointed voices of the Lord, and I guess I was starting to think of him that way too, despite myself. Though I didn't like him or trust him I sensed he had a special power. When everybody was praying for the Sign I prayed too, not so much because I thought it would come about but just to avoid trouble with Lucy, but I did put my heart into the prayer, and when the Earth stopped turning a shiver ran all through me and I got such a jolt of amazement that I thought I might be having a stroke. So I apologized to Lucy for all I had said about Thomas.

I still suspected he was a madman and a charlatan, but I couldn't deny that he had something of the saint and prophet about him too. I suppose it's possible for a man to be a saint and a charlatan both. Anything's possible. I understand that one of these new religions is saying that Satan is actually an incarnation of Jesus, or the fourth member of the Trinity, or something like that. Honestly.

Well then all the riotings and burnings began when the hot weather came and the world seemed to be going crazy with things worse not better after God had given His Sign, and Thomas called for this Day of Rededication, everybody to go down to the sea and wash off his sins, a real old-time total-immersion revival meeting where we'd all get together and denounce the new cults and get things back on the right track again.

And Lucy came to me all aglow and said, Let's go, let's be part of it. I think there were supposed to be ten gathering-places all around the United States, New York and Houston and San Diego and Seattle and Chicago and I don't remember which else, but Thomas himself was going to attend the main one at Atlantic City, which is just a little ways down the coast from us, and the proceedings would be beamed by live telecast to all the other meetings being held here and overseas. She hadn't ever seen Thomas in person. I told her it was crazy for people our age to get mixed up in a mob of the size Thomas always attracts. We'd be crushed, we'd be trampled, we'd die sure as anything. Look, I said, we live right here by the seashore anyway, the ocean is fifty steps from our front porch; so why ask for trouble? We'll stay here and watch the praying on television, and then when everybody goes down into the sea to be purified we can go right here on our own beach and we'll be part of things in a way without taking the risks. I could see that Lucy was disappointed about not seeing Thomas in person but after all she's a sensible woman and I'm going to be eighty next November and there had already been some pretty wild scenes at each of Thomas' public appearances.

The big day dawned and I turned on the television and then of course we got the news that Atlantic City had banned Thomas' meeting at the last minute on the grounds of public safety. A big oil tanker had broken up off shore the night before and an oil slick was heading toward the beach, the mayor said. If there was a mass meeting on the beach that day it would interfere with the city's pollution-prevention procedures, and also the oil would endanger the health of anybody who went into the water, so the whole Atlantic City waterfront was being cordoned off, extra police brought in from out of town, laser lines set up, and so forth. Actually the oil slick wasn't anywhere near Atlantic City and was drifting the other way, and when the mayor talked about public safety he really meant the safety of his city, not wanting a couple of million people ripping up the boardwalk and breaking windows. So there was Atlantic City sealed off and Thomas had this immense horde of people already collected, coming from Philadelphia and Trenton and Wilmington and even Baltimore, a crowd so big it couldn't be counted, five, six, maybe ten million people. They showed it from a helicopter view and everybody was standing shoulder to shoulder for about twenty miles in this direction and fifty miles in that direction, that's how it seemed, anyway, and about the only open place was where Thomas was, a clearing around fifty yards across with his apostles forming a tight ring protecting him.

Where was this mob going to go, since it couldn't get into Atlantic City? Why, Thomas said, everybody would just march up the Jersey coast and spread out along the shore from Long Beach Island to Sandy Hook. When I heard that I wanted to jump into the car and start heading for maybe Montana, but it was too late: the marchers were already on their way, all the mainland highways were choked with them. I went up on the sundeck with our binoculars and I could see the first of them coming across the causeway, walking seventy or eighty abreast, and a sea of faces behind them going inland on and on back toward Manahawkin and beyond. Well it was like the Mongol hordes of Genghis Khan.

One swarm went south toward Beach Haven and the other came up through Surf City and Loveladies and Harvey Cedars in our direction. Thousands and thousands and thousands of them. Our island is long and skinny like any coastal sandspit, and it's pretty well built up both on the beach side and on the bay side, no open space except the narrow streets, and there wasn't *room* for all those people. But they kept on coming, and as I watched through the binoculars I thought I was getting dizzy because I imagined some of the houses on the beach side were moving too, and then I realized that the houses *were* moving, some of the flimsier ones, they were being pushed right off their foundations by the press of humanity. Toppling and being ground underfoot, entire houses, can you imagine? I told Lucy to pray, but she was already doing it, and I got my shotgun ready because I felt I had to try at least to protect us, but I said to her that this was probably going to be our last day alive and I kissed her and we told each other how good it had been, all of it, fifty-three years together. And then the mob came spilling through our part of the island. Rushing down to the beach. A berserk crazy multitude.

And Thomas was there, right close to our place. Bigger than I thought he'd be, and his hair and beard were all tangled up, and his face was red and peeling some from sunburn—he was that close, I could see the sunburn—and he was still in the middle of his ring of apostles, and he was shouting through a bullhorn, but no matter how much amplification they gave him from the copter-borne speakers overhead it was impossible to understand anything he was saying. Saul Kraft was next to him. He looked pale and frightened. People were rushing into the water, some of them fully clothed and some stark naked, until the whole shoreline was packed right out to where the breakers begin. As more and more people piled into the water the ones in front were pushed beyond their depth, and I think this was when the drownings started. I know I saw a number of people waving and kicking and yelling for help and getting swept out to sea. Thomas remained on shore, shouting through the bullhorn. He must have realized it was all

out of control, but there was nothing he could do. Until this point
the thrust of the mob was all forward, toward the sea, but now
there was a change in the flow: some of those in the water tried
to force their way back up onto land, and smashed head on into
those going the other way. I thought they were coming up out of
the water to avoid being drowned, but then I saw the black smears
on their clothing and I thought, *the oil slick!* and yes, there it was,
not down by Atlantic City but up here by us, right off the beach
and moving shoreward. People in the water were getting bogged
down in it, getting it all over their hair and faces, but they
couldn't reach the shore because of the rush still heading in the
opposite direction. This was when the tramplings started as the
ones coming out of the water, coughing and choking and blinded
with oil, fell under the feet of those still trying to get into the
sea.

I looked at Thomas again and he was like a maniac. His face was
wild and he had thrown the bullhorn away and he was just screaming, with angry cords standing out on his neck and forehead. Saul
Kraft went up to him and said something and Thomas turned
like the wrath of God, turned and rose up and brought his hands
down like two clubs on Saul Kraft's head, and you know Kraft is
a small man and he went down like he was dead, with blood all
over his face. Two or three apostles picked him up and carried him
into one of the beachfront houses. Just then somebody managed
to slip through the cordon of apostles and went running toward
Thomas. He was a short, plump man wearing the robes of one of
the new religions, an Awaiter or Propitiator or I don't know what,
and he had a laser-hatchet in his hand. He shouted something at
Thomas and lifted the hatchet. But Thomas moved toward him
and stood so tall that the assassin almost seemed to shrink, and
the man was so afraid that he couldn't do a thing. Thomas
reached out and plucked the hatchet from his hand and threw it
aside. Then he caught the man and started hitting him, tremendous close-range punches, slam slam slam, all but knocking the
man's head off his shoulders. Thomas didn't look human while he

was doing that. He was some kind of machine of destruction. He was bellowing and roaring and running foam from his mouth, and he was into this terrible deadly rhythm of punching, slam slam slam. Finally he stopped and took the man by both hands and flung him across the beach, like you'd fling a rag doll. The man flew maybe twenty feet and landed and didn't move. I'm certain Thomas beat him to death. There's your holy prophet for you, your saint of God. Suddenly Thomas' whole appearance changed: he became terribly calm, almost frozen, standing there with his arms dangling and his shoulders hunched up and his chest heaving from all that hitting. And he began to cry. His face broke up like winter ice on a spring pond and I saw the tears. I'll never forget that: Thomas the Proclaimer all alone in the middle of that madhouse on the beach, sobbing like a new widow.

I didn't see anything after that. There was a crash of glass from downstairs and I grabbed my gun and went down to see, and I found maybe fifteen people piled up on the livingroom floor who had been pushed right through the picture window by the crowd outside. The window had cut them all up and some were terribly maimed and there was blood on everything, and more and more and more people kept flying through the place where the window had been, and I heard Lucy screaming and my gun went off and I don't know what happened after that. Next I remember it was the middle of the night and I was sitting in our completely wrecked house and I saw a helicopter land on the beach, and a tactical squad began collecting bodies. There were hundreds of dead just on our strip of beach. Drowned, trampled, choked by oil, heart attacks, everything. The corpses are gone now but the island is a ruin. We're asking the government for disaster aid. I don't know: is a religious meeting a proper disaster? It was for us. That was your Day of Rededication, all right: a disaster. Prayer and purification to bring us all together under the banner of the Lord. May I be struck dead for saying this if I don't mean it with all my heart: I wish the Lord and all his prophets would disappear and leave us alone. We've had enough religion for one season.

## 12. *The Voice from the Heavens*

Saul Kraft, hidden behind nine thousand dollars' worth of security devices, an array of scanners and sensors and shunt-gates and trip-vaults, wonders why everything is going so badly. Perhaps his choice of Thomas as the vehicle was an error. Thomas, he has come to realize, is too complicated, too unpredictable—a dual soul, demon and angel inextricably merged. Nevertheless the Crusade had begun promisingly enough. Working through Thomas, he had coaxed God Almighty into responding to the prayers of mankind, hadn't he? How much better than that do you need to do?

But now. This nightmarish carnival atmosphere everywhere. These cults, these other prophets. A thousand interpretations of an event whose meaning should have been crystal clear. The bonfires. Madness crackling like lightning across the sky. Maybe the fault was in Thomas. The Proclaimer had been deficient in true grace all along. Possibly any mass movement centered on a prophet who had Thomas' faults of character was inherently doomed to slip into chaos.

*Or maybe the fault was mine, O Lord.*

Kraft has been in seclusion for many days, perhaps for several weeks; he is no longer sure when he began this retreat. He will see no one, not even Thomas, who is eager to make amends. Kraft's injuries have healed and he holds no grievance against Thomas for striking him: the fiasco of the Day of Rededication had driven all of them a little insane there on the beach, and Thomas' outburst of violence was understandable if not justifiable. It may even have been of divine inspiration, God inflicting punishment on Kraft through the vehicle of Thomas for his sins. The sin of pride, mainly. To turn Gifford away, to organize the Day of Rededication for such cynical motives—

Kraft fears for his soul, and for the soul of Thomas.

He dares not see Thomas now, not until he has regained his

own spiritual equilibrium; Thomas is too turbulent, too tem-
pestuous, emits such powerful emanations of self-will; Kraft must
first recapture his moral strength. He fasts much of the time. He
tries to surrender himself fully in prayer. But prayer will not
come: he feels cut off from the Almighty, separated from Him as
he has never been before. By bungling this holy Crusade he must
have earned the Lord's displeasure. A gulf, a chasm, parts them;
Kraft is earthbound and helpless. He abandons his efforts to pray.
He prowls his suite restlessly, listening for intruders, constantly
running security checks. He switches on his closed-circuit video
inputs, expecting to see fires in the streets, but all is calm out
there. He listens to news bulletins on the radio: chaos, turmoil,
everywhere. Thomas is said to be dead; Thomas is reported on
the same day to be in Istanbul, Karachi, Johannesburg, San Francisco; the Propitiators have announced that on the twenty-fourth
of November, according to their calculations, Satan will appear on
Earth to enter into his sovereignty; the Pope, at last breaking his
silence, has declared that he has no idea what power might have
been responsible for the startling happenings of June 6, but thinks
it would be rash to attribute the event to God's direct intervention without some further evidence. So the Pope has become an
Awaiter too. Kraft smiles. Marvelous! Kraft wonders if the
Archbishop of Canterbury is attending Propitiator services. Or the
Dalai Lama consorting with the Apocalyptists. Anything can happen now. Gog and Magog are let loose upon the world. Kraft no
longer is surprised by anything. He feels no astonishment even
when he turns the radio on late one afternoon and finds that God
Himself seems to be making a broadcast.

God's voice is rich and majestic. It reminds Kraft somewhat of
the voice of Thomas, but God's tone is less fervid, less evangelical;
He speaks in an easy but serious-minded way, like a Senator cam-
paigning for election to his fifth term of office. There is a barely
perceptible easternness to God's accent: He could be a Senator
from Pennsylvania, maybe, or Ohio. He has gone on the air, He
explains, in the hope of restoring order to a troubled world. He
wishes to reassure everyone: no apocalypse is planned, and those

who anticipate the imminent destruction of the world are most unwise. Nor should you pay heed to those who claim that the recent Sign was the work of Satan. It certainly was not, God says, not at all, and propitiation of the Evil One is uncalled for. By all means let's give the Devil his due, but nothing beyond that. All I intended when I stopped the Earth's rotation, God declares, was to let you know that I'm here, looking after your interests. I wanted you to be aware that in the event of really bad trouble down there I'll see to it—

Kraft, lips clamped tautly, changes stations. The resonant baritone voice pursues him.

—that peace is maintained and the forces of justice are strengthened in—

Kraft turns on his television set. The screen shows nothing but the channel insignia. Across the top of the screen gleams a bright-green title:

## ALLEGED VOICE OF GOD

and across the bottom, in frantic scarlet, is a second caption:

## BY LIVE PICKUP FROM THE MOON

The Deity, meanwhile, has moved smoothly on to new themes. All the problems of the world, He observes, can be attributed to the rise and spread of atheistic socialism. The false prophet Karl Marx, aided by the Antichrist Lenin and the subsidiary demons Stalin and Mao, have set loose in the world a plague of godlessness that has tainted the entire twentieth century and, here at the dawn of the twenty-first, must at last be eradicated. For a long time the zealous godly folk of the world resisted the pernicious Bolshevik doctrines, God continues, His voice still lucid and reasonable; but in the past twenty years an accommodation with the powers of darkness has come into effect, and this has allowed spreading corruption to infect even such splendidly righteous lands as Japan, Brazil, the German Federal Republic, and God's own beloved United States of America. The foul philosophy of coexistence has led to a step-by-step entrapment of the forces of good, and as a result—

Kraft finds all of this quite odd. Is God speaking to every nation in English, or is He speaking Japanese to the Japanese, Hebrew to the Israelis, Croatian to the Croats, Bulgarian to the Bulgars? And when did God become so staunch a defender of the capitalist ethic? Kraft recalls something about driving money-changers out of the temple, long ago. But now the voice of God appears to be demanding a holy war against Communism. Kraft hears Him calling on the legions of the sanctified to attack the Marxist foe wherever the red flag flies. Sack embassies and consulates, burn the houses of ardent left-wingers, destroy libraries and other sources of dangerous propaganda, the Lord advises. He says everything in a level, civilized tone.

Abruptly, in midsentence, the voice of the Almighty vanishes from the airwaves. A short time later an announcer, unable to conceal his chagrin, declares that the broadcast was a hoax contrived by bored technicians in a satellite relay station. Investigations have begun to determine how so many radio and television stations let themselves be persuaded to transmit it as a public-interest item. But for many godless Marxists the revelation comes too late. The requested sackings and lootings have occurred in dozens of cities. Hundreds of diplomats, guards, and clerical workers have been slain by maddened mobs bent on doing the Lord's work. Property losses are immense. An international crisis is developing, and there are scattered reports of retribution against American citizens in several Eastern European countries. We live in strange times, Kraft tells himself. He prays. For himself. For Thomas. For all mankind. Lord have mercy. Amen. Amen. Amen.


## 13. The Burial of Faith

The line of march begins at the city line and runs westward out of town into the suburban maze. The marchers, at least a thousand of them, stride vigorously forward even though a dank, op-

pressive heat enfolds them. On they go, past the park dense with
the dark-green leaves of late summer, past the highway cloverleaf,
past the row of burned motels and filling stations, past the
bombed reservoir, past the cemeteries, heading for the municipal
dumping-grounds.

Gifford, leading the long sober procession, wears ordinary class-
room clothes: a pair of worn khaki trousers, a loose-fitting gray
shirt, and old leather sandals. Originally there had been some talk
of having the most important Discerners come garbed in their
academic robes, but Gifford had vetoed that on the grounds that
it wasn't in keeping with the spirit of the ceremony. Today all of
the old superstitions and pomposities were to be laid to rest; why
then bedeck the chief iconoclasts in hieratic costume as though
they were priests, as though this new creed were going to be just
as full of mummery as the outmoded religions it hoped to sup-
plant?

Because the marchers are so simply dressed, the contrast is
all the more striking between the plain garments they wear and
the elaborate, rich-textured ecclesiastical paraphernalia they carry.
No one is empty-handed; each has some vestment, some sacred
artifact, some work of scripture. Draped over Gifford's left arm is
a large white linen alb, ornately embroidered, with a dangling
silken cincture. The man behind him carries a deacon's dalmatic;
the third marcher has a handsome chasuble; the fourth, a splendid
cope. The rest of the priestly gear is close behind: amice, stole,
maniple, vimpa. A frosty-eyed woman well along in years waves a
crozier aloft; the man beside her wears a mitre at a mockingly
rakish angle. Here are cassocks, surplices, hoods, tippets, cottas,
rochets, mozzettas, mantellettas, chimeres, and much more:
virtually everything, in fact, save the papal tiara itself. Here are
chalices, crucifixes, thuribles, fonts; three men struggle beneath
a marvelously carved fragment of a pulpit; a little band of marchers displays Greek Orthodox outfits, the rhason and the sticharion,
the epitrachelion and the epimanikia, the sakkos, the epigonation,
the zone, the omophorion; they brandish ikons and enkolpia,

dikerotrikera and dikanikion. Austere Presbyterian gowns may be seen, and rabbinical yarmulkes and tallithim and tfilin. Farther back in the procession one may observe more exotic holy objects, prayer wheels and tonkas, sudras and kustis, idols of fifty sorts, things sacred to Confucianists, Shintoists, Parsees, Buddhists both Mahayana and Hinayana, Jains, Sikhs, animists of no formal rite, and others. The marchers have shofars, mezuzahs, candelabra, communion trays, even collection plates; no portable element of faith has been ignored. And of course the holy books of the world are well represented: an infinity of Old and New Testaments, the Koran, the Bhagavad-Gita, the Upanishads, the Tao-te-ching, the Vedas, the Vedanta Sutra, the Talmud, the Book of the Dead, and more. Gifford has been queasy about destroying books, for that is an act with ugly undertones; but these are extreme times, and extreme measures are required. Therefore he has given his consent even for that.

Much of the material the marchers carry was freely contributed, mostly by disgruntled members of congregations, some of it given by disaffected clergymen themselves. The other objects come mostly from churches or museums plundered during the civil disturbances. But the Discerners have done no plundering of their own; they have merely accepted donations and picked up some artifacts that rioters had scattered in the streets. On this point Gifford was most strict: acquisition of material by force was prohibited. Thus the robes and emblems of the newly founded creeds are seen but sparsely today, since Awaiters and Propitiators and their like would hardly have been inclined to contribute to Gifford's festival of destruction.

They have reached the municipal dump now. It is a vast flat wasteland, surprisingly aseptic-looking: there are large areas of meadow, and the unreclaimed regions of the dump have been neatly graded and mulched, in readiness for the scheduled autumn planting of grass. The marchers put down their burdens and the chief Discerners come forward to take spades and shovels from a truck that has accompanied them. Gifford looks up; helicopters hover and television cameras bristle in the sky. This event will have extensive coverage. He turns to face the others and intones, "Let this ceremony mark the end of all ceremonies. Let this rite usher in a time without rites. Let reason rule forevermore."

Gifford lifts the first shovelful of soil himself. Now the rest of the diggers set to work, preparing a trench three feet deep, ten to twelve feet wide. The topsoil comes off easily, revealing strata of cans, broken toys, discarded television sets, automobile tires, and garden rakes. A mound of debris begins to grow as the digging team does its task; soon a shallow opening gapes. Though it is now late afternoon, the heat has not diminished, and those who dig stream with sweat. They rest frequently, panting, leaning on their tools. Meanwhile those who are not digging stand quietly, not putting down that which they carry.

Twilight is near before Gifford decides that the trench is adequate. Again he looks up at the cameras, again he turns to face his followers.

He says, "On this day we bury a hundred thousand years of superstition. We lay to rest the old idols, the old fantasies, the old errors, the old lies. The time of faith is over and done with; the era of certainty opens. No longer do we need theologians to speculate on the proper way of worshiping the Lord; no longer do we need priests to mediate between ourselves and Him; no longer do we need man-made scriptures that pretend to interpret His nature. We have all of us felt His hand upon our world, and the time has come to approach Him with clear eyes, with an alert, open mind. Hence we give to the earth these relics of bygone epochs, and we call upon discerning men and women everywhere to join us in this ceremony of renunciation."

He signals. One by one the Discerners advance to the edge of the pit. One by one they cast their burdens in: albs, chasubles, copes, mitres, Korans, Upanishads, yarmulkes, crucifixes. No one hurries; the Burial of Faith is serious business. As it proceeds, a drum roll of dull distant thunder reverberates along the horizon.

A storm on the way? Just heat lightning, perhaps, Gifford decides. The ceremony continues. In with the maniple. In with the shofar. In with the cassock. Thunder again: louder, more distinct. The sky darkens. Gifford attempts to hasten the tempo of the ceremony, beckoning the Discerners forward to drop their booty. A blade of lightning slices the heavens and this time the answering thunderclap comes almost instantaneously, *ka-thock*. A few drops of rain. The forecast had been in error. A nuisance, but no real harm. Another flash of lightning. A tremendous crash. That one must have struck only a few hundred yards away. There is some nervous laughter. "We've annoyed Zeus," someone says. "He's throwing thunderbolts." Gifford is not amused; he enjoys ironies, but not now, not now. And he realizes that he has become just credulous enough, since the sixth of June, to be at least marginally worried that the Almighty might indeed be about to punish this sacrilegious band of Discerners. A flash again. *Ka-thock!* The clouds now split asunder and torrents of rain abruptly descend. In moments, shirts are pasted to skins, the floor of the pit turns to mud, rivulets begin to stream across the dump.

And then, as though they had scheduled the storm for their own purposes, a mob of fierce-faced people in gaudy robes bursts into view. They wield clubs, pitchforks, rake handles, cleavers, and other improvised weapons; they scream incoherent, unintelligible slogans; and they rush into the midst of the Discerners, laying about them vigorously. "Death to the godless blasphemers!" is what they are shrieking, and similar phrases. Who are they, Gifford wonders? Awaiters. Propitiators. Diabolists. Apocalyptists. Perhaps a coalition of all cultists. The television helicopters descend to get a better view of the melee, and hang just out of reach, twenty or thirty feet above the struggle. Their powerful floodlights provide apocalyptic illumination. Gifford finds hands at his throat: a crazed woman, howling, grotesque. He pushes her away and she tumbles into the pit, landing on a stack of mud-crusted Bibles. A frantic stampede has begun; his people are rushing in all directions, followed by the vengeful servants of the Lord, who wield their weapons with vindictive glee. Gifford sees his friends fall, wounded, badly hurt, perhaps slain. Where are the police? Why are they giving no protection? "Kill all the blasphemers!" a maniac voice shrills near him. He whirls, ready to defend himself. A pitchfork. He feels a strange cold clarity of thought and moves swiftly in, feinting, seizing the handle of the pitchfork, wresting it from his adversary. The rain redoubles its force; a sheet of water comes between Gifford and the other, and when he can see again, he is alone at the edge of the pit. He hurls the pitchfork into the pit and instantly wishes he had kept it, for three of the robed ones are coming toward him. He breaks into a cautious trot, tries to move past them, puts on a sudden spurt of speed, and slips in the mud. He lands in a puddle; the taste of mud is in his mouth; he is breathless, terrified, unable to rise. They fling themselves upon him. "Wait," he says. "This is madness!" One of them has a club. "No," Gifford mutters. "No. No. No. No."

## 14. The Seventh Seal

1. And when he had opened the seventh seal, there was silence in heaven about the space of half an hour.

2. And I saw the seven angels which stood before God; and to them were given seven trumpets.

3. And another angel came and stood at the altar, having a golden censer; and there was given unto him much incense, that he should offer it with the prayers of all saints upon the golden altar which was before the throne.

4. And the smoke of the incense, which came with the prayers of the saints, ascended up before God out of the angel's hand.

5. And the angel took the censer, and filled it with fire of the altar, and cast it into the earth: and there were voices, and thunderings, and lightnings, and an earthquake.

6. And the seven angels which had the seven trumpets prepared themselves to sound.

7. The first angel sounded, and there followed hail and fire

*mingled with blood, and they were cast upon the earth: and the third part of trees was burnt up, and all green grass was burnt up.*

*8. And the second angel sounded, and as it were a great mountain burning with fire was cast into the sea: and the third part of the sea became blood;*

*9. And the third part of the creatures which were in the sea, and had life, died; and the third part of the ships were destroyed.*

*10. And the third angel sounded, and there fell a great star from heaven, burning as it were a lamp, and it fell upon the third part of the rivers, and upon the fountains of waters;*

*11. And the name of the star is called Wormwood: and the third part of the waters became wormwood; and many men died of the waters, because they were made bitter.*

*12. And the fourth angel sounded, and the third part of the sun was smitten, and the third part of the moon, and the third part of the stars; so as the third part of them was darkened, and the day shone not for a third part of it, and the night likewise.*

*13. And I beheld, and heard an angel flying through the midst of heaven, saying with a loud voice, Woe, woe, woe, to the inhabiters of the earth by reason of the other voices of the trumpet of the three angels, which are yet to sound!*

## 15. The Flight of the Prophet

All, all over. Thomas weeps. The cities burn. The very lakes are afire. So many thousands dead. The Apocalyptists dance, for though the year is not yet sped the end seems plainly in view. The Church of Rome has pronounced anathema on Thomas, denying his miracle: he is the Antichrist, the Pope has said. Signs and portents are seen everywhere. This is the season of two-headed calves and dogs with cats' faces. New prophets have arisen. God may shortly return, or He may not; revelations differ. Many people now pray for an end to all such visitations and miracles. The Awaiters no longer Await, but now ask that we be spared from His next coming; even the Diabolists and the Propitiators cry,

Come not, Lucifer. Those who begged a Sign from God in June would be content now only with God's renewed and prolonged absence. Let Him neglect us; let Him dismiss us from His mind. It is a time of torches and hymns. Rumors of barbaric warfare come from distant continents. They say the neutron bomb has been used in Bolivia. Thomas' last few followers have asked him to speak with God once more, in the hope that things can still be set to rights, but Thomas refuses. The lines of communication to the Deity are closed. He dares not reopen them: see, see how many plagues and evils he has let loose as it is! He renounces his prophethood. Others may dabble in charismatic mysticism if they so please. Others may kneel before the burning bush or sweat in the glare of the pillar of fire. Not Thomas. Thomas' vocation is gone. All over. All, all, all over.

He hopes to slip into anonymity. He shaves his beard and docks his hair; he obtains a new wardrobe, bland and undistinguished; he alters the color of his eyes; he practices walking in a slouch to lessen his great height. Perhaps he has not lost his pocket-picking skills. He will go silently into the cities, head down, fingers on the ready, and thus he will make his way. It will be a quieter life.

Disguised, alone, Thomas goes forth. He wanders unmolested from place to place, sleeping in odd corners, eating in dim rooms. He is in Chicago for the Long Sabbath, and he is in Milwaukee for the Night of Blood, and he is in St. Louis for the Invocation of Flame. These events leave him unaffected. He moves on. The year is ebbing. The leaves have fallen. If the Apocalyptists tell us true, mankind has but a few weeks left. God's wrath, or Satan's, will blaze over the land as the year 2000 sweeps in on December's heels. Thomas scarcely minds. Let him go unnoticed and he will not mind if the universe tumbles about him.

"What do you think?" he is asked on a street corner in Los Angeles. "Will God come back on New Year's Day?"

A few idle loungers, killing time. Thomas slouches among them. They do not recognize him, he is sure. But they want an answer. "Well? What do you say?"

Thomas makes his voice furry and thick, and mumbles, "No, not a chance. He's never going to mess with us again. He gave us a miracle and look what we made out of it."

"That so? You really think so?"

Thomas nods. "God's turned His back on us. He said, Here, I give you proof of My existence, now pull yourselves together and get somewhere. And instead we fell apart all the faster. So that's it. We've had it. The end is coming."

"Hey, you might be right!" Grins. Winks.

This conversation makes Thomas uncomfortable. He starts to edge away, elbows out, head bobbing clumsily, shoulders hunched. His new walk, his camouflage.

"Wait," one of them says. "Stick around. Let's talk a little."

Thomas hesitates.

"You know, I think you're right, fellow. We made a royal mess. I tell you something else: we never should have started all that stuff. Asking for a Sign. Stopping the Earth. Would have been a lot better off if that Thomas had stuck to picking pockets, let me tell you."

"I agree three hundred percent," Thomas says, flashing a quick smile, on-off. "If you'll excuse me—"

Again he starts to shuffle away. Ten paces. An office building's door opens. A short, slender man steps out. *Oh, God! Saul!* Thomas covers his face with his hand and turns away. Too late. No use. Kraft recognizes him through all the alterations. His eyes gleam. "Thomas!" he gasps.

"No. You're mistaken. My name is—"

"Where have you been?" Kraft demands. "Everyone's searching for you, Thomas. Oh, it was wicked of you to run away, to shirk your responsibilities. You dumped everything into our hands, didn't you? But you were the only one with the strength to lead people. You were the only one who—"

"Keep your voice down," Thomas says hoarsely. No use pretending. "For the love of God, Saul, stop yelling at me! Stop saying my name! Do you want everyone to know that I'm—"

"That's exactly what I want," Kraft says. By now a fair crowd has gathered, ten people, a dozen. Kraft points. "Don't you know him? That's Thomas the Proclaimer! He's shaved and cut his hair, but can't you see his face all the same? There's your prophet! There's the thief who talked with God!"

"No, Saul!"

"Thomas?" someone says. And they all begin to mutter it. "Thomas? Thomas? Thomas?" They nod heads, point, rub chins, nod heads again. "Thomas? Thomas?"

Surrounding him. Staring. Touching him. He tries to push them away. Too many of them, and no apostles, now. Kraft is at the edge of the crowd, smiling, the little Judas! "Keep back," Thomas says. "You've got the wrong man. I'm not Thomas. I'd like to get my hands on him myself. I—I—" *Judas! Judas!* "Saul!" he screams. And then they swarm over him.

# Things Which Are Caesar's

## GORDON R. DICKSON

*Gordon R. Dickson was born in western Canada, the son of a mining engineer, but has lived for much of his life in Minnesota. His first stories, many of them written in collaboration with Poul Anderson, saw print in 1950; his steady rise to literary prominence was capped by the publication nine years later of his novel* Dorsai, *which established him as a major science-fiction writer. His many subsequent novels include such well-received titles as* Soldier, Ask Not; The Tactics of Mistake; *and* The Alien Way. *He was a Hugo winner in 1965 and received the Nebula award two years later. From 1969 to 1971 he served as President of the Science Fiction Writers of America.*

*"I know you," Jamethon said. The dark skin of his face was like taut silk. "You are one of the Deniers of God."*

*"An incorrect name for us," answered Padma. "All men deny and believe at the same time—and each builds to his own heaven."*

Soldier, Ask Not (Childe Cycle: revised)

Men and women born of cities find it hard to realize how utter a dark can come, outdoors, when the last of the sunset goes and the moon is not yet up. For a long hour of gradually fading twilight, the meadow between the road and the lower woods had been almost as visible as in full daylight. Now, suddenly, it was all dark as an unlit cave. The few people already camped in the meadow moved closer to their fires or lit lanterns inside their tents.

A few were caught away from the camping spaces they had rented, visiting either at the store trucks selling food and supplies alongside the road, or at one of the temporary chemical toilets set up on the road's far side, where the ground lifted in a wooded slope to the near horizon of the hilltop. These stumbled and felt their way back to where they thought they should be, not helped much by the limited beams of flashlights, even if they were lucky enough to be carrying such.

The only one who did not fumble his way was Ranald. With neither sunset nor flashlight to help him, he kept moving at a normal pace over the now invisible ground. In the first breathing of the night wind his full, sandy beard blew back around his neck under his chin. He did not stumble over anyone, even those couples lying together in darkness. To his ears, each person there was a beacon of noise in the obscurity. Even those who were not talking, breathed, gurgled or rustled loudly enough to keep someone like himself from walking into them; and, even if they had not been so loud, he could smell each of them and their belongings from ten or fifteen feet away. Possessions or people, they all smelled, one way or another. Even those who thought of themselves as extremely clean stank of soap and dry-cleaning fluids and city smokes.

Ranald passed them by now; and he passed by their fires. Almost to a man or woman, these early-comers to the campground were loaded with outdoor gear of some sort or another. Most had brought food of their own, as well—the store trucks had barely begun to do the business their owners expected to do tomorrow or the next day. Ranald himself carried no camping equipment. But under each arm he had a chunk of log from a dry sugar maple. Behind him, now, he could hear some follower, someone heavy-footed and unsure, using him as a guide through the dark. Ranald grinned a little sadly in his beard and breathed deeply of the night breeze. Among and beyond the smells of the campers, he scented pine and spruce trees from downslope, swamp soil, and running river.

His searching gaze settled at last on one small fire and his nose found the reek of it right. Turning to it, he detoured around four city-dressed adults who were lying, talking in the total dark like children backyard camping for the first time. He came up to the small fire. It was a narrow blaze, fed by the ends of five pieces of oak limb, pointing to the burning area like wagon spokes to a hub. Just beyond the flames was a lean man, himself the color of peeled, old oak, dressed in Levi's and a red-and-white-checked wool shirt. He sat on an unrolled sleeping bag with a poncho staked at a rain slope above it.

He and Ranald looked at each other like strange dogs across the plains.

"Hard maple," said Ranald, dropping his two pieces of wood beside the fire. "Burns slow."

The other man stared for a moment at the chunks of wood, then reached off into the darkness behind him with his right hand and came back holding an aluminum coffeepot with its base blackened from the fire. "Tea?" he asked.

"I thank you," said Ranald. He sat down cross-legged himself; and he and the man behind the fire regarded each other in its light. The man who owned the fire was easily a foot taller than Ranald and looked competent. But Ranald, under his thin, worn leather jacket, was oddly wide across the shoulders and heavy-headed under a mass of sand-colored hair and beard, so that in a strange way he looked even more competent than the man with the fire.

"Dave Wilober's my name," said the man with the fire.

"Ranald," said Ranald.

The distance separating them across the flickering red flames was too far to reach across easily for the shaking of hands. Neither man tried.

"Pleased to meet you," said Dave Wilober. His accent was Southern and twangy. Ranald spoke almost like a Midwesterner, except for a slight rhythm to his phrasing—not the singsong of someone with a Scandinavian inheritance of speech, but a patterning of words and emphasis that was almost Irish. The two looked at each other examiningly.

"And you," said Ranald.

The coffeepot on the white-glowing wood coals in the fire's center was beginning to sing already. Dave reached out and turned the pot to expose the curve of its other side to the greatest heat.

"I was thinking I'd probably sit by myself here," he said, half to Ranald, half to the fire. "Didn't guess anyone neighborly might come by."

"There'll be others," Ranald said. He frowned at the fire, with his beard blowing about his face in the night breeze. In the unrelieved darkness behind him, he heard an uncertain shuffling of heavy hiking boots, and there was the sound of embarrassed breathing.

"Others?" Dave frowned a little. "Don't know about that. I'm not great for company."

"There'll be others," Ranald repeated. "There were the first time."

"The first time?" Dave raised an eyebrow and lifted the coffee-pot off the coals. Inside it now, they could both hear the boiling water hammering at the metal sides. "There been a Sign in the Heavens before this? When?"

"Far back," said Ranald. He was tempted to say more, but the years had made him taciturn. "Long since."

Dave watched him for a moment. Ranald only gazed back.

"Any case," said Dave, taking the top off the hot pot with a quick, clever snatch of his fingers, and dropping it inside-up on the ground beside him. He poured some tea leaves from a bag into the pot. "Likely most anybody coming to something like this'd be churchy. I'm not."

He paused to glance at Ranald again.

"You neither?" he asked.

"That's right," said Ranald, softly. "There's nothing for me in god-houses."

Dave nodded.

"Not natural," he said, "going into a box—for something like that."

He half rose, to turn and produce a couple of plastic cups before sitting down again. As he did so, a small chinking noise came from him—so slight a noise that only ears like Ranald's could have caught it. Ranald cocked his head on one side like an interested bird, staring at the lower half of Dave's body, then raised his gaze to find Dave's eyes steady and unmoving upon him.

"Brother," said Ranald, peacefully, "you go your way, I go mine. Isn't that so?"

Dave's gaze fell away, back to the fire.

"Fair enough—" he began and broke off, turning his head to the right to look off into darkness. From the direction in which he stared came plainly now the noise of two pairs of feet, two breathing bodies, heavily approaching. After a moment a pair of people loomed into the illumination of the fire and halted, staring down at the seated men.

They were male and female—both young. The man was only slightly taller than Ranald, and slighter of build. Like Ranald, he was bearded; but the dark-brown hair on his face was sparse and fine, so that with the wind blowing it this way and that it seemed as if he were only bearded in patches. Above the beard and narrow cheekbones his brown eyes had the dark openness of a suffering, newborn animal. Below the beard, his narrow body was thickened by layers of clothing. He walked unsurely. Beside him, the girl also was swollen with clothes. She was smaller than he, with long, straight-hanging blond hair, and a mere nub of a nose in a plate-round face that would not have looked old on a girl of twelve. But her arm was tightly around his waist. It was she who was holding him up—and she was the one who spoke.

"We've got to get warm," she said; and her tone of voice left no choice in the matter. "We've got to sit down by your fire."

Ranald glanced across at Dave. In the flickering firelight Dave's features were like a face carved in bas-relief on some ancient panel of dark wood. He hesitated, but only for a moment.

"Sit," he said. He reached behind himself once more and came back this time with two more plastic cups and an unopened can of vegetable beef soup.

The girl and the young man dropped clumsily down before the fire. Seated now, and clearly shown in the red light, the man was shivering. The girl kneeled beside him in her baggy, several layers of slacks; and placed the palm of her small, plump hand flat on his forehead. Her nails were top-edged in black; and to Ranald's nose she, like the young man, reeked of old dirt and sweat.

"He's got a fever," she said.

They were both wearing packs of a sort, his hardly more than a knapsack, hers sagging, heavy and large, with a blanket roll below the sack. She helped him off with his, then shrugged out of the straps that bound her, and opened up the blanket roll. A moment later she had him wrapped with a number of thin, dark-blue blankets, most of them ragged along their edges, as if something had chewed them.

Dave had opened the can of soup and emptied it into a pan on the fire. He rinsed out the can with water from a white plastic jug, then filled the can and the three cups with tea from the coffeepot. He handed the cups to Ranald and the other two, keeping the can for himself.

The girl's eyes had gone to Ranald as the cups were passed out. She had put her own cup down; and it was cooling beside her as she continued to urge tea into the young man. Ranald gazed back at her without particular expression, all the time Dave had been in constant activity.

"He's sick," the girl said to Ranald.

Ranald only continued to watch her, without moving.

Behind him, there was a sudden rush. The hiking boots that had followed him here, and which had been fidgeting in the background since, came forward with a rush, carrying a man in his mid-to-late thirties into the firelight. The light of the flames played on the boots, which were new-looking, with speed lacings, fastened tight to the tops of the thick corduroy pants above them with leather straps around the pant cuffs. He was zipped up in a plaid jacket, with a large back pack of yellow plastic strapped to an aluminum pack frame that glinted brilliantly in the firelight.

He smiled eagerly at them, turning his head to include everybody. His face was softened and his waist thick with perhaps thirty pounds of unnecessary fat. His hair was receding, but what was left was black and curly. Only his long sideburns were touched with gray. He ended his smile upon the girl and squatted down beside her, getting out of his pack.

"I've got some antibiotics here . . ." he chattered, digging into the pack. "I couldn't help hearing you say your friend was sick. Here . . . oh, yes . . ."

He brought his fist out with a tube of bicolored capsules, red and black in the firelight. The eyes of both the young man and the girl jumped for a moment at the sight of the capsule-shapes, then settled back to quiet watching again.

"What's that?" asked the girl sharply.

"Ampicillin." The man in boots tilted one of the capsules out of the tube into the palm of his left hand, offering it to the girl. "Very good . . ."

She took the capsule and pushed it between the lips of the young man.

"Take it with the tea," she told him. He swallowed.

"That's right. And keep him warm—" the man in boots started to hand the tube of capsules to the girl, whose back was turned. He hesitated, then put the tube back in his pack. "Every six hours. We'll give him one. . . ."

He looked across at Dave and ducked his gaze away as Dave looked back. He glanced at Ranald, and looked away from Ranald back to Dave, almost immediately.

"My name's Strauben," he said. "Walt Strauben."

"Dave Wilober," said Dave.

"Ranald," said Ranald from the other side of the fire. Walt Strauben turned his face to the young man and the girl, expectantly.

"Letty," said the girl, shortly. "He's Rob."

"Rob, Letty, Dave . . . Ranald. Myself . . ." said Walt, busily digging into his pack. He came up with a heavy black thermos bottle and held it up. "Anyone care for some coffee—"

"Thanks," said Dave. "We've got tea."

"Of course. That's right. Well, I'll have some myself." Walt unscrewed the cap of the thermos and poured the cap half full of cream-brown liquid, closed the bottle again and put it away in his pack. He dug into his pack and came out with a folded newspaper. "Did you see today's paper? They're camping out all over the world just like us, waiting. Listen— *'The promise of a Sign from some supernatural power on the day of the vernal equinox has already, today, sent literally millions of people out into the fields all over the world to await the evidence of faith that rumor has promised for tomorrow. Expectation of some sort of miracle to celebrate the Christian year 2000, or simply to reward those who've been steadfast in their beliefs in any faith, continued to mount through the morning. All over the globe ordinary business is effectively at a standstill. . . .'* "

"That's all right," said Dave.

Walt stopped reading, lowered the paper and stared at Dave. The paper trembled a little in his hand. His heavy lower lip trembled a little as well.

"No need to read," said Dave. "You're welcome—for now."

"Oh all right. I just thought . . ." Walt cleared his throat and refolded the newspaper. Its pages crackled in the stillness as he thrust it back into his pack.

"Thank you," he said, speaking more into the packsack than in any other direction. "I appreciate . . ."

The girl, Letty, had been staring at him. Now, nostrils spread, she turned sharply to Dave as if to say something. Dave's eyes met her, still and steady. She turned back to Rob without speaking.

"Is that soup ready yet?" asked Rob. He had a sharp, high-pitched voice, with a ring to it that sounded just on the edge of excitement or anger.

"Soon, baby," said Letty to him, in a different voice. "Soon."

Dave sat drinking his tea from the soup can. Walt worked with his pack, unfolding an air mattress, blowing it up and unrolling a sleeping bag upon it. After a little while Dave took the pot holding the soup off the coals. Letty passed over the cup from which Rob had been drinking tea and Dave emptied the last of the liquid in it on the fire. It hissed and disappeared. Dave filled the cup with soup and handed it back to Letty.

"Thanks," she said, briefly, and held the cup for Rob. He sucked at it, not shivering visibly anymore.

". . . All the same," said Walt, now lying on his sleeping bag and beginning to talk so quietly that his voice came at the rest of them unexpectedly, "it's an amazing thing, all the same. Even if no miracle happens, even if no Sign is shown, everybody coming out to watch for it, like this, all over the world, has to count for something more than just hysteria. . . ."

Neither Dave nor Letty nor Rob answered him. Ranald watched him unmovingly, listening; but Walt, as he talked, avoided Ranald's eyes.

". . . So many people of different religions and cultures, getting together like this everywhere, has to be a Sign in itself," said Walt. "Spiritual values are beside the point. Personal weakness hasn't anything to do with it. We've all been *called* here when you think about it, in a sense. . . ."

Ranald's head lifted and his head turned. He listened and sniffed at the darkness behind him. After a second he got up and moved off away from the firelight so quietly that not even Dave's head turned to see him go.

Once he was well away from the fire, the pastureland between the road and the woods took shadowy form in his eyes. The moon was barely up above the hill, now—a fairly respectable three-quarters moon, but blurred by a high, thin cloud layer. Through this layer it spread enough cold light to show the upright objects in the pastureland as silhouettes, but left the ground surface still deep in obscurity.

Over this obscurity Ranald followed his nose and ears to a scent of perfume like lilacs, and an almost voiceless sound of crying. He came at last to a shape huddled on the ground, away from any fire or tent. Nose and ears filled in what his eyes could not see in the little light there was. Seated alone was another young woman or girl, tall, wearing shoes with heels made for hard cement rather than soft earth, a dress thin and tight for indoors, instead of out, and a coat cut for fashion, not warmth. Besides these things, she had nothing with her—no pack, no blankets, no lantern or shelter materials.

She sat, simply hunched up on the open ground, arms around her legs, face in her knees, crying. The crying was a private, internal thing, like the weeping of a lost child who has given up hope any adult will hear. No ears but Ranald's could have found her from more than six feet away; no other nose could have located her, huddled there in the darkness of the ground.

Ranald did not touch her. He sank down silently into a cross-legged sitting position, facing and watching her. After a while, the girl stopped crying and lifted her head, staring blindly in his direction.

"Who's there?" Her whisper was shaky.

"Ranald," said Ranald, softly.

"Ranald who?" she asked.

He did not answer. She sat staring toward him without seeing him in the darkness, as seconds slipped away. Gradually the tension of fear leaked away and she slumped back into the position in which he had found her.

"It doesn't matter," she said, to the darkness and to him.

"It always matters," said Ranald; but not as if he were answering her. He spoke out loud but absently, to himself, as if her words had pressed a button in him. "Every spring it matters fresh. Every fall it begins to matter all over again. Otherwise, I'd have given up a long time ago. But each time, every time, it starts all over again; and I start with it. Now and now."

"Who *are* you?" she asked, peering through the darkness without success.

"Ranald," he said.

He got softly to his feet, turned, and started back toward Dave Wilober's fire. Behind him, after a few steps, he heard her rise and follow the moon-limned silhouette of his body. He went with deliberate slowness back to Dave's fire, and all the way he heard her following. But after he had sat down he heard her come only to the edge of the thick shadow his own body cast from the fire flares. Having come that far she sat down, also, still slumped but no longer weeping.

". . . What does someone like you know about it?" Rob was saying sharply to Walt. "What do you understand?" Rob had straightened up and even thrown off most of his blankets. His face was damp and pink now above the beard, and the beard itself clung damply to his upper cheeks under the brown, yellow-lit eyes.

"Very little, very little. That's true. . . ." Walt shook his head.

"You talk about how fine it is, everyone getting together out here, and every place. But what do you really know about it? What makes you think you know anything about why people are here? You don't know why Letty and I are here!"

"No, that's true. I don't deny it," said Walt. "Who can know? No one knows—"

"Not 'no one'! You!" said Rob. "*You* don't know. You and the rest of the dudes. You don't know anything and you're scared to find out; so you go around making it big about nobody at all knowing. But that's a lie. I know. And Letty knows. Tell him, Letty."

"I know," said Letty to Walt.

"I believe you. I really believe you," said Walt. "But don't you see, even if you think you're positive about something, you've got a duty to question yourself, anyway. You have to consider the chance you're wrong. Just to make sure—isn't that so?"

"Hell it is!" said Rob. "It's just a lot of junk you pile up to hide the fact you haven't got guts enough to face life the way it really is. Not other people. *You*—"

He broke off. Another pair of booted feet that Ranald had already heard coming toward the fire from the nearest fire down-slope stepped into the firelight, and the flames showed them.

"No. That's a mistake, of course," Walt was saying in a voice that shook a little but was calm. He folded his hands together and closed his teeth gently on the middle knuckle of the first finger. "You don't—"

He caught sight of the boots and broke off in turn, raising his gaze to the man who had just joined them.

"All right, all of you. Let's see your permits."

As the firelight painted him standing there against the black frame of the darkness, the lawman now looming over them was shiny with leather. He was agleam with white motorcycle helmet, brown boots, and black jacket, unzipped in front to show the straps of a Sam Browne belt supporting a holstered revolver, glittering handcuffs and the dark, bloodsucker shape of a black leather sap. He had a heavy-boned, middle-twenties face with a short-bristled, full moustache, so light-colored of hair it was almost invisible in spite of its thickness.

"I said, permits," he repeated. His voice was a flat tenor.

Without saying anything, Dave reached behind himself once more and brought out a piece of printed blue paper. The man took it, looked at it, and handed it back. He took a similar paper from Walt Strauben, read it, and gave it back. His eyes slid along to Ranald, who had not moved, neither to produce a paper nor anything else. Eyes still locked with Ranald, the lawman reached down to take the piece of paper upheld by Letty. With a sudden effort, then, he broke his gaze from Ranald's and looked down at Letty's permit.

He handed it back to Letty and looked at Rob.

"All right," he said to Rob. "Where's yours?"

"We're together," said Rob. His voice had thinned from the note it had held talking to Walt. The yellow glint was out of his brown eyes, leaving them dark and flat.

"He's my guest," snapped Letty. "The permit's good for a space ten feet by ten feet. That's all we take up, together."

"One person only to every ten-by-ten plot." The lawman turned back to her. "This isn't one of your garbage-heap camping grounds. The place is clean—it's going to keep clean. If your friend wants to stay, he'll have to get another permit."

"Who're you?" said Rob. His face seemed narrower now. It was pale and damp with sweat; and his voice was still thin. "This is private property."

"Pig," said Letty, strongly. She got to her feet. Standing, she looked no more than half the size of the lawman. "It's nothing to do with you. We'll talk it over with the owner."

"Now if you want trouble," said the lawman, answering her without lifting his voice, "you just keep on. There's deputies enough of us here on special duty from the county sheriff's office to keep things orderly. I'm not going to waste time arguing. You can buy another camping permit for twenty-five dollars; or one of you is going to have to clear out."

He stood, still holding the paper Letty had given him.

"Make your mind up," he said.

"He's sick, you bastard!" snarled Letty. "Sick, don't you understand? He can't clear out."

"All right," said the deputy, in the same tones. "Then we'll give him a ride into the hospital in Medora. If he's sick, they'll take care of him there. But nobody camps here without buying a permit."

"Do you buy and sell people the chance to know God exists?" asked Walt. But his voice trembled a little and was so low-pitched that what he said went ignored by both Letty and the deputy.

"What about *him?*" Rob said suddenly, nodding in the direction of Ranald. "Why just us? You aren't giving him a hard time for his permit!"

Ranald did not move. The deputy's eyes flicked a little in his direction, but not far enough for their gazes to lock together again.

"Never mind anyone else here," he said to Rob. "I'm talking to you. Get a permit to stay, or get on your feet and get moving."

He stepped forward and reached down as if to pull Rob to his feet out of the cone of blankets that swathed him.

"Wait! No, wait . . ." The words came tumbling out of Walt. "Here, officer. I'll take care of the permits. Just a minute now . . . wait. . . ."

He was digging into a side pocket of his corduroy pants. He came up with a wallet and thumbed out bills, which he handed up to the deputy.

"I'll take two of them," Walt said. "Fifty dollars—that's right?"

"Two." The deputy, still holding the bills, took out a pad of blue papers and a pen, scribbled a date and initials on two of the papers and tore them from the pack. He handed both to Walt, who passed one over to Letty and held out the other to Ranald.

"All right," said the deputy, putting money and pad of permits away. "Remember to keep the grounds clean. Pick up your own trash. And the comfort stations are across the road. Use them. That permit doesn't entitle you to make a nuisance of yourself. Any trouble by anyone and you'll still go out."

He stepped back into darkness and everyone there heard his boots going away.

Ranald reached out to take the permit Walt was still holding. He examined it for a moment and then turned to hand it to the girl he had found crying, and who all this while had hidden, crouched behind him.

"Who's that?" demanded Walt, twisting to stare at her.

"I'm . . . Maybeth Zolovsky," the girl said. Her voice was thin, as Rob's had been.

Walt opened his mouth and saw Ranald mildly watching him. Walt's eyes shifted; he closed his mouth and turned back to find himself facing the round, childish, hard features of Letty.

"The world's as much ours as anyone else's," she said. "He's got no inherent right to keep us off any part of it, when we aren't doing any harm, any more than we've got a right to keep him off."

Rob said something inarticulate, endorsing. Walt shook his head and looked away from them down into the flames of the fire.

"*You* thank him, if you want," said Rob, turning to Ranald. He added, "But I guess you don't need to. You weren't going to get asked for a permit anyway, were you? How come? Why didn't he ask you?"

Ranald looked back at him silently, the night breeze blowing in his beard.

"Don't want to tell us?" said Rob. "All right. But I'd like to know. What makes you a special case?—You don't want to tell me, is that it?"

Dave snorted a little, filling his soup-can cup again from the teapot. Rob looked back across the fire at him.

"Now you're laughing," Rob said. "How about letting the rest of us in on the joke?"

Dave lifted his soup can, drank some hot tea, and looked across the rim of the container at the younger man.

"You want to know why that deputy didn't ask a man like him for a permit?" Dave said. "Whyn't you find out for yourself? He gave the permit away to the young lady there. Whyn't you just go try to take it back from her?"

Rob stared at Dave.

"What?" he said, after a moment.

"I said," Dave went on, "you want to know why the deputy done what he done, you go do something like it. Go take the permit back from"—he hesitated, looking at the dark-haired girl— "Maybeth?"

She nodded back at him, only half-sheltered now behind Ranald.

"Take it away—" Rob's voice cracked. "What do you think I am? Why'd I want to do something like that?"

"To learn," said Dave.

"Learn? You mean learn how to be like that?"

"No." Dave looked directly at him. "Learn why you'd never try to do it, even if you wanted to—no more than that deputy'd try it. Look at him—." Dave's voice went a little harsh. "I say, look at *him!*"

Rob turned and stared again at Ranald. Ranald gazed back, sitting quietly bathed by the moving firelight. In its red and yellow light he was a short man in a thin leather jacket; but he was strangely wide across the shoulders and heavy-headed under his mass of sand-colored hair and beard. His blue eyes watched Rob without blinking.

For several seconds Rob looked at him in silence. Then he gave something like a start and a shudder combined, and jerked his gaze back to the fire. He sat hunched toward the flames and muttered something under his breath.

Letty lifted one of the dropped blankets to wrap about him, again, meanwhile throwing a brief, fierce glance first at Ranald and the dark-haired girl, then at Dave. She tucked the blanket about Rob's huddled shape.

"Baby . . . ?" she murmured, feeling his forehead once more. Rob pulled his head back from her touch.

"Never mind!" he said. "I tell you, never mind!"

"You see?" said Dave, from across the fire. "It'd have been more trouble to a man, than it was worth—for that deputy to mess with Ranald—or for you to."

"Or for you," muttered Rob to the flames.

Dave looked down at his tin-can cup for a second without speaking.

"Could be," he said, quietly.

A silence came down on them all, which lasted several minutes. Then Walt Strauben stirred. He turned to his pack and dug out a blue-and-white blanket three times the thickness of any of the dark blankets wrapping Rob. He held the blanket out to Maybeth Zolovsky.

"Come in next to the fire?" he said.

Maybeth hesitated, glancing at Ranald. But he looked back at her with no particular expression. She got up and came forward to sit down beside Walt, wrapping the blanket around her, hugging it to her.

"Thanks," she whispered.

From across the fire, Letty gave her a grim glance.

"Coffee?" Walt said, pouring from his thermos.

"Thank you," she said. She turned to Dave. "Thank you."

"Welcome," said Dave.

"You must have made up your mind to come out here on the spur of the moment. . ." Walt said to her.

They fell into low-voiced conversation. Dave let them talk, only feeding the fire from time to time. Ranald sat back in silence, listening to other sounds of the evening. After a while, Letty began to rearrange the blankets enclosing Rob, until she and he were wrapped up together in a sort of cloth cocoon that was bed and tent in one for them both. A little after that, Walt produced another blue-and-white blanket and made up a bed of sorts for himself, turning his own sleeping bag over to Maybeth. The three-quarters moon traveled upward, burning its way slowly through the low-lying cloud layer and climbing at last into a star-clear sky, so that the pastureland with its people and tents and pinpoints of fire or lanternlight showed up like the negative of a photograph taken by daylight.

When the moon was almost straight overhead, Dave stirred from where he had sat feeding the fire all this time, reached back behind him to come up with some middle-sized, dark object, and rose to his feet. He went off toward the woods at the lower end of the pasture.

Ranald silently got up and followed the taller man.

The moon was bright enough now so that Dave walked almost as surely as Ranald had walked earlier in full darkness. Dave threaded his way between the fires, and to anyone's hearing but Ranald's, his going was utterly silent. But to Ranald's ears, each stride of the taller man produced the same faint chinking noise Ranald had heard earlier by the fire.

Dave went downslope across the pastureland to its lower edge and moved in among the trees. He went some little distance, until the ground under its layer of dead grass and leaves began to feel soft—if not yet damp. The sound of the running river was close, now. In a little open space, in the moonlight, Dave sat down on a dead and fallen tree trunk. For a second or two he simply sat; not exactly slumped, but with his back gently curved like the back of a man who has been carrying a heavy pack through a long day.

Then he stirred, lifted the shape he had carried away from the campground, and unscrewed the top of it.

The moonlight showed the shape of a large bottle in black silhouette against the stars as he drank. He lowered the bottle, sat again for a moment, then recapped it and put it aside. Leaning forward, he began to rake together some of the ground trash and fallen twigs before him. Once or twice Ranald heard the small snap of a dead branch, breaking.

In a pool of moon-shadow cast by a twisted oak-trunk, Ranald sank into a squatting position on his heels. The darkness around him hid him utterly as he watched Dave's hands, like independent small creatures squirrel-busy at some instinctive task, glean the makings of a fire from ground that hardly appeared to bear anything worth burning. Once, Dave stopped to drink again from his bottle, but otherwise the craft of his hands seemed a reflexive, automatic thing—as if wherever he went, there had to be fire.

After a little, he finished. A match scratched and spurted yellow light in the darkness. The flame caught among the twigs and other stuff of the little conical pile of twigs before the log on which he sat. The flame spread and rose. In its new light, Dave got up briefly to go a few steps aside for larger pieces of dead branch, which he returned and fed into the fire, end-on, as he had done with the fire above in the pasture.

This was a smaller fire, however, than that earlier one. A private fire. Still, its light pushed back the shadows; and, as Dave lifted the bottle to drink a third time, the flickering of the flame illuminated Ranald, squatting at the base of the oak.

Dave drank and lowered the bottle.

"You?" he said. "I came here to get away from the crowd."

Ranald said nothing.

"True," said Dave, "you're not like the rest. Come to the fire."

Ranald rose, approached the other side of the flames and squatted again. There was a naturalness and ease about the way he sat on his heels, as if he could remain that way for hours with as much comfort as another man in an armchair.

"Drink?" said Dave. He held out the bottle.

"I thank you," said Ranald. He lifted the bottle and swallowed. Its contents was store-sold bourbon. Not the best, perhaps, but store-sold and distillery-made, a half-gallon bottle heavy against the firelight.

He handed the bottle back to Dave, who drank again.

"It's happened before," Dave said, setting the open bottle down to one side of the fire, but equidistant between them. "You said that. You told me there'd been a Sign in the Heavens before. Long ago. How long? Fifty years?"

"Longer," said Ranald.

"A hundred? Five hundred? A thousand—"

"About that," said Ranald.

"But you remember it?" Dave gestured to the bottle. "Help yourself."

Ranald reached for the bottle, drank and replaced it exactly where it had sat a moment before.

"You remember?" repeated Dave.

"I remember," Ranald answered.

"Could be," said Dave, looking at him across the fire. "Could be—anything. But here you are with the rest of us; and you said there was nothing for you in god-houses."

"I've found nothing there. That's true," answered Ranald. "But there's no telling. Maybe I'll go to a god-house in the end, to die."

"Maybe they'll bury me out of a church someday, too," said Dave, thoughtfully. "Maybe . . . And here we are, all of us sitting out here, waiting for a great Sign of Faith. God, his own self, is going to come down and walk among us in glory, amen. Tonight, maybe, or tomorrow. All over the world at once, there's going to be proof it's been true, all this time and—then what?"

"I don't know," said Ranald.

"But you've seen it once before, you said." Dave made a motion toward the bottle. "Drink. Drink when you feel like it. I can't go drinking myself, with you waiting for an invite each time."

Ranald reached out and drank.

"All these people," said Dave, drinking after him. "That Letty and Rob. That Walt Strauben. That deputy even, and that Maybeth girl you pulled out of a hip pocket—that deputy sure didn't want to make trouble with you, now, did he? Mighty queer how a man can get to be the way you are, and another man just know it without being told. No one ever monkeys with you, do they?"

"Odin," said Ranald, "had one eye."

"Odin?"

"Another god," said Ranald. "He gave his eye for wisdom, they said. But any man who wants to give the price for anything, can buy, like that. Having bought, it shows on him. And so it goes. Each buys his own want and pays the price. That part never changes."

"What changes, then?" asked Dave. His tongue stumbled a little on the *ch* sound.

Ranald shook his head.

"I don't know," he said. "Every season, every year, the thought of living comes fresh and new to me. Fresh and new—and I go on again. But nothing changes. Over a thousand years, now." He looked across the fire to Dave. "Why do I keep on starting and starting again, if there's no change? If you can, tell me; and I can rest."

"Nothing I can tell you. Take a drink," said Dave. "It'll help you think."

Ranald drank.

"Thanks," he said, "I give you thanks." His tongue had not thickened as had Dave's; but there was a different note, of something like an echo chamber's echo of melancholy in his voice.

"Welcome, brother," said Dave, lifting the bottle himself. "Welcome and rest yourself. Tomorrow the Sign comes, the papers say—and the world changes. We'll all change—"

He put down the bottle and began to sing, a little hoarsely but in key with a light baritone voice.

*"There was a rich man and he lived in Jerusalem.*
*Glory, Hallelujah, hi-ro-de-rum!*
*He wore a top hat and his clothes were very spruce-ium.*
*Glory, Hallelujah, hi-ro-de-rum!*

*Hi-ro-de-rum, hi-ro-de-rum!*
*Skinna-ma-rinky doodle-doo, skinna-ma-rinky doodle-doo,*
*Glory, Hallelujah, hi-ro-de-rum!*

*Now, outside his gate there sat a human wreckium.*
*Glory, Hallelujah, hi-ro-de-rum!*
*He wore a bowler hat in a ring around his neckium.*
*Glory, Hallelujah . . ."*

"Sing!" Dave interrupted himself to say to Ranald. Ranald cocked his head on one side, listening, as Dave started a new verse.

*". . . Now the poor man he asked for a piece of bread*
*and cheesium—"*

"*Glory, Hallelujah, hi-ro-de-rum!*" sang Ranald along with him. Dave nodded. ". . . *The rich man said, I'll call for the police-ium,*" Dave went on. "*Glory, Hallelujah, hi-ro-de-rum!*" They sang together:

*"Hi-ro-de-rum, hi-ro-de-rum!*
*Skinna-ma-rinky-doodle-doo, skinna-ma-rinky-doodle-doo!*
*Glory, Hallelujah, hi-ro-de-rum! . . ."*

The singing, the firelight, the bottle passing back and forth, made something like a private room for them in the midst of the darkness. They went on through other verses of the same song and other songs after that, while the fire burned down toward the coals and they came back to talking again. Or rather, Dave came back to talking.

". . . that Walt," he was saying, no longer stumble-tongued, but with a deliberate slowness of pronunciation. "I smell preacher on him. Maybe not now he's a preacher, but he's been one. So, that's why he'd be here. He'd come to see a Sign because he needed one to preach. But that Letty and Rob—what do they want with a proof of God?"

"To know, perhaps," said Ranald.

"To know?"

"To find out what actually is. —For themselves, as men and women always do each generation, over and over again."

"And Maybeth? What do you say for that Maybeth girl?"

"Lost," said Ranald, "with nowhere else to go. Maybe she came here, hoping."

"Hoping?" Dave said. "Come here praying, you mean. Praying for a miracle, to set everything right for her without her having even to lift a finger for herself."

"A broken finger," Ranald looked across the dying flames at him, talking in a voice that showed no trace of effect from the liquor, "lifts hard. Broken legs don't run easy nor broken wings fly, brother."

"Can't fly or run, you can walk. Can't walk, can crawl. I been there. I know."

"You know," said Ranald, softly. "But do you know all there is to know?"

"Enough," said Dave. "Been there, I say. Could have given up anytime. Never did. You know why? Even with everything else gone, broke or rotted—there was still air, dirt, and water. Air to breathe, dirt to grow in, water to wash life down into the dirt. Running water. Rain. Black dirt. Green stuff. Trees."

"Yes," said Ranald, his eyes going past the fire and Dave for a moment. "New and new—each fresh season. I know that part, too."

"And I damn near lost it all," said Dave. "Things nearly turned me away from that part of it." He lifted the bottle to his lips, but it was empty. He stared at it for a moment, then set it down care-

fully. "Three sisters of mine, four brothers, all died before they
were old enough to go to school. My daddy died. I got born last,
after he was put in the ground."

"A sickness?" Ranald said.

"Yes. No. Killed." Dave stared hard across the fire coals at Ranald. "Worked too hard, they said. Mine—coal mine and then field-
work. No. People killed him. Other people killed him, taking him
away from dirt and water, and air. . . ."

> "*—Down in the mountain, in a fall of the coal,*
> *Buried in the mountain is O'Shaunessy's soul . . .*"

"—they buried my daddy aboveground, but his soul was buried
down in the mine like O'Shaunessy's, just the same. All the people
of the world, with their mines, their coal, their things—they put
my dad down in a mine to kill and bury him; and when I asked
why, they sent me to church for answer. Church!"

The breath of his last word fanned the red coals of the fire momentarily white.

"Looky here," said Dave. He bent forward and rolled up his
right pants-leg, uncovering what looked like a bulky white band-
age covering his leg from the ankle to low on the calf. "I was the
last alive of the children. Ma near on frantic to keep me from
the chance of dying too and making it all for nothing—babies and
husband, all in the grave. Now, she was one believed what people
told her. She asked around and they said, 'Take the boy to church.
Take him to the preacher. Ask help of the Lord.' So she took me."

Dave started to reach for the now-empty bottle, checked his
hand halfway there and let it drop back on his knee.

"She took me to a preacher and he prayed over me," Dave
went on. "Middle of the week too. Just into May; apple blossoms, peach blossoms on the trees, and all. No one in the church,
but we three went and knelt there before the altar with the windows open and the bird noise sounding all around outside. 'Guard
this boy, Lord. The last of the flock. . . .' And then we all

waited for an answer on our knees, with the preacher's eyes closed, Ma's eyes closed—mine supposed to be, too, but I got tired holding them shut. . . ."

Dave's voice ran down. Ranald sat perfectly still, watching him and listening—not just like someone who is merely attentive, but like someone waiting, and who has been waiting a long time for an answer.

"Preacher opened his eyes, at last," Dave went on, suddenly. "I got mine closed again just in time. 'God has answered,' he told Ma and me. 'There's a way to make this boy of yours safe, but only one way. Straight and narrow is the road to the gate. Straight the road he must walk. You got to give him to the Lord; and he must know the Lord is with him, the hand of the Lord is on him, guiding him, night and day. . . .' And Ma believed him; and—looky here."

Dave reached down and began to unwind the cloth around his leg and ankle. It fell away, so that Ranald saw a section of limb just above the ankle that looked blackened and crusted—as it might have been by dirt, but was not. The darkness and the ribbed skin were the markings of callouses and old scars, very nearly solid callous and scar tissue for six inches from the ankle upward. And what had caused this still circled the ankle—a loose loop of tractor chain with two-inch links, shiny with age and rubbing against itself and the leg it encircled.

Dave turned his ankle to the firelight and the chain slipped, chinking as Ranald had heard it chink earlier.

"It would come off," said Ranald, looking at the chain. "A hacksaw, a file—even a good knife. It wouldn't be hard to take off."

Dave laughed. It was only the second time he had laughed in Ranald's hearing.

"Oh, I had it off," Dave said. "Ma died when I was sixteen; and I took out for other places. First night away from home, I had it off me. Crowbar and hatchet. Stuck a crowbar end through a link, chopped the link open with a hatchet, then buried the chain in some woods. Five years I walked around with no weight on my ankle."

"Then what?"

"No 'then what,'" answered Dave. "Bit by bit it come back on me. I moved around; but everywhere I went—city, town, farm or backwoods—there wasn't no notch, no wrinkle, no fold, no place for me to back myself into like everybody else was backed into and settled. Bit by bit, then, I come to understand. That chain hadn't been just something I could chop off and throw away. It was part of a deal my ma had made for me with someone that wasn't there, far as I was concerned. But the fact that someone wasn't there for me, though, didn't make no difference. Takes two to make a bargain; and there had been a bargain made. Only I hadn't kept my end."

"Odin gave his eye," said Ranald.

"Like that. I'd taken, but I hadn't given. My not believing didn't matter, long as I wore the chain; because the chain stood for what I hadn't got to give—that believing I couldn't do, no matter how much my ma wanted me to. But when I took the chain off . . ."

Dave sighed.

"So," he said, "I put it back on, without nobody telling me to. Just like you see now. And then things began to straighten out for me. I found my way back to my own country; and I found out how it was I had to live. Alone with the fields, the barns, and all; and got along with neighbors all right, long as we didn't visit together too much. But I had my honest dirt, water, and plain air —and peace out of it all."

He stopped talking. For nearly a minute the silence filled the moment between the little cracklings of the dying fire.

"Now, it was *my* mother," murmured Ranald, looking at the red and white wood coals, "said I would never find my way home again, if I went. But our ships sailed out that spring; and I was twelve. I went with them; in time, to many places. But, when years later I sailed north again, I could not find where I'd been born. It

had been a small place always; and maybe some other ships had
put in to raid and burn there, killing or making slaves of all—and
afterwards it went back to forest. Or maybe it was only that all the
old people I'd known there were dead; and I did not recognize
the place when I saw it again, remembering it only the way a boy
remembers things, bigger than they are. But my mother was right.
I'd gone, and after that I could never find home again."

He hesitated, gazing at what was left of the fire.

"That's when I first thought I would die, because there was no
reason for me to live longer," he said, softly. "But I found I could
not bring myself to it; and since, I go on and on."

He raised his head from its tilt toward the cooling embers and
looked across at Dave. Sometime since, Dave had slid from his
seat on the log to a seat on the ground, with his back against the
thick round of the log from the dead and fallen tree. Now his
hands were limp, palms-upward on his thighs. His chin was down
on his chest and his eyes were closed.

Ranald lifted his head and sniffed the night air. The moon was
low on the far horizon, and the breeze blew from a different direction, bringing a chill with it. Ranald made no attempt to build up
the fire, but lay down on his side and drew his arms and legs in
toward his body, curling up animal-fashion. Like Dave, he slept.

Dawn woke them both. They rose without conversation, left
the dead, small fire, and went back to the campground. There,
Dave silently revived the earlier fire he had left unattended and
cooked them both a breakfast of bacon and pancakes. As they
were finishing this, the others—Maybeth, Letty, and Rob—began
to wake and stir in their various bed-shelters. These looked with
attention at the remains of breakfast; but Dave made no move to
invite them to eat. It was Walt, struggling out of his blankets with
a stubble of a twenty-four-hour beard gray on his face and under-
chin, who finally produced a small Coleman stove, cookware, and
breakfast materials for himself and the other three.

As the morning warmed, the pastureland rapidly began to fill.
There was a steadily growing feeling-in-common above the tents

and shelter-halves and groundsheets that blossomed all about. A feeling like excitement, but not like a holiday sort of excitement. A tense thread of apprehension laced like a red vein through the body of eager expectancy that enclosed them all, there between the comfort stations and the woods stretching below down to swamp and river. It was a cloudless day, promising to become hot.

As it warmed and grew close to noon, the pressure of the tensions in the people increased; as if they were all under water that was becoming steadily deeper. By eleven o'clock it was hard to believe that any space in the pasture remained unsold; and there were a number of deputies of the local county sheriff to be seen, sweating under their equipment and uniforms. The particular deputy who had checked those around Dave's fire for permits the night before now passed by frequently, as if their space were within an area he had to patrol. In the daylight he looked much younger than he had the night before; and it was possible to see that he wore not only a star-shaped gold badge, but a nameplate below it with white block letters spelling out TOM RATH-KENNY on a blue background.

In the daylight, some of the certainty he had shown during the dark hours earlier was missing. He no longer stood out among the crowd of people who had bought space in the pastureland, but seemed more to fit in among them—a little shorter and less heavily-boned, a little more of flesh and less of leather. Sweat gleamed on his chin in the sunlight and his glance shifted more frequently from person to person as he walked past.

Just past eleven thirty, the pressure broke. The universal ocean-wash of voices was interrupted by a moving wave of silence that traveled across the pasture and, on the heels of that moving silence, a man walked among them.

". . . him"—the word erupted everywhere in the crowd as the man passed—". . . him . . . him . . . him . . ."

He went by not fifteen feet from Dave's fire, walking swiftly and apparently alone; a thin, brown-faced man, beardless, with shaven head and eyes spaced widely above sharp cheekbones. He was barefoot and wearing what seemed to be only a loose gown of coarse and heavy brown cloth, the skirt of which rippled with the length of his strides. Beneath the hem of that skirt, his feet were mottled with dirt.

". . . *him*," echoed Walt as the voices took up after the man had passed. "The prophet. The one who promised the world a Sign. But what brings him here, out of everywhere else on the Earth? Why to this one little place? Him . . ."

"Him . . . him . . ." said Letty and Rob and Maybeth, and all the other people crowding in the wake of the one who had passed. "Here . . . here of all places. *Him* . . ."

Dave had gotten to his feet with the rest. Now he sat down again to face Ranald, who had not risen.

"Why's he here?" Dave asked. "Is there something special here?" He looked steadily at Ranald. "It's not because of you?"

Ranald shook his head.

"Was he really here?" said Ranald. "Perhaps they're seeing him everyplace where people have gotten together to wait for the Sign."

"What're you talking about?" Walt turned suddenly to stand above Ranald. "He was here. I saw him. We all saw him. Didn't you?"

Ranald shook his head again.

"I saw, but that was all. I heard no one passing. I smelled no one," he said.

"Heard?" echoed Rob. "Smelled? In this crowd? Who could hear or smell anyone in a crush like this?"

Ranald glanced at the younger man.

"In any case," Ranald said, "he would only be a messenger."

"You can't know that," Letty said. "He could be the Sign, himself. Maybe that's what he was."

Ranald looked at her, almost mildly.

"When Signs come," he said, "there's no question."

And there was none. Just at noon, just as Ranald remembered from the time before, there was a shock that went through everyone and everything. A shock like that of a great gong being struck in a place where no sound was permitted—so that the effect was not heard, but felt, in great shudders that passed through all living and nonliving things like light through clear water. And when the shock had passed, a knowledge of sorts came into them all, as if a part of their minds which had been asleep until this moment had now been awakened to report what it witnessed. Above them, the sun had ceased apparent movement. They felt the fact that it no longer moved. It stood still in a sky without clouds.

Earth, also, stood still under their feet. They could feel its new lack of motion, as well. The laws of the universe were no longer touching sun, or Earth, or people. Something like a hand was now holding them apart from such things.

In the pasture, the crowd too was stilled. No one moved or spoke. In the woods downslope no birds sang, no insects hummed. Even to the ears of Ranald, the river seemed to have ceased its murmur. Matters were as he remembered them happening that earlier time, before he had learned that he could never find his way home again—back when he had been already far from home. He sighed silently inside himself, now, lowering his head and closing his eyes; and, sharp as a burn, fresh-branded on his inner eyelids, was suddenly the image of that home as he remembered it in the moment just before he sailed. The shore, the ships, the log buildings in the green clearing by the sea came back to him across more than a thousand years, with such immediate pain that he could almost believe he might open his eyes to see it there after all, alive again instead of lost forever.

He got to his feet, still holding his eyes tightly closed to keep the picture to him. Moving by sense of hearing and smell alone, like a blind man with radar, he drifted through the silent, unstirring crowd toward the sanctuary of the woods. It was not until he had left the crowd behind him and felt the shade of the trees on his face and his exposed lower arms and hands that he paid any attention to the fact that once more boots had followed him, familiar boots.

This time, however, they caught up with him.

"Forgive me . . ." said the voice of Walt, trembling and a little breathless behind him. "But I have to talk to you. You *knew*, didn't you? You're a Messenger yourself, aren't you—or something more than mortal?"

Ranald stopped. The picture on the inner surface of his eyelids was already fading. His shoulders sagged. He opened his eyes.

"No," he said.

"Oh, but I know you are.—Aren't you?" Walt came walking around to face him. They stood, surrounded by thick oaks, dappled themselves with oak shade in the hot, still air. "I mean—if you are, I don't want to intrude. I don't want to pry. If you don't want to say anything about yourself, that's all right. But I have to talk to you about myself. I have to explain to . . . a part of God, anyway, to some man who's part of God Eternal."

Ranald shook his head again.

"I'm no god, nor god-man," he said.

"But I was," said Walt eagerly. "I was a God-man—or at least, a man of God. That's what makes talking to you now important. It's as if this has all happened just between God and me. Do you understand what I'm saying?"

Ranald sat down wearily cross-legged on the ground with his back against an oak trunk.

"Yes," he said.

"Then you can see what it means—." Walt squatted also, facing Ranald, but found the position awkward and ended up sitting down clumsily with an unsuccessful effort to cross his legs as easily as Ranald had, "—means to me. And if it means that much to me, what it must mean to the whole world. I don't flatter myself it was just for me, of course. But that's the essence of miracle, that it works for everyone as if it were just for him, alone. Isn't it?"

Ranald shook his head, without answering. Walt made a wide gesture at the sky and the unmoving noontide sky overhead.

"Now we've had the Sign," Walt went on. "Now we'll never be the same again—each of us, as individuals, never the same again. Now all our doubts are answered, finally and completely. And now that my own doubts, my special doubts, have been answered, I can see how little, how shameful, how sinful they were. Do you know what my particular sin and crime was? Doubt itself. Not just plain doubt—simple doubt—but doubt for doubt's sake. Can you imagine that?"

Ranald nodded.

"Yes," said Walt, his face pink-brown in the pinto shade-and-sunlight. "I played a game with the Creator. Even my choosing religion as a lifework was part of that game. I knelt and prayed '*I believe, Lord,*' but the words were a lie. What I meant was '*Prove to me that I should believe, Lord.*'"

He paused, looking at Ranald; but Ranald only sat watching.

"You understand?" said Walt. "I had to be continually testing God. Not only God directly, but God as He was made manifest in the world—in other men and women, in the things man had built, in nature itself. *Render unto*—do you know the verse from Matthew, Chapter twenty-two, Verse twenty-one—"

"Yes," said Ranald. "I was a slave in a monastery for a while, and I served the tables while they ate and one read to the others."

"There were no slaves in monasteries," said Walt. "Matthew twenty-two, twenty-one has to do with the questioners that the Pharisees sent to test Jesus. What do you think their question was?"

"Whether it was lawful to give tribute to Caesar or not," said Ranald.

"They asked Him whether it was lawful to give tribute to Caesar or not," said Walt. "And you know what He answered? '*Why tempt me, ye hypocrites?*' He made them show Him the tribute money with the image of Caesar on it, and told them, '*Render unto Caesar the things which are Caesar's—*'"

"Render *therefore* unto Caesar—" murmured Ranald.

"'—And unto God the things that are God's,'" continued Walt. "Two thousand years ago He said those words; but all down those millenniums this has been our major confusion. We confuse our duties to Caesar with our duties to God. In essence, we tend to think of God as just another Caesar—to be paid tribute, if necessary, but also to be questioned. This has been my sin, in particular; a sin which men like you and Dave, gifted with a simple response to nature, have learned instinctively to avoid. Now, you two are naturally free in this respect, so free neither of you even suspected I had something like that in me. But that young man Rob did. You remember how he kept saying it was *my* particular fault, my own lack, that I saw in the world and other people. —You remember that, yesterday?"

"Yes."

"Well," said Walt, slapping the pants-cloth stretched tightly over his bent right knee, "he was right! Absolutely right. That's been my missing part all along, a lack of simple faith. Faith like you have, and Dave Wilober has. But now I have it, like everybody else; and now that I *know* this, I can do something about it, I can learn—from people like you and Dave."

He leaned forward, eagerly, his heavy shirt creasing over his belly.

"Talk to me," he said. "Tell me how you see the world."

He stayed leaning forward, waiting. Ranald gazed at him for a long moment, then shook his head.

"No," he said, getting to his feet.

"Wait . . ." Walt began to scramble to his own feet. "What do you mean—'No'?"

"It's no use," said Ranald.

He turned and went off through the woods. Behind him, he heard Walt calling him by name and trying to follow, but the other man crashed noisily among the trees, tripping over roots and blundering into bushes; and Ranald soon left him behind.

Once he was free again, Ranald turned and went back to the pasture. On the way, he met others of the campers, wandering under the unmoving sun, as if the suspension of physical laws had suspended all responsibility as well; and there was no longer any requirement upon them but to follow the whim of each second, through a noonday pause that was unending.

The sound of a steady metal-on-metal hammering drew him back to the campfire he had shared with Dave and the others. Dave was seated on his bedroll, singing to himself, cutting with a chisel and hammer through a link of his ankle chain, laid upon a hatchet-blade for support. Maybeth was half seated, half kneeling beside him, watching. Across the now small fire, with flames nearly invisible in the bright sunlight, were three people close together. The deputy, Tom Rathkenny, was huddled up on the ground with his head in Letty's lap. She was stroking his short, pale-blond hair soothingly; and the new-softened weapon of her gaze was turned on him, rather than Rob, who was standing, looking down at the two of them.

". . . The whole world's changed," Rob was saying to Letty. She did not look up at him.

". . . *Now the poor man died*," sang Dave in tune to the clink of his hammer on the head of the chisel. . . .

"*. . . and his soul went to Heavenium.*
*Glory, Hallelujah, hi-ro-de-rum!*"

"Are you listening to me, Letty?" demanded Rob.

"*. . . He danced with the angels till a quarter past elevenium . . .*"

"—I said, are you listening?"

But Letty did not answer him. Her head was bent forward, her hair falling over the head in her lap.

"Poor baby," she was murmuring. "All right, baby. All right. I'm here . . ." She interrupted herself to speak briefly to Rob. "Go to hell! Can't you see I'm busy?"

*"Skinna-ma-rinky doodle doo! Skinna-ma-rinky doodle doo!*
*Glory, Hallelujah, hi-ro-de-rum . . ."*

"All right," said Rob.

He straightened up. In the noonday heat, he had shed more of his layers of clothing. The antibiotics seemed to have conquered his illness and his fever. With his beard no longer plastered to his face by the wind and his face no longer damp with sweat he looked slim, but supple and strong, in both determination and body. He turned and walked over to stand above Maybeth, who looked away from Dave and up at him.

"Come on," said Rob to her.

She hesitated and looked back at Dave. But Dave was occupied only with his chiseling and his singing.

*". . . Now the rich man died, and he didn't fare so wellium . . ."*

"I said, come on!" repeated Rob.

Maybeth looked at him again, and from him to Ranald. Ranald met and returned her gaze with the same open, uncommenting stare with which he had dealt with her from the beginning.

"It's happened, don't you understand?" said Rob to her. "It's the New Age. We've had the Sign and it'll never be the same again. Now, everyone *knows;* and the world's going to be completely different. Don't you understand? Some of us don't want to face that. Letty there, she doesn't—and look at that mess over there in her lap, scared out of his wits because what really *is* has caught up with him. It's too much for him and her—but not for people like you and me. For us it's the New Age of Actuality; it's the Garden of Eden really for the first time. Come on! What're you waiting for? You don't belong here with a couple of failures, and two old men."

Maybeth looked down at the ground before her. Slowly she got to her feet without looking again at Dave or Ranald. She went off with Rob and they disappeared among the moving figures of the crowd that was still in the pasture.

"... *couldn't go to Heaven, so he had to go to Hellium.*
*Glory, Hallelujah—*"

With a final *clink* the chisel cut through the link on which it had been biting; and Dave broke off his song. The chain parted and slithered snakelike from around Dave's scarred and calloused ankle to the hard, heel-beaten ground of the pasture. Dave picked up the links and laid them, with the hammer and chisel, carefully back into his pack behind his sleeping bag. He looked up at Ranald and laughed.

"Sing!" he said. "I got me religion at last. Don't need no chain anymore to stand for no faith I never had. All it took the Lord was a little old stopping of the sun at midday to set me free—from that, anyhow. Now I can give to folks without thinking I'm paying back for something."

"You always could," said Ranald. "And did." His mind was half lost in time.

Dave frowned for a second.

"What?"

"'For owre ioye and owre hele. Iesu Cryst of hevene,'" said Ranald, "'In a pore mannes apparaille pursueth us evere . . .'"

"What?" repeated Dave. "Say it again?"

"It's part of a poem," said Ranald, "that the priests used to use for a text in sermons. All week long, up and down hall, the priest was nothing to the gentles. But on Sunday all the good families around would come into chapel and the priest could say his sermon with a god's voice, paying them all back. And so he would tell them how Piers the plowman was closer to God than they. And those listening used to weep to hear it—people do not believe that now, but all were more open with weeping in those days. They wept, knights, ladies, all matter of warm-dressed folk. But later, after chapel, it made no difference you could see."

Dave fingered his chin, which was now lightly shadowed by twenty-four hours of beard.

"I've plowed," he said. "But I'm no 'pears-to-be-a-plowman.' I'm Dave Wilober."

"That, and more too," said Ranald. "But all of us are something more, with the sun straight overhead the way it is now."

Dave glanced briefly at the unmoving daystar above them.

"Could be. Could well be," he said. He laughed again. "Never mind, I'm free."

"Let's go get something to drink, come back and talk."

Tom Rathkenny lifted a crumpled face from Letty's knees.

"There's no alcoholic beverages out here," he said in a choked voice. "Every truck's been told . . ."

"Still, always something around," said Dave. He jerked his head at Ranald. "Come on, brother."

They went off to the line of trucks by the road; and, the third truck they came to was occupied by a drunken driver-owner who first tried to share his own half-empty bottle; then offered to give them an unopened one, but only if they would take it for nothing. Quietly telling the man that he took things for nothing only from neighbors or friends, Dave tucked bills unnoticed into the pocket of the driver's shirt and accepted the fresh bottle.

He and Ranald went back to their camping place. Letty and Tom Rathkenny were gone, now. Rob, Maybeth, and Walt had none of them returned. Ranald and Dave sat down on opposite sides of the fire with the bottle to one side of them, uncapped. But although Dave poured cups half full of the tepid, blended whisky, neither of them drank. It was hot and the air was without movement. They forgot the liquor and became lost in talk; which went down mines, up mountains, and from the California shore to the Ob River half a world away. Their words swung them through all sorts of places and seasons; from winter through summer and fall and back to winter again. Meanwhile, the sun stayed in place above them and the hours without time went by.

". . . A knife like that with a deer-antler handle," Dave heard himself saying at one moment. "I had a knife like that, and lost it commercial fishing—handlining sharks at the mouth of the Tampico River down in Mexico."

"Sharkskin soon spoils any knife edge," said Ranald. "Sponge-dredging off the Libya coast . . ."

Unremarked, alone, Maybeth crept quietly back to join them, sitting down back a little from the fire and listening. She nodded after a while, lay down with her head just on a corner of the foot of Dave's sleeping bag, and fell asleep.

Later, yet, Rob came back by himself. He glanced at the sleeping Maybeth without smiling and then lay down on the pile of blankets he and Letty had occupied the night before. Shortly, he began a light, easy snoring.

It was some hours later that Letty returned with Tom Rathkenny. The former deputy now wore only shirt, motorcycle breeches, and boots, and the shirt was open at the neck. While the shadow of beard on Dave's lean face stood out darkly in the sunlight, Tom's blond features looked as clean-shaven as they had the night before. Letty took one of the thin blankets not pinned to the earth by the weight of Rob's sleeping body and, with Tom helping, set it up on two sticks as a sloping sunshade to keep the eternal noontide glare out of their eyes. In the shadow of this, they both also lay down and slept.

Similar things were happening all about the pasture. People were yielding everywhere to the weariness of the unchanging noon day. Like wilting flowers, they were returning back to the earth beneath them and falling into deep, unmoving slumber. The sound of the voices of those left awake slowed, diminished, and fell silent at last; and that same silence crept in the end even between Dave and Ranald.

"Me, too," said Dave, at last looking around at the pasture full of unconscious figures. "Whatever comes next, for now there's got to be some time to rest." He glanced back at Ranald. "How about you?"

"Soon," said Ranald.

Dave picked up his untouched cup and poured the liquor in it back into the bottle without spilling a drop. Ranald picked up the cup from which he himself had not drunk and began to pour its contents back as well.

"You don't have to do that," said Dave. "Keep the bottle with you."

"Later," said Ranald. "Now's no drinking time."

"Maybe right," Dave answered. He turned, saw the head of May-beth on the corner of his sleeping bag and carefully stretched himself out on it without disturbing the girl. He put his hand up to his face to shield his eyes from the sunlight. "Talk to you later, then."

"Yes," said Ranald.

Ranald closed his eyes. Smoke-thin across the inner lids, misty and unsubstantial, drifted the vision of home that had been so clear to him before. The heat of the sunlight beat on his closed eyes like the silent shout of a god demanding to be heard. He dozed.

—And woke, with animal instinct, a second before her hand touched him. Maybeth had crept close until she was seated just beside him and her fingers were inches from the fingers of his right hand. At the sight of him, awake, she drew back and looked down away from his pale-blue gaze.

"I'm sorry . . ." she whispered.

"There's no magic in me," said Ranald. "Touch me if you like, but nothing will change."

Her head bent lower on her neck until she looked only at the earth.

"Why won't you like me?" she said, barely above her earlier whisper.

"There's no magic in that, either," said Ranald. "In time, even love and hate wear out. Not all the way out . . . each new season a little comes back again. But near out. Your god has spoken above you. Turn to him for magic."

She lifted her face to him at that.

"But He's your God, too," she said. "Now that He's proved Himself. Isn't He?"

"No god have I," said Ranald.

"But He's stopped the sun at noon. He's stopped the Earth."

"Yes," said Ranald. "But I neither thank nor curse him for it. It's long since I hardly remember giving up praying at every sound of thunder, or touch of the dry, hot wind that threatens drought. Gods may stop Earths and suns, but none of them can give me back my home again, or make me what I was—and it's I, not he or any other, that keeps me going on, and on, from season to season, when I see no sense in it any longer. I do that to myself, against myself, and don't know why. But no god has any hand in it."

She sat, staring at him.

"You aren't afraid—" she began.

But at that moment Walt Strauben came back to them. He was flushed and panting, barefoot now and stripped to the waist, the hair on his head and the rolls of fat on his chest and belly grayed and darkened with what looked like dirt. Trickles of sweat had cut streaks of meandering cleanliness down his upper body. In his right hand he carried a cardboard sign nailed to the neck of a cross made of two pieces of lath; and on the sign in grocer's crayon was written "RENDER UNTO CAESAR . . ." In his left hand he carried a newspaper which he threw down between Ranald and Maybeth as he collapsed, panting, into a sitting position on the ground beside them.

"Look—" he gasped.

They looked. Two words filled the upper half of the front page of the paper—SUN EVERYWHERE. Below that headline, the page was black with type with no pictures showing.

"Everywhere!" said Walt. "The sun's at noon everywhere around the world. Every place there were people gathered together, they saw the Messenger, just the way we did here. The sun's stopped at noon all over the Earth."

"Everywhere?" asked Dave. He had woken up and now lay propped on one elbow, watching them. "Don't make sense. Earth's round, isn't it? Has to be dark on one side."

"Can you ask a question like that after what you've seen happen here?" Walt turned on him. "If it's true here, why not everywhere? Why not anything? Why not?"

"Have to show me something more than a newspaper," said Dave. He shut his eyes and lay down again.

"There'll be some lacking enough faith—even now," said Walt, turning back to Ranald and Maybeth. "But read the paper. Read it. A few people stayed with their jobs to make sure it was printed; and because of that we know that God has indeed touched this Earth with a Sign of His power. Not just for our few numbers here in this meadow—but for everyone, everywhere."

He reached out clumsily to the edge of the dead fire and scraped up a handful of ashes, which he added to what was already thickening his disordered hair.

"Glory, glory!" A good share of the ashes he had scraped up had clung to the palm of his sweaty hand instead of falling on his head. He wiped the hand clumsily on the hard ground beside him. "I'm my God's man now, truly, at last!"

He met Ranald's eyes directly for the first time, with a glint of defiance.

"This was all it took, this news about the sun everywhere," he said, "it cleared up my last shred of doubt."

Ranald looked back at him without answering.

"But not people like Dave! Not you—" Walt's voice rose. "You don't believe in Him, do you? Even now, you don't believe He exists!"

"I believe," said Ranald.

"It's a lie! You—"

"It's not a lie," said Maybeth, out of nowhere. "Of course he believes. It's just that he doesn't have to be jolted, or shook up, or frightened, like we do. He just takes God for granted."

"Sin—sin! Blasphemy!" shouted Walt, pounding the butt end of his sign's post on the ground. "To take God for granted—"

"Walt," said Ranald.

Walt looked defiantly back at him; and this time Ranald caught and held the other man's eyes with his own.

"Walt," he said, "look around. All these people here are tired. So are you. You need sleep. Sleep now."

He held Walt's eyes unmovingly with his own.

"I . . ." Walt began, and broke off as his mouth, opened to speak, opened wider and wider into an enormous yawn. "I said . . . I . . ."

His eyelids fluttered and closed. He leaned sideways to the ground and half curled up there, hugging his sign to him. Within five breaths he was inhaling and exhaling deeply in slumber.

"We need sleep, too," said Ranald.

He lay down and closed his eyes once more against the sunlight. He heard Maybeth lie down near him; and a second later he felt the touch of her hand creeping into his.

"If you don't mind," he heard her murmur, "I'll hold on, anyway."

This time Ranald fell into full sleep.

He woke, briefly and instinctively, some time later. His body had felt a sudden cutting off of the sun's heat, and he opened his eyes to look up into a night sky full of stars. Once again, from the woods and the river he heard bird and water sounds, and the whisper of a breeze. He went back to sleep.

The next day found the people in the meadow more normal after their night's sleep, but still under the influence of the timeless noontide that had held them awake to the point of exhaustion. They were like people who had been stunned, and were now conscious again, but unsure of themselves, as if at any moment dizziness might make the ground rock beneath their feet. In the meadow, this unsureness showed itself in the reluctance of those there to leave their encampment and go back to whatever place it was from which they had come.

—And there were other aftereffects.

Walt was not the only one with something like ashes in his hair and a sign or cross or other symbol in hand. There were a number like him; and they were mostly busy speaking either to small groups in near-privacy, or from stumps or boxes to any who would listen. Many listened, others had withdrawn into meditation or trance, ignoring the noise around them. There were those who sang and prayed together; and those who sang and prayed alone. There were those in the store trucks parked along the roadway who had given away all their goods, and those like the driver-owner from whom Dave had bought drink the day before, who still sat numb with drink or drugs in their vehicles and indifferent to anyone who wanted to help himself to what was there.

Letty and Tom Rathkenny had gone off once more by themselves early. Walt, still holding his sign and smeared with the dirt of ashes, was wildly preaching to a group farther down the meadow. Rob, either high on something obtained from one of the trucks or self-hypnotized into a near-trance state, was engaged in a meditative process, seated cross-legged on the ground by himself, staring at the few grass blades upon the trodden earth between his knees.

"This is too much holy for me," said Dave finally, when a natural noon sun had passed its high point in the sky. He looked around the meadow and back at Ranald and Maybeth. "Far as I'm concerned, a hallelujah or two in the morning ought to take care of it, and then a man could get down to other things. I'm going to walk off a piece. How about you two?"

Ranald got to his feet and Maybeth followed. The three of them wove their way through the crowd downslope, into the trees and away through the trees, skirting the soggier spots until they came to a firm bank opening between trees on the clear-running water of the river. It was a middle-sized stream, perhaps two hundred feet across at this point, and shallow with mid-summer dryness so that the pebble shoals could be seen under the clear water reaching out for some distance from the bank. They came to a halt there and stood watching the running water. Insects buzzed by their ears; and now and then a bird call sounded not far from them. It was cooler here, down by the river and under the thick-leaved branches.

"Never stops running, does it?" said Dave, after a while. "Some-where, always, there's water running downhill to the sea."

"I think it may have stopped yesterday," said Ranald. "When everything else was stopped, too. I didn't hear it."

"Held up a bit was all, probably," said Dave. There was almost a loving note in his voice as he spoke about the moving river. He bent, picked up a pebble and threw it far out to midstream. The pebble made a single neat hole in the water, going in, and then there was no sign it had ever fallen. "Stopped for good is dead. Like with that shark-fishing, down in Mexico. *Finito*, and you're through for the day; *acabo*, and the sharks got you. This river just got finitoed along with everything else, for a little while. That was all."

"You're not afraid of things, either of you, are you?" said Maybeth, unexpectedly. "I've always been afraid. I tried to pre-tend I wasn't for sixteen years, and then, when I got away from home, I didn't have to pretend any more and I faced it."

"If you faced it, what's the difference?" said Dave. "I can get scared like anybody."

He looked over at Ranald. But Ranald shook his head.

"Not often for me, any more," he said. "I was telling her— things wear out. Love, hate . . . also fear."

"You don't understand, either of you," said Maybeth. "I'm always afraid. Of everything. It's a terrible feeling. I keep hunting for something to stop it. I thought this would, but it didn't. Even stopping the sun didn't do it. I'm just as afraid as ever. What if there is a God? He doesn't really care about me."

"Nobody used to expect gods to care without reason," said Ranald. "It's only the last few hundred years—" He stopped speaking rather abruptly. Something or someone was crashing through the underbrush in their direction. Ranald stepped forward to the riverbank, bent down and picked up a handful of sandy soil. As he straightened up, Tom Rathkenny, carrying a revolver, burst through the leaves of the brush behind them to join them.

"What'd you do with her?" the young deputy sheriff shouted, pointing the revolver at them. "Where'd you—"

At this point, he saw the handful of sand, which Ranald had already flung, coming at him through the air like a swarm of midges. The flung soil fell well short, but Tom ducked instinctively and the revolver went off, pointing at the sky.

Before he could pull its muzzle and his gaze back to earth again, Ranald had reached him—running very quickly but effortlessly with what looked like abnormally long strides—and as Tom tried once more to aim the revolver, Ranald hit him. It was a blow with clenched fist, but as odd in its way as Ranald's method of running. The fist came up backhand from the region of Ranald's belt level in a sweep to the side of the other man's jaw. It snapped Tom's head around sideways; and he took a step backward, fell, and lay apparently unconscious. Dave, who had come up meanwhile, reached down and picked up the revolver.

"What got into him?" asked Dave. He squatted down comfortably on his heels beside Tom, holding the gun loosely on one knee with his right hand and waiting for Tom to come to.

"Letty," said Maybeth. "Maybe he thought she was with you instead of me."

Tom opened his eyes, blinked stupidly at them all, and tried to sit up, reaching for the revolver. Dave pushed him back to the ground.

"Can't go shooting around like that," Dave said. "Lay there for a minute and cool off. Then maybe you can tell us what got you worked up."

"She isn't here?" Tom said. "Letty isn't?"

"Last I saw of her she was with you," Dave said.

Tom let himself go limp. His head rolled back on his neck so that he stared bitterly at the sky. He lay for a moment.

"She went off," he said, then. "She expects me to read her mind. For God's sake, I don't know what she's thinking!"

Dave, Ranald, and Maybeth watched him.

"She got mad," Tom said to the sky. "She wants me to change; but she's got all these crazy ideas of what I am. And I'm not. How can I change from something I'm not? How can I tell what she's thinking when she doesn't tell me?"

He waited, as if for an answer. None of them offered any.

"Guess you can get up," said Dave, getting to his own feet. Tom scrambled upright. His eyes went to his gun, now tucked into the belt of Dave's Levi's.

"That's mine," he said hoarsely. "Give it back."

"Guess I will," said Dave, "when I figure you can be trusted with it again."

"That's stealing," said Tom. "I could arrest you for that."

"You still a sheriff's man?" Dave said. "You don't look it much, right now. Anyway, how do you know there's still a sheriff?"

He stood. Tom leaned forward a little as if he might try to take the revolver back, but kept his arms down. He turned, suddenly, and plowed off into the brush.

"We'll just hold on to this for now," said Dave, patting the revolver butt fondly. "He'll be all right once he gets his head clear. How if we move on down the river?"

He turned and led the way along the bank, downstream. Ranald and Maybeth went with him.

"She's like you two," said Maybeth, a little bleakly as they went. "She's not afraid of anything. That's why it always happens to people like her."

But as they moved on beside the river, her mood improved.

Some time later, the two men even heard her humming almost inaudibly to herself. They followed the curving stream until the bank began to rise and they found themselves at last on what was actually a small bluff, looking through a screen of birch and maple trees down a vertical drop of perhaps eighty feet to a small open area like a valley. There a road emerged on the right below the bluff to run straight ahead, until the trees of a wooded slope to its right seemed to move in and swallow it up in the distance; and the river emerged on the left to run right beside the road with only a small strip of bank between them.

"That'll be the farther part of the road from back where we're camped," Dave said. "This way must be the way to Medford. Let's go back. Thought I saw a pool up a ways with some fish in it."

They went back the way they had come for perhaps an eighth of a mile to the pool Dave had seen. He produced a fishing hand-line and hooks from a leather folder in his right hip pocket and discovered some earthworms under a log. He turned the line and worms over to Ranald and went to build one of his reflexive fires. By the time he had it going and burned down to a useful set of coals, Ranald had, in fact, caught four middling-sized brook trout.

"Let me do that," said Maybeth, when the fish were cleaned and spitted on twigs over the coals.

There was actually nothing more for her to do but watch the fish and turn them occasionally. But she sat keeping an intent watch on them and the two men heard her humming once more to herself.

When the fish were done, they ate the flaky, delicate flesh with their fingers, using some salt Dave produced in a fold of wax paper from the same leather folder that had contained, and now contained again, the fishline and hooks. The four trout made next to nothing of a lunch for three people, but by this time the day had heated up to noon temperature and none of them were very hungry. After eating, they put the fire to rest with river water and walked back upstream.

It was quite warm. Maybeth took off the sweater Walt had lent her and carried it. Dave took off his jacket, folded it, and tucked it under the belt of his Levi's, in back. Only Ranald stayed dressed as he was, indifferent to the temperature.

They passed the spot where they had first come upon the riverbank and Tom had burst out on them with his revolver. They went on up the river's edge, detouring only here and there when some small bay or close stand of brush barred the direct route. Returning from one of these small detours, they heard ahead, through a stand of young oak and elm trees, a sound of voices in relaxed and comfortable argument.

"That's Rob and her, now," said Maybeth.

They came up through the stand of young trees and looked out on a wide, shallow stretch of the river. Letty and Rob were there in the water, naked in the sunlight. Rob was seated on a fallen log that had its upper edge barely out of the river's surface; and Letty, standing behind him, was washing his hair. Up to her knees in water, she worked her fingers industriously and had succeeded in raising a good lather. The sun gleamed on her pale, compact back and firm buttocks; and wads of lather dripped from Rob's narrow and bent, but sinewy, shoulders to float off like foam flecks on the current downstream.

". . . that's your trouble," Rob was saying, "you always want to run things."

"Like hell I do," she answered.

"The hell you don't."

"The hell I do—sit still, you son of a bitch," said Letty. "Anyway, hold your head still."

"This log . . ." said Rob, shifting his weight uncomfortably.

Dave laughed softly.

"Just as well I kept that Tom's gun," he said, low-voiced. He turned away. They went off from there without any further words.

"I think I'll go back," said Maybeth unexpectedly, when they were once more out of sound of the voices from the two in the river. She was not humming now, and her face had gone back to its old expression. She turned, and stopped. "Which way is it?"

Ranald pointed through the woods.

"Just keep the sun at your back," said Dave. "If you don't hit the meadow, you'll run into the road. If it's the road, turn left and the meadow'll be down a ways, only."

She left.

"Well, now," said Dave, looking after her. "And I was just about figuring she'd come out of it."

"Nothing changes," said Ranald. "As I said."

Dave glanced at him.

"You really hold to that," Dave said.

"I'd like to believe it's not so," said Ranald. "But it's what I've learned. All that's left to know is why I go on, knowing it, getting a new start each time spring turns to summer, summer to fall— to winter—to spring again."

"Go on because you're wrong," said Dave. They were walking on together, once more, following the riverbank upstream. He pointed to the moving water. "See there? Riverbed's changing all the time. No spring's like any other spring. No two trees alike. That tree there"—he pointed to a young birch—"there never was one like it before. After it's grown big and died and fallen, never be another like it. There never was another like it, from the beginning of the world until now. Same with people. Anyone, he dies, no one just like him's ever going to come again."

"What profit in that?" Ranald said, "—if all he does is what men have always done—no more, no less. What gain is there in his special differences if he comes from nowhere just to walk the same treadmill in one spot before going back into nowhere again?"

"Why bother to argue it with me if you think that's so?" said Dave. "If you're so sure of it and we're just saying what's been argued all out, time and again, before?"

"Because I wish you were right and I was wrong. Still," said Ranald. "That's the one thing I can't understand. Why I go on, why I still hope. —Also, you aren't like most men, brother."

"That's a kind word," said Dave. "Well, listen to my side of it,

then. You're wrong thinking people never get nowhere. We've
come a long ways. Apes once, wasn't we?"

"Or something like that. What of it?" said Ranald. "As apes we
walked in the woods like this and the sun made us hot, like this.
Where are you and I different, now? What difference Rob and
Letty, naked in the river? They were naked there as apes, also."

"Not washing hair."

"Grooming each other. As apes and monkeys do, today."

Dave laughed.

"Might be right about that," he said. "But even if you're winning the argument, you're still not changing my mind. I still feel
you're wrong—know you're wrong."

"You have your god," said Ranald. "That may be the
difference."

"Have Him?" Dave said. "I believe He's there, sure enough. I
can't hardly say no to that after seeing the sun stopped over my
head the way it was. But *have* God? No more than I ever had
when He was just a chain around my ankle."

"He'll be a chain around your ankle again," said Ranald. "Nothing changes."

"What it is I believe in, that says you're wrong," said Dave,
"that's not God or religion. That's what I got from what I've seen
—everything I seen all my life long. I tell you a tree lives and dies
and there never was nothing like it before, nor can't anything ever
be like it again—nor it don't make sense things ever be the same
after it's once lived and died. Trees, everything's that way. People can't be any different—and they're not. I know it by feel, inside me."

"I felt like that once—now only my foolish self goes on acting
as if I did," said Ranald. " '*Render therefore unto Caesar the
things which are Caesar's.*' That's the verse Walt's taken for his
text. '*—and unto God the things that are God's.*' Meaning that
when all the dues of the world are paid, faith remains. But what
if one pays all dues and then finds no faith, nothing left over?"

They walked on a little way without talking, their feet finding level and uncluttered space without conscious thought on either man's part.

"You told me you went through this once before," said Dave. "The sun stopped—"

"No," said Ranald. "That time it was a matter of darkness at midday. A hand held the light of the sun away from the earth."

"Eclipse, maybe?" suggested Dave.

Ranald shook his head.

"A hand," he said. "We were made to know it. The sun was there, unmoving as it was this time. We could see it. But a hand held its light from reaching us and the other things of Earth. And so matters stayed for some time, for about as long as it happened in the meadow to you and me and the rest. But afterward, there was no difference. Just as there was no difference a little later after the gentlefolk had wept at chapel at hearing that Piers Plowman was closer to God than they. Soon afterward, no man or woman stayed changed."

"Everyone's been changed this time, far as I can see."

"At first. It seemed all those there were changed, too, that earlier time. But it was like in the chapel, for a small time only. Very soon after the hand was gone, any difference it had made was gone from those who had seen it."

"Maybe," said Dave. "Got to see it myself to believe it. Got to see it *in* myself, to believe it."

They went on a few more miles up the river, then turned and came back to the meadow in the midafternoon. Maybeth was not by the dead ashes of their campfire, nor Letty, Rob, or Tom. But Walt was there, no longer preaching, sitting on his sleeping bag, still dirty and shirtless with his sign face down on the ground by him. Newspapers were spread around him; and he pushed front pages from these into the hands of Dave and Ranald as they came up.

"Read!" he said. "The counterattack of those who hate God. The lies of the atheists."

Headlines on the sheet in Ranald's hand took up nearly half the available white space there.

### ACT OF GOD
### OR
### ACT OF NATURE?

The paper Dave had been given had smaller headlines.

### MIRACLE MAY BE AN ILLUSION

"Not all," said Walt, "could testify to the truth. There had to be those few who had to try to tear it down." He waved his hand at the snowdrift of other newspapers scattered around him. "All these other papers are honest, reporting the new era as it is." His voice trembled a little. "But among the sheep there have to be a few goats—a few wolves, wolves would be a better name for them; and they're tearing at the truth, trying to tear it down. Pity them, as I do. Pity them!"

"Says here," said Dave, bending his head over the newssheet he held, "the whole thing could have been the result of massive auto-hypnosis. Guess not. I don't hypnotize well. Man tried it once on me some years back, then said I kept fighting him. I wasn't fighting; just sitting there waiting to see what it felt like. He said that was the same thing as fighting."

Ranald was reading below the headlines on the page in his hand. . . .

"*We owe at least this much to nearly three millennia of scientific thought and work,*" Nobel Prize winner Nils Hjemstrand said today, "*not to throw out all possibility of a natural explanation for this apparent miracle before a thorough investigation is made by competent physicists, astronomers, and students of any other scientific disciplines which might have been involved in what seemed to happen. . . .*"

"Their investigation won't work," said Walt, looking up at Ranald's face. "They'll learn that."

Ranald handed the paper back down to him and looked over at Dave.

"Tomorrow you'll begin to see it for yourself," he said to Dave. "It'll begin."

"Fools," muttered Walt, staring down at the paper Ranald had just given back to him, "doubting fools, clinging to a superstition called science. . . ."

That night Maybeth rejoined them, and the praying and the singing of religious songs was louder in the meadow than it had ever been. But at dawn there were gaps among the line of store trucks parked along the road and the number of campers in the meadow was noticeably less. During the morning, Walt washed himself, put on a clean shirt, and gathered an audience around him. Standing on a wooden egg crate, he lectured his listeners earnestly on the chance, now, to form a new society, a new world. Maybeth stood in the audience with Walt's other listeners for perhaps an hour, then she left and came back to the campsite where Dave and Ranald, Rob and Letty were turning a loaf of bread and two cans of corned beef into lunch.

She sat down, but made no move to reach for the bread and meat. Her shoulders were curved and she stared down at the gray-black ashes where the fire of last night had glowed.

"Walt's right," she said, without looking at any one of them in particular. "It shouldn't be lost, what we all know happened here. The people who went through it ought to get together and change things."

"Not his way," said Rob. "People tried it his way for hundreds of years—and look what it led to. He just wants to set up more of the same. But that won't work—anymore."

Maybeth looked at him as if she would argue, then gazed back at the ashes without saying anything.

"You don't believe me?" Rob got to his feet. "I'll prove it to you—it's not going to work."

He went off toward the road and the store trucks. Letty started to rise and follow him, then sat back down again. She looked for a moment hard at Maybeth, but Maybeth was still staring at the fire's dead ashes.

It was over an hour before Rob returned; but when he came he brought with him almost as many newspapers as Walt had surrounded himself with the day before. They were a new day's editions, and he dumped them on the ground before the seated Maybeth.

"Read those," he said. "Half of them, anyway, have already switched over. Half of them don't believe any more it was a miracle. They're full of articles by scientists saying how it could have happened without anything supernatural about it."

"But there was!" Maybeth said. "Don't you remember? It wasn't just the sun stopping, it was what we all felt. Remember? We all *knew* it was God doing it, then."

"What if we did? What if it was?" Rob said. "What matters isn't what happened, but what people are going to think happened, a year from now."

"Oh, no!" said Maybeth.

"Oh, yes," he said. "You damn right, yes. That's how things happen. You just have to face it."

She looked hopefully at Dave and Ranald. Dave, however, was occupied in using a wire pad to clean fire-black from the bottom of his soup pan, and did not even see the glance she gave him. Ranald met her eyes in open, unresponsive silence.

She looked down again at the headlines on the newspapers before her.

"I'm no good arguing," she said. "Walt'll answer you. Why don't you try to make him believe it's going like that?"

"That's what I'm sitting around here waiting for," said Rob, the yellow glints showing in his eyes. "Just that."

It was early afternoon before Walt gave up his efforts long enough to come back to the place where the rest of them were, to make himself a sandwich and a cup of coffee. All the others,

though they had strayed some little distance away from time to
time since Rob and Maybeth had talked, came drifting back to
their common campsite when Walt sat down with his coffee cup
and a pressed-ham sandwich.

He ate and drank hungrily, saying nothing. Rob spoke to him.

"It's not working, is it?" Rob said.

Walt looked at him and bit into the sandwich without
answering.

"It isn't, is it?" said Rob. "I mean, you talking to them. It's
not doing any good, not keeping them from changing their
minds?"

Walt swallowed the last of his sandwich. His back was bent as
Maybeth's shoulders had been bent, earlier.

"Forgive me," he said. "I'm all talked out for the moment."

"Are you? Are you?" Rob, who had been sitting down, got to
his knees and walked several steps on his knees clumsily to bring
himself right in front of Walt and only half a body's length away.
"You sure it's not just you don't want to discuss it—I mean, really
discuss it, not just stand up there and shout while people pretend
to listen?"

"I think," said Walt, holding his voice very even, "some at least
were listening."

"The ones who want to be brainwashed, you mean?" Rob said.
"Look around, for Christ's sake. This place hasn't got half the
people it had yesterday, or when it happened."

"Then you admit it happened," said Walt heavily.

"Happened? Happened? It happened, all right," said Rob, leaning forward. "But what's 'happened' mean? According to you it's
supposed to mean something great, is that it? Well, it doesn't.
*Nothing*—that's what it means!"

"You don't believe in God," said Walt. "That's what makes you
talk this way."

"Believe? I don't not-believe and I don't believe. I don't give a
damn one way or another. Because it doesn't *matter*—don't you
understand? Haven't you seen these latest papers?"

"I looked," said Walt, not looking at them. "There's nothing new there. A few dissenters—"

"Not a few," said Rob. "A lot. Half of them, at least. And even the ones who're still shouting miracle are starting to tone down and go cautious on it—keeping an open mind, that's how they put it. But toning down, all the same!"

"I repeat," said Walt, slowly and deliberately, "you don't believe in God. If you believed in Him, then what you saw here would have been a revelation for you, too."

"Revelation!" Rob laughed. "Do you know what it was to me? You never saw anything like the sun stand still in the sky before. That was really something for you, wasn't it? And so you think it had to be really something for everybody else, too. Well," Rob leaned even closer, "I'm telling you now, it wasn't; no matter what people like you want to make out of it. I'll tell you what it was. An experience—that's all. A trip, man! And you never had one before, so you thought it was something to turn everybody in the world inside out."

Walt shook his head and turned to face away from Rob. Rob scrambled around on his knees to keep them nose to nose.

"You think that's the first time I saw something like the sun standing still?" Rob demanded. "I've seen lots of things—things you couldn't even dream up; and not just from being high, either. A trip, that's all it was; and there's all kinds of trips. I don't care where this one came from. It was a trip, that's all. Just that and nothing else."

"The two things," said Walt, staring at him now, "don't compare in any way. What you're talking about is subjective. What we all saw here was objective."

"All right, call it objective. You think that makes any difference? God exists and He made the sun stand still," said Rob. "You think that impresses me with Him? If He wanted to get to me, why didn't He feed a million people that are starving right now in the world? Now, that's something I've never seen done. Why didn't He clean all the smog out of the air everywhere and make it that there couldn't be any more? Why didn't He stop the wars and the killing and heal everybody in the hospitals and out of the hospitals who're sick or hurt?"

"These are our own sins," said Walt, heavily. "We have to cure them ourselves."

"But we're already curing them, old man." Rob sat back on his heels. "We. Us. —Not you. We're already not making smog, or polluting, or killing people. It's people like you who keep on doing that, talking one thing and doing another. You and your 'Render unto Caesar—' How'd you like your own quotations to turn around and bite you? What was it Jesus was supposed to say when they came to ask him that question about what was Caesar's and what was God's? '. . . Why tempt ye me, ye hypocrites?' Wasn't that it? Who do you suppose the hypocrites are now, with this miracle business—Us? Or you people?"

Walt jerked the last coffee in his cup out onto the dead ashes, staining the gray dust black. He put the empty cup in his packsack and got to his feet.

"You're twisting things," he said, "and you know it. You're doing it quite deliberately. I think you know you're not being fair or honest."

He walked away. From the other side of the campfire ashes, Letty looked at Rob.

"You stink, every so often," she said. "You know that?"

Rob did not look back at her. He had picked up a small stick and was digging one sharp end of it furiously into the ground before him, watching the dirt break and move.

"Shut up," he said. "Will you just for once shut up?"

That night, though at least half of the original crowd had gone, the singing and praying in the meadow was as loud as it had been the night before. If anything, the prayers were more sonorous and the songs more shouted. There were also more intoxicants in evidence. Several times during the early evening, when all the campfires were alight, fights broke out and there were men and women to be seen staggering about, or lying sprawled and thickly breathing in unlikely or inconvenient places.

The late editions of the newspapers, when they reached the meadow, contained many stories that backed off even farther from putting the name of miracle to what had happened. Now, less than a third of the press took for granted that a Sign of some kind had been given to the people of the Earth. And there were news stories in opposition to the idea of miracle that used words like "gullible" and "frenzied" in their descriptions of those who might still be wholeheartedly believing.

Meanwhile, as the evening grew, Dave had been sitting by the evening fire, seeming to become bonier of jaw and more bleak of eye as the noise and activities in the meadow increased. Now, a few hours after full dark, he rose suddenly and disappeared into blackness in the direction of the woods lower down. This time Ranald did not go after him. Instead, he stayed by the fire with Maybeth, who was the only other person still there. When Dave left she moved closer to Ranald, who sat cross-legged now, in the midst of the meadowful of noisy people, with the light of the flames playing yellow variations on the rusty colors of his beard, like a magician surrounded by the demons and other dark figures of his conjurations.

"This is going to be the last night here, isn't it?" she asked him.

He did not answer.

"You know," she said, after a little while, "I think I really have been changed."

His face lifted then, and he turned his head to look at her. His gaze was completely unblinking and the firelight reflected from his eyes as if they had themselves caught fire. She had never faced such a brilliant and piercing look in her life; and after a second she looked away from him, down at the ground.

"Never mind," he said. "You meant well. But after these many years I've learned the ways people look when they lie."

"I—" She had intended to speak out loud, but her throat hurt so from tears she did not dare let loose, that her voice could only come out in a whisper. "—just wanted to give you something."

"I know," he said. "And you have, as much as anyone can. But no one person's changing can be an answer to my trouble. The answer I need has to be one that fits everybody. If I can know why I want to go on living, then I'll know why the whole race wants to keep on living when it rejects all gods and keeps trying the impossible as if it were possible."

"But maybe it *isn't* impossible," she said. "Maybe it's possible and you just can't see it."

"I?" he asked; and the single questioning syllable tore to dust rags the fine fabric of the argument she was forming in her mind. Without an argument and without hope, she went on talking, anyway.

"It could be because you're different," she said. "After all, you're immortal."

"No," he answered. "I've only lived a long—a very long time. And that's the problem of it. I'm mortal, all men and women are mortal, the human race is mortal. That's why it makes no sense. An immortal would want to keep the eternal life he had. But people are like climbers on a cliff too high even to imagine. Each knows he can struggle up only a little distance before he dies and drops off and another climber takes his place. —Still, when a god comes winging close like some great bird, ready to carry at least some of them toward the top, they reject him—turn their heads away and insist they're alone on the cliff."

"But, as you say," she said, "you've lived so long. Maybe it looks different to you from how it really is for the rest of us."

"No, it doesn't look different," he said, staring at the flames, "and I'm no different. I turn my back on gods, just like the rest. I want to climb, too."

"Instinct," she said.

He shook his head.

"Instinct's to find a safe notch in the cliff face and stay there. To climb goes against that."

"Maybe, then," she said, "that's what they mean by 'soul.'"

"A soul is a god-thing," he replied. "A soul would reach for the god who comes swooping by just like the instinct-part would try to find a safe spot and live there without pain and effort. But in spite of soul and instinct, the climbing goes on."

He rocked a little on his hips. It was the first physical sign of emotion she had ever seen in him.

"And still I keep going on," he said. "And on. And on."

Two dark figures broke from the clutter of the crowd in the darkness downslope and came running toward their fire, a larger shape chasing a smaller. As they broke into the firelight the pursuer grabbed for the smaller figure, which dodged with the easy smoothness of much faster reflexes and cut around the fire to stand behind Ranald and Maybeth. Panting on the other side of the fire, the pursuer showed himself to be Tom Rathkenny.

"Yellow—" he gasped. "Why don't you stand still? You, doing all that talking about not being afraid of anything—anybody."

"Who's—afraid?" said the voice of Rob, behind Ranald and Maybeth. "You just want me to give you all the advantages. If I weighed forty more pounds, I'd stand still. So, I don't. So, let's see you catch up with me."

"I'll kill you," panted Tom.

"Sure—you will." Rob was getting to be breathing almost normally. "That's all you can do. You can't win the argument, so you'll kill me. You can't catch me, so you'll kill me. Sure, pig, come kill me!"

"Yug—" It was a sound without words. Tom started straight ahead through the fire at the two seated people and direction of Rob's voice.

Ranald got to his feet without touching his hands to the ground, so suddenly that his appearance in Tom's path was almost like a stage trick.

Tom checked, the flames licking about his boot tops.

The heavy-boned young man swayed on his feet for a second like an animal caught in a trap. Then he turned and plunged off down the slope into the darkness and the crowd. From behind Ranald and Maybeth came a long, slightly shuddering outbreath.

"Woo," said Rob, gustily. He came around and dropped down at the fire in a sitting position facing them. Ranald reseated himself.

"I'm not afraid of him," said Rob, in a calm voice. "Not afraid of him at all. That's something somebody like him can't understand. I'm not afraid of"—he glanced at Ranald, then hesitated slightly and looked back at the fire—"hardly anything."

"You shouldn't drive him crazy like that, anyway," said Maybeth.

Rob looked at her.

"Well," he said. "The great silent one speaks."

"I'm just telling you," said Maybeth. "It's dangerous to get anybody—anybody, even—that mad at you. If people get mad enough they don't care what they do." He grinned and she turned to Ranald. "You tell him."

Ranald looked at her and at Rob, but said nothing.

"Please," she said. "Tell him. He'll believe you.—And shouldn't someone tell him?"

Ranald looked directly at Rob.

"He'll kill you," Ranald said.

"Kill me?" said Rob; but, eye to eye with Ranald, he did not grin. "Maybe he might even try it, at that. But he'd have to catch me first."

"I did not say what he might do," said Ranald. "I said what he will do."

Rob stared at him. Face to face across the fire, both short and wiry, silky beard and high white forehead facing full beard and brown skin faintly wrinkled about the eyes, the flames made them look for a moment like older and younger brothers. Then Rob jerked his head aside and scrambled to his feet.

"No," he said, "you don't—"

He broke off. Letty was coming upslope into the firelight to join them. She stopped in front of Rob.

"I got him to promise to stay away from you," Letty said, flatly. "And you're going to stay right here the rest of the night. I promised him that."

"You, too?" said Rob. "Oh, Mama!"

He sat down again with a thump, as if all his muscles had given way at once. Letty knelt beside him and put an arm around his shoulders.

"You can't help being a bastard," she said tenderly. "I know you can't. But he's a straight. He doesn't understand; and he could hurt you."

"Mama, Mama," said Rob. "No—*Aunt* Letty." He looked across the fire. "Mama Maybeth. Daddy Ranald."

"Will you stop it?" said Letty. She put her other arm around him and tried to pull him over backwards. After a second he gave in and they both fell back on the ground intertwined. The firelight played on the soles of their boots, but the upper parts of their bodies were in shadow. Rob laughed and muttered unintelligibly.

"Who cares?" said Letty, indifferently.

Maybeth looked sideways at Ranald. But Ranald's gaze went through and beyond the two on the other side of the fire as indifferently as if they had been half-sketched figures in some old drawing that familiarity had made practically invisible.

His face had shown little but calmness in the time she had known him; and there were no explicit lines of emotion on it now. But a shadow of sadness seemed to have appeared like a visor over his eyes; and he stared off into the distance at nothing, or at least nothing she could see. Timidly she rested a hand on his arm; but he neither moved nor spoke to her. It was like touching a carving in wood.

The fire burned down to red coals and Dave did not return. But close to midnight, Walt came heavily back to join them and dropped into a sitting position on his sleeping bag. After a minute, he reached out for some of the thicker pieces of dead oak limbs Dave had collected in a neat pile nearby, and put them on the coals. Little flames licked up immediately, feeding on the loose bark but leaving the heavy center wood no more than darkened.

"How many did you convert tonight?" Rob asked, from across the fire.

Walt ignored him, staring at the pieces of oak branch with the little flames feeding with temporary ease on the rough bark.

"Didn't hear me?" said Rob, raising his voice. "I asked you—"

"I heard you," said Walt. He sagged, a roll of belly bulging his shirt out above his belt as he sat on the sleeping bag. He still did not look up; and his voice was hollowed by weariness. In the new light of the little flames, his eyes showed bloodshot.

"But you didn't answer me."

"If you don't mind," Walt said with great effort, still not looking up, "I'm not in much shape to talk, right now."

"Hey, that's too bad," said Rob.

Walt sat silent and unmoving.

"I said," said Rob, "that's too bad." He raised his voice again. "Too bad—I said."

"Why don't you quit talking?" said Letty.

"Yes, that's a shame," said Rob. "Shows how little real faith there is in people. God says one thing and the newspapers say another; so naturally, they take the word of the newspapers. Here, instead of the converted growing in numbers, they've been staying just the same. —Or maybe they've even been falling off the bandwagon. Is that right?"

He paused; but Walt still did not respond.

"Come to think of it, it seemed to me there were fewer people standing around listening to you and the rest preach tonight, than there were earlier today. —To say nothing of last night. The congregations've been getting smaller and smaller all along, here. In fact, haven't the people been peeling off until there wasn't anyone left for you to talk to at all? —Walt?"

Walt stirred. He did not look up from the pieces of oak limbs which were now beginning to catch fire in the true sense and to grow rows of little flames flickering and running along their undersides. But he shifted his weight on the sleeping bag and the ground on which the bag was lying.

"God is not mocked," he said.

"No, of course not," said Rob.

Maybeth, still seated beside Ranald, tugged a little at his arm. "Ranald . . ." she whispered.

Ranald's full attention came back slowly, as if from a thousand miles and a thousand years, away. He looked at her, and around the fire at Walt, Rob, and Letty, and back to her again. Then he went away once more into distance and time.

Maybeth dropped her hand strengthlessly to her lap.

"God can't be mocked," Rob was saying, "because that wouldn't be right. Or do I mean 'righteous'? That's right, I mean righteous. It wouldn't be righteous for God to be mocked; the way He is here when people begin to decide they don't believe in Him even after His stunt with the sun—"

"They believed," said Walt in a near whisper, staring at the fire.

"Of course they believed," said Rob. "After all, it happened, didn't it? And they should have gone on believing. You ought to have made sure they go on believing. After all, that was your job, wasn't it?"

"Please," said Walt, staring at the fire. "If you don't mind . . ."

"But I mean that really hurts me, those people who listened to you acting like this," said Rob. "They should have gone off in every direction after hearing you, like a batch of disciples, to spread the faith. And here they do just the opposite. They back off from the faith themselves, dropping away one by one until you haven't got anyone there listening to you. How could that happen? How could you let it happen?"

Walt was no longer looking even at the fire. His head hung down now, so that he stared directly at the barren, heel-trampled earth between his thighs.

"Leave him alone," said Letty, getting to her feet. "Come on."

"No," said Rob, not looking around at her, watching and speaking only to Walt, "I can't let something like that happen without trying to understand it. Something that rotten can't happen without a reason, some big reason. I mean—something besides the newspapers must have been working on those people listening to you, to drive every one—every single one of them—away from you, like that."

Walt shuddered a little, but he still sat without answering, staring at the ground.

"Rob," said Letty.

"Be with you in a minute, Let," said Rob, not moving from the ground. "I just want to find out how anybody could have a hundred percent failure, like that. Even the law of averages ought to give one or two converts, shouldn't it? Here now, it's almost as if Walt had been preaching against their believing in the miracle, instead of for it. Hey, do you suppose a man actually could do something like that? I mean, subconsciously? Say one thing, but say it so the people listening realized he was really lying to them? Like, for example, he would be saying out loud to them, 'Abandon doubt, believe and enter the kingdom of heaven . . .' but at the same time the way he'd say it he'd actually be telling them that even if they thought they were positive about something, they had a duty to question themselves about it anyway. —As if he was telling them sort of behind his words that they really had to consider the chance they were wrong. As if they ought to try doubt on for size, just to make sure—"

Walt made a choking sound. Then another. It was suddenly clear that he was sobbing, crying where he sat, making no effort to move or wipe away the tears.

"After all," said Rob, raising his voice a little over the sounds Walt was making, "it's true enough. —I don't see how any thinking person can deny it. You've got a duty to keep an open mind, no matter how much faith you have. That's the only good way, the enlightened way—"

"LEAVE HIM ALONE!"

The fury of Letty's scream was incandescent. Like a sudden eruption of white light in darkness, it left them all momentarily numb and dazzled; and it silenced not only Rob, but everyone in the meadow for fifty yards in all directions. Having exploded, Letty said nothing more, but stood waiting until Rob, after a moment, scrambled to his feet. Then she turned and stalked away. He went after her.

Walt looked after them, then turned to Maybeth and Ranald with a face in which the lines seemed to have deepened like the eroded gullies in some dry desert riverbed.

"He's right," Walt said. "I preached doubt to them. I preached my own doubt, after all. From the second day—right after those newspapers began to doubt, I began to doubt again, too."

"You shouldn't care," said Maybeth. "You did it in spite of what you were thinking. That's harder than doing it with no doubts at all. Doing something in spite of yourself is the hardest thing there is."

He shook his head and went back to looking down at the earth. She looked bleakly at the ground, herself. It had been no use, like throwing a kiss to a starving man; but it was all she knew to say to him.

The noise dwindled in the meadow and at last, with the moon small and high overhead and the fires low, there was silence. It was then that Dave came back and found all of them asleep but Ranald, who was still sitting as he had been.

"Two bells, and all's well," said Dave, sitting down and tossing one of the oak limbs on the once more nearly dead fire. A scent of whisky came across the fire with his words to Ranald. Just as in the woods, only a deliberateness about Dave's speech backed up the evidence reaching Ranald's nose.

"Party's over, I take it?" asked Dave.

Ranald stirred and came back, as he had briefly for Maybeth earlier, from the distance of his mind.

"Tomorrow everyone will go," Ranald said. His eyes went to the bottom pants leg covering that ankle of Dave's he had seen dark with scar and callouses.

"No," said Dave, following the direction of Ranald's gaze, "I didn't put it back on. Don't intend to, either; but I don't know as it makes any difference. Turned out the covenant between me and the Lord wasn't something you could put on and off like a chain, anyhow."

"So," said Ranald, almost to himself, "like the gentlefolk leaving chapel, like these around us here, there's to be no change for you either, brother?"

Dave frowned.

"Don't know," he said. "I won't know until I get the sight and stink of this place out of my eyes and nose." He reached into his pocket and pulled out the cut chain. It glittered like a living metal thing in his grasp. "The day comes I can throw this away, I'll know I found something here—found it for good."

He turned, unzipped his sleeping bag and opened it. He lay down in it, throwing the unzipped top flap loosely over him.

"Paying Caesar never really worried me none," he said, looking up at the night sky. "It was paying God. Actually, a man ought to be able to pay them both off—and be free. I'll see about that after I'm clear of this place. Well, party's over. Night."

"Farewell," said Ranald.

In a moment Dave was asleep and the meadow held only one waking mind under the moon and the stars.

Dawn rose on a meadow empty of more than nine tenths of the crowd that had filled it when it was most full. And these that were left now went about the business of leaving, themselves. Even before the sun was above the hill beyond the road where the trucks had lined up, most of the last few campers were gone or on their way; and, now that the meadow was clearing, it was possible to see the signs they had left behind them.

The crowd had been good about collecting their litter and trash in the beginning. But the last couple of days, all order had begun to disintegrate. Now that the surface of the meadow was no longer hidden by people, it showed all sorts of discarded material, as if the ground had sickened with a disease called humanity; and the illness showed now in a rash of useless items. Torn newspapers, unclean plastic and paper plates, empty cans, abandoned, punctured air mattresses in various gaudy colors, bits of tents and clothing, shoes and garbage, all blotched the gentle slope where sparse but tough green grass had covered loose, brown soil. Above, the morning sky was high and blue with clouds as fluffy and clean as if they had just been born out of the pure upper air. It was cool, with a fair, small wind blowing from the northwest, from the hill down toward the unseen river.

Around Dave's campfire, they were also getting ready to leave, packing up along with the two dozen or so other people remaining in the meadow. There were two of the sheriff's deputies in uniform going from group to group. One of these was Tom Rathkenny. He came up to the fire with a paper in his hand, as shiny in leather helmet, boots, and Sam Browne belt as he had been the first time they had seen him. Only the holster at his belt was empty, though the fact that the holster flap was closed and buttoned down helped to disguise its emptiness.

"I'll take my gun back," he said to Dave, holding out his free hand.

Dave, seated as he filled his pack, looked at the hand for a second, then reached into the pack, pulled out the revolver and handed it up. Tom unbuttoned his holster and put the weapon into it; but he did not button down the flap again. He held the paper up.

"This is a legal notice," he said. "Your license to camp here has expired and the county court orders you to vacate the premises, after cleaning up any litter you have left, repairing any damage you have done, and returning the area you have occupied to the condition it enjoyed before you occupied it."

"I never was much for being able to grow grass in one day," said Dave.

The younger man ignored him. Tom was looking at Rob only, and running the thumbnail of his right hand back and forth along the top curve of his unbuttoned holster flap. Rob, busy packing the tattered blankets he owned with Letty, ignored the attention he was getting. Ranald, the only one of them unmoving, still seated as if he had not even shifted once from his position the night before, watched both of the younger men.

"Yang and Yin," said Ranald to Tom, without warning, "love and hate. *'Abou Ben Adhem, may his tribe increase, awoke one night from a great dream of peace; and saw within the moonlight of his room—'* "

It was a moment before they all realized he was reciting verse; and, when they did realize, they continued to listen—for the moment all stopped from what they were doing—as if caught by the magic of primitive people listening to an incantation.

*"Making it rich,"* Ranald went on, as if no one but Tom were there.

> *". . . and like a lily in bloom,*
>     *An angel writing in a book of gold.*
> *Exceeding peace had made Ben Adhem bold;*
>     *And to the presence in the room he said,*
> *'What writest thou?' The Vision raised his head;*
>     *And with a look made of all sweet accord,*
> *Answered, 'The names of those who love the Lord.'*
>     *'And is mine one?' asked Abou. 'Nay, not so,'*
> *Replied the Angel. Abou spake more low,*
>     *But cheerily still, and said, 'I pray thee, then,*
> *Write me as one that loves his fellow men.'*
>     *The Angel wrote and vanished. The next night,*
> *He came again with a great wakening light;*
>     *And showed the names whom love of God had bless'd;*
> *And lo! Ben Adhem's name led all the rest."*

". . . and there are others," Ranald said, without pause or change in his voice. *'Le temps a laissé son manteau, De vent, de froidure, et de pluie . . .'* Also, *'He prayeth well who loveth well both man and bird and beast . . .'* But it doesn't matter. I was too young the first time this happened. Each one must build or break his own god. —And I, like all . . ."

Then, as they still watched and waited, his attention went away off from them again into time and space, as it had the day before. They sat or stood, still without speaking—there was something in the air, something fearful promised to whoever might break the silence first.

"What was that about?" asked Dave.

He asked the question of Ranald, but Ranald did not answer and he looked around at the others.

"That . . . that last bit about praying was from Coleridge— 'The Ancient Mariner,'" said Walt, unsurely, staring at Ranald. "The French bit was from the fourteenth-fifteenth century—a poem about how wonderful spring was, written by a man who'd been locked in prison for years, I think . . . Charles d'Orléans. That first verse is by some nineteenth-century poet." He looked at Maybeth and Letty and Rob in turn. "I can't remember who. Do you know?"

They stared at him, and shook their heads.

"All three things he quoted have something to do with loving— people or things . . ." Walt said. "I . . . don't understand."

Dave looked at Tom Rathkenny. Tom's features were pale and tight. It was impossible to tell whether his expression was one of fear, or rage, or only of simple embarrassment. He wore a statue's or an idol's face; and, as Dave's eyes hit him now, Tom turned and plunged away, off down the slope of the meadow toward another group of late departees.

Rob looked after him for a moment, then turned back to stuff the last blanket into the pack he, himself, would be carrying, and buckled it closed. Getting to his feet, he put the pack on. Letty already bore hers.

"Well," said Rob, half turned to go. He hesitated, looking at Maybeth and Walt. "We've got the promise of a ride in the last panel truck down there. The driver wants somebody along to help him change tires. He could take some more people besides us."

Walt got slowly to his feet, then shook his head.

"No," he said. "I've got to be alone—a while."

He snatched up his pack and went off away from the road, downslope, but not in the direction Tom had taken, until he disappeared into the woods between meadow and river. They watched him go; and neither Tom nor the other sheriff's deputy was watching as he went.

"Well," said Rob, after he had gone, "anyone who wants a ride better come along in a hurry. That trucker's ready to pull out."

He and Letty took their gear and went toward the road. Maybeth looked after them, hesitated, and looked back at Dave and Ranald.

Ranald's eyes, once more lost on the view of his inner vision, looked through and past her. Dave returned her look.

"Better go," Dave said.

"I can't stay with you," she said, "even a little longer?"

Dave shook his head slowly.

"Not me," he answered. "Someday, maybe, if it turns out this changed things, I may want a woman around steady, neighbors in to dinner, and all the rest of it. But that's someday."

He buckled tight the last buckle of his pack on its pack-frame and stood up, sliding his arms through the straps. Maybeth looked at Ranald.

"Good-bye, Ranald," she said.

He came a little way back from where he had gone, to speak to her.

"Go with a god," he said. "Your god, if may be. But any god will do."

She turned abruptly and almost ran after Rob and Letty, who were now standing talking to a short, brown-shirted man beside the left front door of a somewhat battered blue panel truck—the only vehicle left in the meadow except for two motorcycles of the sheriff's deputies. Dave looked after her for a moment as she joined them, and they all got into the truck. It pulled away, back down the route up which they had all come.

"The other way, for me," said Dave, "up that road alongside the river we saw, into Medora or whatever they call it. A day or so's walking'll clear my head."

He looked back at Ranald.

"So long, then," Dave said. "Maybe we'll run into each other again."

"I don't think so," said Ranald. His voice and eyes were a little strange because of his being only partway back. "I will turn away a little, then turn back and find you are dust. Unless . . ."

"Unless?" Dave stared at him curiously.

"Unless . . ." said Ranald, still from the in-between of two places, "you turn away, then turn back to find me dust. I was too young the first time I saw this."

"You figuring on dying?" said Dave, bluntly.

"No. Yes—eventually. Maybe, soon . . ." Ranald came almost all the way back and looked up at Dave with strangely clear eyes. "I do not know if I want to. I do not know if I should. I don't know if I will."

Dave stared at him.

"What makes you so sure anything'll happen?" he asked.

"Always," said Ranald. "People always do the same things. A curse makes a blow—makes—wounding—makes a killing."

Dave grunted slightly under his breath.

"Man ought to know what's he doing."

"I belong to no god," said Ranald. "And no more do I belong to any people, so that their ways are a law to me. I belong, though, to myself—to Ranald; and I do not know what Ranald is going to do. It's a little thing to die after three score years and ten. To die after much longer is a hard problem. How can I be sure this moment is so worthwhile? Will it be worth all those other times before when I refused death, fought it off and said—'Not yet'?"

Dave hesitated. Then he took a step closer and held out his hand.

"Luck," he said.

Ranald reached up and took hold; but with his hand grasping Dave's forearm above the wrist, so that Dave had no choice but to fold his own fingers around Ranald's forearm in return. They let go.

"If I'm to die soon," said Ranald, "I'd like to see you free first, Brother Piers." He added, almost muttering under his breath, " '*Cessez, cessez, gens d'armes et piétons—de piller et manger le bonhomme . . .*' "

"You're full up with poems, today," said Dave.

"It's Walt and his question about Caesar that opened my memory to them," said Ranald. "Walt was right. His question is the question, after all. . . ."

He stopped talking as if he had run down.

"As I say, luck, then," said Dave after a second. But this time Ranald did not answer. Dave shook his head, turned, and went off with a loose, swinging stride toward the far end of the meadow where the trees came together, hiding the road to Medora.

Near the middle of the road beside the openness of the meadow, the two deputies watched him go. Then they turned back. Ranald was the last left amidst the litter of the open space, sitting cross-legged and unmoving. One of the deputies started toward him; but the other, who walked like Tom Rathkenny, caught the first by the arm and turned him around. They went to their motorcycles, the other got on his and left in the opposite direction Dave had taken, back toward the city. Tom started his own bike after a minute and slowly followed. Ranald was alone in the meadow.

Now that there was no human activity around to retreat from, he came all the way back into the present, opening all his senses to the land around him and its inhabitants. Already half a mile distant, the other sheriff's deputy droned on his motorcycle back toward his headquarters. Tom Rathkenny, just out of sight beyond the meadow, had pulled his machine off the road behind a willow clump and stopped. He put the kickstand down carefully and got off.

A few hundred yards beyond and out of sight on the winding road from Tom, the panel truck had stopped with a flat tire, which Rob was just now replacing with a spare from inside the truck, while the driver stood by and watched.

In the opposite direction, already out of sight beyond the meadow, Dave swung along the people-empty route to Medora, the sound of his bootsoles in the loose gravel on the shoulder of the roadway noisy in the noon silence. Down beside the river, beyond the woods and not moving—possibly on his knees—Walt was praying out loud.

". . . I'm this way because this is the way You made me, Lord," he was praying. "No, I don't mean to put all the responsibility on You; but You ought to share in what I am. . . ."

All these things—the rushing of the river, the rustling of tree leaves, the drone of a nearby wasp—came clearly and unavoidably to Ranald's acute hearing. There was a flutter of wings, and a male Western song sparrow came to a perch on the end of a leaning tent-pole near Ranald, a tent-pole abandoned, but still stuck in the earth and semi-upright. The song sparrow threw back his head and sang, and Ranald understood. Like the intentions of humans, the messages of birds and animals had become clear to him through long time and familiarity. But he had never understood a bird as clearly as this one, at this moment.

"*I am me!*" cried the song sparrow. "*Me. Me! And this meadow is mine! Mine—and no other's! Mine—and no other's!*"

". . . Lord," Walt was praying to a God in whom he had no trust, no hope, "You should help me. . . ."

". . . All right," Rob was saying to the driver of the panel truck, "suppose you get something into your head. We came along to *help* with your flat tires; not do all the work while you stand around juicing! The next tire that goes flat, you're going to do as much fixing as we do!"

"That's what you get for trying to do favors," said the driver, climbing back into the front seat of the truck. "To hell with you. Just to hell with you! You can walk into town!"

He closed the door of the truck, started the panel up and drove off.

"Wait—" Maybeth called after him.

"Let him go," said Rob. "They're all alike. I ought to've known."

Dave had begun to whistle as he strode along. Walt was still praying. Tom Rathkenny had left his motorcycle and was walking down the curve of the wooded road toward Rob and the others, although he could not yet be close enough for them to see him. The breeze blowing against the left side of Ranald's face ceased for a moment. Abruptly, he sprang upright; and headed down the road in the direction everyone but Dave and Walt had taken, breaking into a run.

He ran with some oddly long strides he had used down by the river when he had taken the gun from Tom. His running was effortlessly swift, so that he seemed to soar slightly with each step, the way a deer soars with each bound. He crossed the road and headed on a direct line through the trees, toward that spot beside the road where Rob and Letty were dividing up some of the load in their packs, so that Maybeth could help them carry it on foot back into town.

Ranald ran. Up ahead of him, out of sight beyond the trees, Tom Rathkenny came around a curve and walked up to the three as they were redistributing the load they had to pack.

"So, you're still here," said Tom.

Rob's answer was lost to Ranald. He was in full stride, now. He coursed the woods like a wild animal, hurdling fallen logs and small bushes in his path as if some instinct deep within him told him when to go over, and when to around. The slope of the hillside and its sun-dappled tree trunks swam around him; and the late morning breeze was cold on face and neck where he had begun to sweat. Ahead, talk between Tom and the others had become some kind of an argument between Tom and Rob; and as Ranald rocketed down the wooded slope, close to the others now, Rob's voice reached clearly through the leaves and pine needles.

"You and Letty?" Rob was saying. "Oh, sure . . . You know what she does? She collects cats, man; and squirrels; and birds with half a leg missing. But she doesn't keep them."

They were all right ahead of Ranald now, although the trees still hid them. He burst through that last screen and came out only a few running steps from them. Maybeth and Letty stood back by the side of the road with the opened packs, and one blanket that had been tied up to make it into a sort of packsack. Between the girls and the trees Tom stood facing Rob with perhaps eight feet of space between them. Rob's back was arched; the narrow, tight muscles of his shoulders under their shirt were thrust forward. Tom was stiffly upright and pale, with the sweat rolling down his face. In his hand he held his revolver, pointed at Rob.

"Go ahead," Rob said. "Let's see you shoot me. You've been talking about it long enough—"

Running at full speed, Ranald came between them, turning his upper body toward Tom just as the revolver went off. The battering-ram impact of the heavy revolver slug high on his left side spun him around. He tried to carry the spin on around in a full circle and stay on his feet. But his legs staggered and dropped him. He lay on his back on the soft roadside earth, looking at the clouds.

The blow of the bullet had left him without breath to speak. There were voices above him, and faces, looking down—Letty and Maybeth, particularly Maybeth. His eyes met hers. He could not remember a woman who had looked at him so.

Both she and Letty were kneeling over him, one on each side. Letty ripped his jacket and shirt open, popping buttons as if they had been sewn with paper.

"It's down there," said Letty, staring at his bare chest. "He needs a doctor. He's got to have a doctor, quick."

"I didn't," Tom was saying. "I didn't pull the trigger. I wasn't going to hurt anyone. It just went off. It—exploded. By itself. I wasn't going to shoot anyone. . . ."

"God . . ." Rob said. His voice was like the thick voice of a drunk. "God, you bastard . . ."

"We've got to get help," said Maybeth, looking up. "An ambulance!"

"Where's his motorcycle?" Letty asked. She had torn off a portion of Ranald's shirt and wadded it up. She was holding this against the bullet hole in his chest. "It's hardly bleeding at all. Maybe he's bleeding inside."

"Please . . ." said Maybeth, almost crying. She had lifted Ranald's head softly onto her knee and was trying to wipe dry his forehead with the edge of her skirt. "Please, will somebody please go get an ambulance?"

"It just went off," Tom said. "I was holding it like this—I didn't even have my finger—"

"Where's your cycle?" Letty asked over her shoulder. "Get on it and get going. Can't you see we need some help?"

"You don't understand. It's not supposed to go off unless it's cocked," said Tom. "Well, I mean you can pull the trigger, but unless it's cocked . . . I didn't have it cocked. I don't think I—"

"That iron's got to be back where we were camped. He walked here just now." Rob's voice was still thick, but sensible. "I'll go find it. I'll ride the thing."

"No, I'll go . . . I'll go," said Tom's voice, moving away. "It's just back around the curve, there. I'll ride up the other way to Medora. That's where the hospital is."

"You'll go someplace else . . ." said Rob, thickly. "You'll let him die—we all saw it, how you shot him!"

"No—I'm going . . ." There was a sound of boots running off. Tom's voice floated back. "Over the hill, there—down a ways—a farm. Maybe you can get to their phone before—"

He did not finish, running off.

"The farm—you go, Rob!" said Letty. "You—" Her face jerked for Maybeth. "Run back to the camp. Maybe there's somebody still there, or still near, who can help. Get going, damn it, will you both?"

Rob turned and went running into the trees up the hillside.

"No," said Maybeth, not moving, "I won't leave him. You go. Hurry!"

Letty lifted the wadded shirtcloth from the wound. It had all but stopped bleeding. For a second it looked as if she were about to hit Maybeth with the fist holding the cloth. Then she shoved the cloth instead into Maybeth's hand.

"Watch him!" Letty said, and scrambled to her feet. She started off at a trot back toward the meadow.

Left alone with Ranald, Maybeth pressed the cloth gently against the hole in his chest and let her head drop until her face was hidden by the long mass of hair that spilled forward like a dark wave onto the leather-brown skin of his lean chest. He had recovered his breath now; and he felt only something like an emptiness, a heavy emptiness, where the bullet had gone in and stopped.

"Do not mourn," he said to her, a little faintly, "this is a great moment. I'm like the rest of them, after all. I did what any one of them would do."

She lifted her head and shook her hair back so that she could see his face, and he, hers. Her face was simply a face, now, but very still. She, who had been able to cry so easily, could make no tears in this moment.

"You'll be all right," she said. "Don't talk."

"I am all right," he said. "And why not talk? I came here knowing what would happen. Men and women do always the same things. It happened; and I will fall from the cliff now, leaving some other climber my handholds and my footholds."

"Don't talk like that," she whispered, as if her throat were raw. "As if it was nothing—as if you were just being wasted."

"That is man," he said, "who can waste himself. It's a gift. The small birds and all other creatures don't know how."

She twisted as if a bullet had just entered her own body.

"No!" she said. "Don't agree with me like that. You saved Rob's life with your own, and he isn't worth it!"

"There is no worth," he said. "What is paid to God, or paid to Caesar, has only the value the giver gives it. A man must choose which one to pay, though, even though he's like me and needs neither of them. I was wrong about that. I had to choose; and I chose to pay the least foolish of the two."

"No!" she said. "No—you saved someone's life. You threw away your life after all this time to save somebody else. Because you love people, you really do. You just won't admit it."

"Do I?" he asked. "Even if I do, it doesn't matter. Man loves man. They love each other—that's the important thing, even when they don't know it. Look at them; they love each other even when they hurt and kill each other. It's their pride. Which is why they will accept no god-help."

She shook her head.

"All this," she said, "just to satisfy yourself! All this!"

"No, no," he said. "To find home, again. I was a wanderer and I've discovered my own place, again. I was a stranger and I've found my people. You—and Dave, and Rob and Letty and Tom and all the others."

He closed his eyes for a second, looking for the image of the green clearing and the log houses, but they were gone for good. He felt Maybeth's hands, suddenly frantic on his face.

"No," she was saying. "Don't . . . hold on. . . . They'll have help here in just a minute. . . ."

He opened his eyes.

"I'll have to be going now," he said. "Walt is down by the river. Go to him."

"Walt!" She went suddenly from her knees to a squatting position with her feet under her, ready to rise. "He's probably got things in his pack. Maybe he knows—where is he?"

"You remember where Dave and you and I came first to the edge of the river," he said. "Close to there. Go there and call him. He'll hear you."

"Oh, yes—" She started to rise, then stopped. "But I can't leave you."

"It makes no difference whether you leave me or not," he said.

"It does! But—" She looked back toward the meadow and the woods. "If Walt can help . . . I've got to go. Maybe he knows something about medicine, or he was a medic in the army once, or something. Don't move, I'll be right back—"

She started to rise. He caught her arm with surprising strength for a wounded man and held her for a moment while he spoke.

"I'll lie still a while," he said. "But things don't hurt me easily. It takes more to kill me than most imagine. If we don't speak again, remember to trust yourself as you would have trusted me."

"Don't talk like that!" She pulled away and he let her go, to her feet and running back toward the meadow. He lay still for a little, listening until the intervening trees softened the sound of her footfalls.

The sun was warm upon him, the heavy emptiness was only a little larger within him. He rose on his left elbow, rolled to his side, and climbed to his feet. For a moment he swayed and tottered, a little off balance. Then he put out one foot before the other and began to walk.

He went in the same direction in which Maybeth had left, running. But once more, his path was a straight line, and soon it took him away from the road and back into the trees of the hillside. He walked more surely now, and faster. Soon, he began to run— at first only at a slow trot, staggering a little, but then with more speed and balance.

Still, it was a slow and clumsy pace he made, compared to his earlier soaring run. The easiness was gone from his coursing. His legs, which had been weightless and instinctive, now were heavy and needed to be driven, one past the other, by the push of his will. At the same time, it was not all work and weakness. The sun flicked at him through the treetops, the breeze cooled his face, and the woods gathered around him as he went. He passed through the trees above the road by the meadow, hearing Maybeth, now out of sight toward the river, calling for Walt, and Walt answering.

He ran on, leaving the meadow and the two of them together, behind. A Western song sparrow flew past him, perched on a low-swung sugar maple limb and watched him pass, cocking its head at him.

He ran on. Angling downslope now—until the straight line he followed once more intersected the road, so that he crossed it and went on into the woods on that same side as the meadow had lain, a way back. He could hear the river growing louder, now, as it swung in toward the road and him; and the angle of the ground on which he ran bent into an upslope, for he was coming close now to that point of land from which he and Maybeth and Dave had looked beyond to river and road running side by side toward Medora.

The heaviness was larger in him now; but now it made no difference. He had had some doubts earlier, but now he knew that even the stubborn will to live could be slain. He ran now almost as he had run before, not as lightly but nearly as fast as he had run to meet the slug from Tom Rathkenny's revolver. The woods swam past him and the song sparrow flew steadily to keep up with him.

Now, the meadow was more than a short distance behind and the heaviness in his chest was grown large enough to make him stagger again for all the length of his strides and his speed. It was done now. To stop would end it. He could hear not only the river loudly now but, even more loudly, Dave, whom he had caught up with and was now passing, above, and out of sight among the trees.

He passed Dave and saw the end of the woods, the edge of the cliff overlooking the partnering of river and road. His head spun, and his chest felt as heavy as if it contained a cannonball. He staggered to a stop and dropped to his knees at the edge of the cliff, looking out through a screen of low bushes and popple saplings at the road below. Dave, below and a little behind him now, had begun to sing:

> *"There was a rich man and he lived in Jerusalem.*
> *Glory, Hallelujah, hi-ro-de-rum."*

He seized the pencil-thin stem of one of the saplings to hold himself upright on his knees. For a moment doubt chilled him with something like terror; but his body cried the truth to reassure him. It was a hard body to kill; but there was a limit to any flesh and bone and the cunning toughness of a thousand years. This last run had finished what the revolver bullet had started; and the cliff that only he could see was growing misty and insubstantial before his inner vision, as the life-hold of his will upon its craggy surface slackened.

He swayed on his knees, still managing to stay upright; and caught hold of another popple stem with his other hand to support himself. The song sparrow perched on a narrow young limb not a foot from his eyes.

"Gods," he said, "I am overdue, long overdue, but I won't disappoint you. Watch me fall, like the others."

". . . *Now the poor man died,*" Dave was singing as he strode along the road down below, his voice growing stronger as he drew level with the high point where Ranald knelt above him, "*and his soul went to Heavenium.*"

> *"Glory, Hallelujah, hi-ro-de-rum.*
> *He danced with the angels till a quarter past elevenium.*
> *Glory, Hallelujah, hi-ro-de-rum."*

"Gods," murmured Ranald, "mourn that you can only fly; and were not born a human who knows what it is to climb."

He swayed, almost going down, but held up by his grip on the saplings. Dave was almost in sight now; and as Ranald held grimly on, the foreshortened, pack-laden figure came into view below, emerging by the river, singing . . .

*"Now the rich man died and he didn't fare so wellium.*
*Glory, Hallelujah, hi-ro-de-rum.*
*He couldn't go to Heaven, so he had to go to Hellium*
*Glory . . ."*

Ranald held to the saplings, watching Dave move off along the road, singing. A little way farther on he stopped, abruptly, both singing and walking, and stepped over to look down into the waters of the river by the bank.

"Now," said Ranald to himself, but unheard to Dave as well, "all men and women do the same things, time after time—only perhaps, just once, my brother . . ."

Dave started to turn back to the road, taking up his song again. But he broke off and swung once more to face the water. His hand went into the right-hand pocket of his Levi's and came out with something which he threw, arcing, out into the middle of the stream. It twisted and glittered like a metal snake as it flew; and a fraction of a second after it had entered the water there was no sign it had ever existed.

Ranald let all the breath out of himself in a deep sigh. He loosened his grip on the popples, and his cupped palms slid down their lengths, roughened and stained by sap from the young torn bark, as he fell forward onto the ground between them. With a last effort, he rolled over on his back to hear Dave's song more clearly as it moved off in the distance.

"Gods . . ." Ranald said; but that was all.

Above him the song sparrow looked down at him, then threw back his head, exposing the white blaze on its chest like a star of great worth, a medal of immeasurable honor, to the hot midday sun.

*"God is Man and Man is God,"* sang the song sparrow above Ranald, *"and I am a Bird!"*

Far and farther away, as the world closed in about Ranald, so that the sun was very close above his head and the song sparrow perched almost on the threshold of his mind, the last of Dave's song chanted faintly to his hearing.

> "*Now, the moral of this story is riches are no jokium.*
> *Glory, Hallelujah, hi-ro-de-rum!*
> *We all will go to Heaven for we all are stony brokium.*
> *Glory, Hallelujah, hi-ro-de-rum . . ."*

—And farther, fainter yet, but invincible still, as Ranald let go his last hold on the cliff and began to fall, the closing chorus followed him down. . . .

> "*Hi-ro-de-rum! hi-ro-de-rum!*
> *Skinna-ma-rinky-doodle-doo!    Skinna-ma-rinky-doodle-doo!*
> *Glory, Hallelujah. . . ."*

1

NNS